RANDOM HEARTS

Warren Adler

MACMILLAN

Random Hearts

PUBLISHING COMPANY • *New York*

Macmillan Publishing Company
866 Third Avenue, New York, N.Y. 10022
Collier Macmillan Canada, Inc.

Library of Congress Cataloging in Publication Data
Adler, Warren.
Random hearts.
I.Title.
PS3551.D64R3 1984 813'.54 83-25613
ISBN 0-02-500290-2

10 9 8 7 6 5 4 3 2 1

Printed in the United States of America

FOR P.L.

All lovers live by longing, and endure:
Summon a vision and declare it pure.

Theodore Roethke,
"Four for Sir John Davies"

RANDOM HEARTS

1

It began to snow at dawn. By noon, Washington looked like a toy village in a department store Christmas window, the people like tiny rosy-cheeked dolls bundled in their winter clothes. The world was shrouded in white, clean and silent. Only the roar of the low-flying planes groaning as they labored to lift themselves through the heavy layer of gray snow clouds brought Lily the message of a harsher reality.

She paid the taxi driver and moved quickly into the airport terminal, her carryall slung over her shoulder. She kept her head down, looking neither right nor left, heading directly toward the Southair gate. After the silence of the snow-covered streets, the terminal was alive with sound.

She could not deny the anxiety that gnawed at her. This journey was a new move, outside their accustomed pattern. She thought of Edward, and her stomach knotted. What she dreaded most was being recognized by someone they both knew. Not now. Not before she was ready. Their objective was to be in control of their lives. Hadn't they managed successfully for more than a year?

Through the crowds, near the numbered Southair gate, she saw Orson leaning against a wall, the collar of his trench coat up, his wavy brown hair moist with melting snow. Like her, he, too, seemed tense. Yet the sight of him calmed her, quickening her heartbeat with anticipation. It had always been that way. From the first moment, his effect on her had been powerful, life-changing.

He did not move forward but stood waiting, gathering her into his arms when she came close enough. He was a head taller, and the heavy coat, smelling of damp as she nuzzled close against it, affirmed his great comforting presence.

"God, I'm scared," she said, her voice muffled as he patted her woolen hat, which was pulled to the eyebrow line over her dark deep-set eyes.

From the pocket of his trench coat he pulled out a single pink sweetheart rose. She took it and smiled.

"Feel better?"

She nodded, inhaling the scent.

"We're delayed. Damned snow. About half an hour at the gate. Another half an hour on the ground."

Picking up his suitcase, one of those compact leather ones guaranteed to fit under the airline seat, he led her to the counter where he produced his tickets for the clerk. They passed through the security check. In the boarding lounge they found seats alone near the window wall, which looked out on a mass of swirling snow. Outside, the Southair 737 was parked like a hoary ghost at the mouth of the passenger chute.

"A few hundred feet up and it's nothing but sun and blue skies," he said. She lay her head on his shoulder and felt the caress of his fingers against her cheek. Reaching up, she stroked the back of his head.

"Four days alone. Imagine," she whispered, her eyes moistening with emotion. "Days." For them, time was always a gift. They were used to measuring their time together carefully—they had only the morning hours at the apartment, their clandestine hideaway. Yet, Lily thought, wrapped in the safety of Orson's arms, even time itself seemed enriched.

"And Edward?"

"He thinks I'll be in L.A. A round of fashion shows. I told him I hadn't found a place to bunk. Besides, he's absorbed in work. They're all busy jockeying for power when the session opens. He'll barely have time to think, much less miss me." Edward was an Administrative Assistant to Congressman Robert Holmes of Iowa, a man with a thirsty ego and soaring ambitions. No. Edward would not be a problem. Poor Edward, she thought sadly. But how could he possibly understand?

"Will he call the store?" Orson asked.

In his mind, she knew, he was the principal creator of scenarios. "No. He rarely does."

"And will you call him?"

"I told him not to expect me to." She had been hesitant on that point but did not expect it to be a problem. Besides, she wanted to strike the worry from her mind. "Let's not think of them. Not for four days." She sighed. "Can we try?"

"We can try. Unfortunately, it's inescapable."

"Where were you six years ago?" she asked.

"Married," he answered softly. "Safe."

"And now?"

"We'll have four days to talk it out," Orson said.

"I know."

Her stomach lurched as she projected the future. Poor Edward, she thought again, helpless, innocent, so perfectly secure in their marriage.

"Viv thinks I'm on the Concorde to Paris."

"Won't that be trouble?" She looked up at him to search his face but could find no trouble there.

"So we're in the clear," she said, relieved.

"For the moment." He sighed, surely thinking of what was impending, of what they still had to go through, perhaps hurting others and themselves. Then, inexplicably, he chuckled.

"What's funny?" she asked.

"On the flight we're Mr. and Mrs. Calvin Marlboro."

"Who?"

"At the ticket counter I saw these signs—Calvin Klein and Marlboro cigarettes. Not very original, but I can't think of anything. Anything but you."

"And I, you."

"Is it possible to love someone so completely?"

"Yes . . ." She paused. "Unfortunately."

"Unfortunately?" he asked, showing a mock pout.

"An error in timing but not in intensity." Lifting her face, she kissed him on the tip of his nose.

"How do you feel?" he asked suddenly.

"Fine. It's too early yet."

Suddenly a voice blared over the speaker: "Fifteen minutes to boarding. Sorry for the delay, folks."

"Good," Orson said. "If things go well, we can be having a cocktail on the beach by five. You'll love the place. The unit looks out on the water."

"Were you there with her? With Viv?" She had wanted to ask

him before but had hesitated, knowing he had been to Key West before with his wife.

"Of course not. This is ours. Once we went there for a party. I remembered the name: Fulton's Beachside."

"Just you and me, kid," Lily said. "Well, almost." Her fingers touched his eyes, which closed automatically. She loved to touch him there, to caress his long lashes.

"Oh, that." He smiled, opening his eyes and showing little nests of happy wrinkles. She started to draw his head down for a long kiss, but he held back, his eyes furtive.

"Coward," she said.

"Cautious."

Above all caution, she thought. It had underscored everything from the beginning. Honored in the breach, she thought wryly. Passion was more powerful than caution, they had learned.

"I know we're ready. We've got to resolve it somehow," she said with exasperation.

"We'll have four days to mull it over."

"And over and over?"

"No. We'll have to decide."

"Until you called, I had resolved not to tell you. To take"—she paused—"well, measures. Then when you said it's time, I knew you had to know."

"When I called you at Trudie's cocktail party, I was certain. Exactly then."

"You took a chance. Edward was still working."

Even telephone calls between them were deliberately rare. She remembered that his voice had frightened her.

He moved his hand along her sleeve until their fingers entwined. Between them, there was never enough touching.

"I was standing there, looking through the fog of smoke, watching the people. I had had three martinis, but I was dead sober. Viv was off in a corner talking to some woman. In the background I heard this buzz of conversation. Someone was saying something to me, but I couldn't hear what he was saying. I just wanted to be with you. Just with you. Always. I ached for you. No point hiding it forever. It must be confronted. We have to think of ourselves, of our love. We'll go away. With clear minds, just the two of us, we'll plan what we must do and how. I remembered Fulton's Beachside, and I called you."

"Here I am."

"I told you I'd always know when the time had come."

"And I'd know."

"Well, it's time."

"You may get sick of me in four whole days. Ninety-six hours. We've never had such continuity."

"And you may get sick of me."

"Never. I'll never be sick of you. Never in ten lifetimes. Because I'll love you through ten lifetimes. No. Through ten eternities."

"There can't be ten eternities."

"Stop being a lawyer."

"That's another thing. I'm going to change that, too."

"What will you be, then?"

"Something I can do that means I'll be around you all day long. Day and night. Something. We'll figure it out at Fulton's Beachside."

"Maybe we can be paid to make love." She laughed. "To each other. Then we don't have to go anywhere, do anything."

They were silent for a moment. She nuzzled a kiss on his neck.

"I'm being overly demonstrative."

"The hell with it."

He bent down and kissed her on her lips. Opening one eye, she saw a woman smile and quickly turn away.

"You electrify me, you know that."

"Uh-huh."

From the very moment she had sat down beside him on the Eastern shuttle, he electrified her. A strange, powerful feeling had surged through her body, a feeling that he, too, admitted experiencing. Like two chemicals in separate containers reacting by osmosis. Was it random selection? Or did it have an inevitability about it, a design? Had it lain embedded, just beneath the level of conscious thought—some life-changing force suddenly revealed through what appeared to be coincidence? Wasn't it everyone's secret wish? Everyone's search? Connecting was like finding the other half of one's self, the missing part. So why couldn't it have happened before we both were married? Why now? Providence playing practical jokes, she had told him. How else to explain it? I don't believe in providence, he had countered. What then? They decided, finally, on Kismet, and the hell with it. It was beyond questioning. It had happened.

She looked into his eyes. They were rich brown, but sometimes in very bright light they were tan, like those of some droopy-eyed puppy, full of innocence. Sometimes long moments, maybe hours, passed as they locked onto each other's gaze and said nothing, as if it were the most concentrated excitement in the world. Which, of course, it was.

Because of the movement of people in the lounge, her eyes drifted. A profile made her heart jump, but when the man turned fully, the face was unfamiliar. She nevertheless ducked her head below his shoulder.

"What is it?"

"I thought it was somebody we knew. God. I wish all that was over."

"Soon," he said.

"Will it be the same without the danger, the sense of adventure?" Thoughts like that troubled her. What happened after was as much on her mind as the impending wounds to be inflicted on Edward and Vivien.

"We'll know when we get there," he teased. It always amazed her that the intensity of their conversation was mostly focused on themselves, their situation, their personal options, their love. As if nothing else was meaningful or existed—not careers or money or things. Only their unfortunate attachments intruded.

They had this single dilemma: hurting Edward and Vivien and, of course, little Ben, Orson and Vivien's son. Affairs like this were usually triangles, another woman, another man. Theirs was a quadrangle. Counting Ben, a pentagon. Five lives. Now six. If only the others were mean-spirited, cruel, uncaring.

"Looks awesome," a man said, standing before the window and watching the swirling eddies of snowflakes. The framed wall reminded her of a huge Jackson Pollock hanging in a vast gallery. It was not all monochromatics; there were colors in it as well, the reds, greens, and blues of airplanes' insignia. Apparently the powers who ran things were undaunted by the blizzard, and the periodic roar told them that planes were flying.

"Maybe it would be easier to go away and never come back. Just disappear. Mr. and Mrs. . . . What was that name again?" She shifted her eyes from the window.

"Calvin Marlboro," he said.

"But what would my name be?"

He looked around the lounge, searching for a name.

"How about Godiva?"

She giggled, looking at the poster on the wall that hawked Godiva chocolates.

"I'd like that. Can I ride through the streets naked on a horse?"

"Only if I'm with you."

"You think we can do it on a horse?"

"Hell, we've done it everywhere else."

That was another marvel of their relationship, the limitless sexual energy. That was why he had finally rented the apartment where they could have a place to be together. Not a moment was ever wasted. They were without inhibitions or secrets or barriers. They shared an intimacy so powerful that sometimes they seemed like one person. They had even tried to express themselves in written words; read aloud, the paper was quickly destroyed. A secret life. That was what they had, a rich, glorious, delirious secret life. When she thought about it, any resolution frightened her. Would what they had resist change? Yet it could not go on like this. Not now. Biology had mysteriously intruded. Had it been oversight or design? Or deliberate forgetfulness? He had asked for no explanations.

"Does this happen to other people?" she asked, after they had been silent for a long time.

"I hope so," he whispered.

For a time it became oddly silent in the lounge, and the snow outside swirled in great clumps of white, obscuring any view.

"Suppose they close the airport?" she asked.

"They fly in this weather. They're fully prepared with all kinds of equipment."

An ear-splitting roar reminded them, once again, that the planes were flying. Groups of passengers began to drift toward the entrance to the passageway. An old woman in a wheelchair was being moved through the knot of people, followed by a woman holding a baby. A group of men in uniform moved into the lounge.

"We're lucky," said one of the men who wore a colonel's insignia. "The Eastern plane was delayed up north."

"We're lucky, too," Lily whispered.

"The luckiest two people on earth."

"God, I'm happy." She tucked her arm under his and pressed closer.

The agent announced that the plane was ready for boarding, and the passengers who were still seated stood up and joined the line near the passageway.

"It's in the eighties in Miami," a woman said. People within earshot smiled, as if the remark had allayed their apprehension.

"No sense getting up until the line thins out," Orson said.

"You're so practical and brilliant," she teased. "That's why I fell in love with you. Your razor-sharp mind."

"I thought it was my body."

"I never noticed."

She slid her hand downward under his raincoat and caressed him there.

"Do you suppose we could figure out a way?" she giggled.

"We've been very resourceful before."

She looked around the lounge as though she were assessing the conditions.

"You're crazy," he said.

"Crazy for you."

She sighed and removed her hand as her eyes roved through the lounge.

"Sometimes I think someone is following us, watching." He followed her gaze, but the lounge was emptying. In their circumstances, she knew, paranoia was a natural condition. "Even though I know I haven't given Edward a single hint, not a moment's insecurity."

"He could pick up vibes. Sometimes I truly believe that Vivien knows."

"But you said you were a good actor."

"It's not an easy part to play."

"Especially in bed."

His forehead wrinkled, but the frown was brief. "We agreed not to talk about that."

"I'm sorry. Sometimes I think about it. You and her."

"And you and Edward."

"I'm not made for all this intrigue, the lies, the dissimulation. It's damned hard work."

"You think I am? You think it's easy being with Vivien and thinking only about you? So far it's been a miracle."

"We keep them secure, that's why."

"And we've been awfully careful." He paused. "Almost."

"It can't go on. Not now."

"No." He shook his head. She could tell he was getting anxious.

"You'd think they'd have gotten suspicious by now."

"That would have been the worst thing that could happen. Not until we're ready to make the final break. Both of us at the same time. Flat-out honest. Cold turkey. We are dealing with two good people, people we once chose to spend our lives with, decent, sensitive people. We agreed that we would not draw out the pain—"

"No matter what, it will hurt." She thought of Edward again and sighed.

"We'd better go," Orson said, getting up, clutching her hand as they walked to the desk and then through the passageway into the plane. Most of the others had already settled into their seats. They chose two, midway in the aircraft. Although the row had three seats, she took the middle seat, leaving the aisle seat empty. She could not bear to be that far away from him.

"The stewardess will think I'm foolish."

"Who cares what she thinks?" he said. He was still edgy from their discussion, and she stroked his thigh while he looked out of the plane's window at the wall of falling snow. In her other hand she still clutched the stem of the little pink rose.

"We met just like this," she said cheerfully. Always, when they discussed the others, it dredged up sadness and guilt. Recalling how they met always cheered them.

The plane lurched slightly as it backed off from the passenger chute. Then the pilot made an announcement.

"Good afternoon, ladies and gentlemen." The pilot's drawl had an air of sarcasm. "It's not like this in Miami, folks. This is no way to live. There'll be at least a thirty-minute delay as we go through de-icing procedures. I'm shutting off the No Smoking sign. I really feel sorry for you Yankees." A wave of laughter passed through the cabin.

"Just get us the hell out of here," a man piped, causing another ripple of laughter.

They could hear the jet's slow lumbering whine and see the backdraft scattering the snow as the plane taxied forward for a long time, finally stopping near one of the large hangars. Outside, men with hoses sprayed the wings with de-icing liquid.

Unfastening her seat belt, Lily stood up, opened the overhead rack, and took out a blanket and two pillows.

"Might as well get cozy," she said, placing the pillows behind them and covering them both with a blanket. "How do you get rid of this damned thing?" she said, referring to the armrest. He fiddled with it and slid it out, leaving no space between them. Turning slightly sideways, she ran her hand over his chest while his hand stroked her earlobe.

"I don't need any de-icing," she giggled.

"Me neither."

"Four days of you. I warn you, I'll give you no rest."

"Idle threats."

"Not so idle." She slid her hand down and caressed his thigh.

The stewardess came by, and Lily closed her eyes, feigning sleep.

"She should see what I have," she whispered.

"You're incorrigible."

"I adore you."

"Just adore?"

"Beyond adore."

"Like love?"

"Beyond even that."

"Beyond that?"

"It's only a word," she said. She hugged him closer. "Will it be like this when we're together?" she asked.

"We are together."

"I mean permanently."

"If not, we'll have gone through a lot of hell for nothing."

He looked down at her. She raised her lips to his, parted them, and they kissed deeply.

"Why you?" she asked.

"Why you?"

2

It was now the central fact of Orson's life, a phenomenon that defied all the laws of logic that normally ruled his cool, analytical lawyer's mind. Lily had become a part of him, an overwhelming need greater than physical hunger, greater than himself. It was impossible to fathom, and endlessly fascinating to contemplate and discuss. How? Why?

"Why you?"

His eyes drifted again to the activity outside the aircraft. A man in a kind of plastic uniform held the nozzle of a large hose, looked upward, and raised his hand, vapor curling from his mouth.

"Because you were there waiting for me," she said again, surely for the thousandth time.

"I was minding my own business. I had just won my biggest case. I was content, happy, a good family man with a devoted wife, a beautiful little boy. I had security, self-worth, substance, self-containment."

"Me, too," she said, "except for the little boy."

"Then why?"

"Because it wasn't true."

Perhaps, just at that moment when she had asked the banal question, Is this seat taken? he had been making inquiries of himself: Is this it? Is this all there is or will ever be? Had he glimpsed the future at that precise point in time?

"I lifted my eyes, and there you were. Everything that I was before self-destructed, and when the parts came together again, I was a different person. And from that mini-second of time all that mattered was you."

"Yes. Yes. Exactly. Everything changed."

"I love you more than life," he said, feeling the pressure of her intimate caress as he returned the gesture in kind.

The plane began a bumping taxi as the pilot's voice told them they were heading for the runway, taking their place in line.

"Won't be long, folks," he said. His tone revealed a faint hint of exasperation. Again, the stewardess passed their seats, and Lily closed her eyes.

The cool and logical part of Orson's mind acknowledged the ridiculousness of the situation. He had always thought of himself as a self-disciplined, civilized man, under control, not foolhardy in his actions. A pragmatic man. A clever man who anticipated events. Then came Lily.

"What is it that you do to me?" he asked.

"All I can."

They could never get enough of each other. It was like peeling away the skin of an onion—there was always another layer underneath. They could never be satiated. It had not been that way with Vivien. Lovely, trusting, good, dependent Viv, the quintessential wife. Sweet Viv. She would have to suffer for his actions. She and Ben.

"A man peaks at seventeen," he often told Lily, marveling at his own capacity. "I'm double that. I should be sliding." With Viv, he could barely find desire. Even at the beginning, that side of his life with Viv seemed tepid, passionless. Never having experienced it, he did not even know it was missing. Nor had he been, as he had come to learn, in love. What he had felt was more like affection—comfortable, bland, without surprises.

They decided finally that what was happening to them could not be explained but simply experienced. Others had felt it—from the beginning of recorded time. Still, they both distrusted its durability. Perhaps it was an aberration that would pass, leaving them sated and sending them running back to their legal spouses, back to real life. But it had not happened, and here they were. Another complication had intruded. In his heart he welcomed it. Wasn't it time?

"Tell me again, my love," she whispered.

"That I love you?"

"That, too. I mean about its being time."

"It's time. No sense postponing the inevitable. Probably next week we'll have to do it."

"It will be the worst moment of my life, up to now."

"For me as well."

"I hope I have the courage. Edward and I planned a whole life. There isn't the tiniest blip on his screen. Maybe it was wrong to do it this way. Maybe he should have been prepared. You know—if I had been nasty, moody, a bitch."

"That's the problem. We're all nice people." Betrayal did not quite fit with his definition, but hadn't he covered that by telling himself that it was impossible to resist?

"Are we really nice? Was it nice doing this? Getting involved?" That, too, needed to be said, if only to admonish. Surely they could not convince themselves absolutely that what they were doing was morally right.

"We couldn't help it."

"But we could have." She paused. "Couldn't we?"

The first time was etched forever in his memory. How could it not be? They had agreed, after sharing only forty minutes of intimacy on the trip from New York to Washington, to meet the next day. Lunch, they both knew, was a euphemism. They were reacting to the power of magnetism, either animal or psychic.

It was late fall, and they drove down George Washington Parkway almost to Mount Vernon. After parking the car, they walked the trail along the river. The day was cloudy, the air slightly chilled. A light fog drifted in from the river, making it seem that they were alone in the world.

"I don't know why I'm here," he told her, knowing even then that he would rather not be anyplace else. "Things like this don't happen in my world. I've been married for seven years. I don't philander."

"Nor do I," she said, lifting her nose, which curved in a slight arc from her high forehead. "I've never been with another man since I met Edward. Before that, briefly, there was one other." His heart pounded. He was certain it was an opening move, which frightened him.

"So we're a couple of innocents," he said lightly.

"I am. I'm sure of that."

"And not so sure of me?"

"Now that you ask . . ."

"I swear to you," he said, hoping she would see his sincerity, "that I've never even contemplated—" He checked himself, not wanting to protest too strongly. Before Vivien there was little to confess. Two, maybe three others.

"I want to believe you," she said.

"Then do."

"I'll try." Like him, she was trying to make their being together unique, an event of significance.

It gave him the courage to open himself to her. He paused in their walk and faced her.

"I don't know why I'm here"—he hesitated—"except that you move me greatly. I've thought of nothing else." A flush rose to her cheeks. There had been no subterfuge. Each knew the other was married.

"Why are you telling me this?" she asked suddenly.

"It's important that I explain myself."

"You mean absolve yourself."

"That, too."

"So we can blame it on some cosmic force, something compelling outside of ourselves. Like a spell."

"That's it," he said, exhilarated by her candor. They had thrown caution away.

She averted her eyes, looking toward the river. "I'm embarrassing myself."

"So am I."

"It's wrong," she said. "This."

"I know."

"Will you always tell me the truth?" she asked suddenly, lifting her eyes to meet his. The "always" frightened him, yet filled him with exquisite joy.

"Yes."

"Then tell me the truth now, the absolute truth"—she cleared her throat—"about what you feel."

"I think I yearn for you."

"In a physical way only?"

"In every way."

"My God."

"What's wrong?"

"I yearn for you. I'm scared to death."

"So am I. It's like I found the other half of my . . . my soul."

"Yes. Like that."

When they touched, it was like being swallowed up by quicksand. His arms engulfed her. Their lips parted, their tongues explored. He was possessed of a physical urgency so compelling and overpowering that it seemed to break into another realm of consciousness. Arms around each other's waists, they went back to his car. Place was irrelevant. They did not make love, they invented the process, he remembered thinking.

Afterward, still embracing him, her shoulders shook, and he felt warm tears against his cheek.

"What is it?" he asked.

"I'm afraid to say it."

"Say what?"

"That I love you."

"Why be afraid to say that?"

"Because it doesn't fully describe what I feel, which is more than that." She hesitated. "And because I don't want my life to change."

"Maybe it won't." He knew immediately that what he had said was not quite the truth, and he admitted it. "I don't want my life to change either. But it's going to, and there's not a damned thing we can do about it."

The aircraft fell in line behind a number of others. Outside, the snow continued to fall and swirl about, sometimes completely obscuring visibility through the windows. Leaning over him, she looked out.

"Are we really going to take off?"

"They know what they're doing," Orson said. A plane's roar split the air. "Listen to that. We'll be in the sunshine two minutes after takeoff."

"When I'm with you, there's always sunshine," she said, caressing him.

The plane's speaker crackled. "The flight tower has given us the go-ahead, folks. Sunny Florida, here we come."

The pilot's voice was followed by that of the stewardess reminding them to fasten their safety belts and put the seats in an upright position. They obeyed the instructions, although they kept the blanket over them.

"I wouldn't care if we just kept on flying to the end of the world, forever," Lily said, entwining her fingers in his.

"That won't solve anything. We'd have to land someday," he said, lifting her fingers to his lips and kissing them.

The aircraft lumbered forward and began to accelerate. Some loose baggage bumped in the overhead racks. The great jets roared, and the plane's body quivered as it charged ahead, flattening them against the seat backs. For an inordinately long time, the plane did not lift.

"Hard getting this baby off the ground," someone said behind them.

Orson felt Lily's fingers squeeze harder as their bodies waited to sense the lift-off. When it happened, her fingers unclasped, and Orson looked out the window into the mass of white. Lily leaned over him.

"Soon," he whispered.

She lifted the rose to her nostrils and breathed in its delicate scent.

Then the plane began to buck and lose altitude. It became deadly quiet; the sudden terror had paralyzed everyone into silence. Even when the big plane sheared a railing off the Fourteenth Street Bridge along with the tops of five cars, there were no screams. Then the plane crashed through the ice with an enormous impact.

3

Sometime in mid-afternoon the falling snow finally made an impression on Edward Davis. He was sitting at his desk, his back to the window, gobbling a chopped egg sandwich and sloshing it down half-chewed with gulps of skim milk, when he swiveled a full 180 degrees in his chair.

"Damn!" he exclaimed, observing the thick white blanket covering the streets and the rooftops. Even the Capitol dome was covered. His reaction was motivated neither by esthetic appreciation nor by the marvels of nature. His principal concern was that the staff would have to be dismissed early, leaving him to bear the brunt of the opening session work load. Such was the bleak fate of a congressional A.A.

He turned, shrugged, and finished his sandwich. With Lily out of town it really didn't matter. Remembering her playful accusations about his being a workaholic, he smiled, then sucked some egg salad from his fingers. It was an accusation that had mellowed with time and circumstances. As a buyer for Woodies, her career took almost as much time away from their marriage as his job and the issue had long ceased to be a bone of contention between them. Besides, he was damned proud of her success.

The telephone rang. It was the Congressman, who was still in Iowa. They went over legislative details and discussed committee assignments, staff matters, a speech that was in the works, the thrust of a press release, and other business.

"Still snowing out there?" the Congressman asked.

"A bitch."

"Will the speech be ready tomorrow?"

"Of course."

After Edward hung up, he felt a flash of irritation, not at the Congressman but at the snow. Jan Peters, a staff assistant, came into his office. She wore a body-hugging turtleneck sweater which set off her full bosom. A tight skirt emphasizing a well-turned bottom added to her blatant sensuality, which she frequently flaunted in his direction. At times she would huddle close enough for him to taste her minty breath, close enough for him to feel a firm breast against his upper arm.

"Why me?" he asked her once. They had been working late, and she seemed to be more tempting than usual. He had expected a denial, if only for propriety's sake.

"You really want to know?" she responded coolly, crossing her shapely legs, the hem of her skirt settling at mid-thigh.

"Not really."

"Then why did you ask?" she inquired, smiling.

"I'm not sure," he said with some embarrassment. Above all he had no desire to stray from Lily.

"You have the look of vulnerability, Edward," Jan explained. "An appeal to the mother instinct. Mine at least. And you're cute and so high-minded about your marriage."

"Is that so rare?"

"From my perch, it is. I welcome a challenge." She got up from the couch and came closer, putting her arms around his neck. "Yes, it definitely is the mother instinct. It turns me on."

Grasping her shoulders, he moved her gently to arm's length.

"I'm committed," he said, holding up his hand to show her his marriage ring.

"You're giving me the finger?"

"You might call it that."

"I'm talking recreation, not a marital earthquake."

"Your kind of recreation creates earthquakes."

"Maybe a bit of noise, but nothing ever breaks," she said, playfully backing away.

"Someday, Jan, I'll explain to you all about honor and loyalty."

"In this place? You're kidding." Jan looked at him and sighed. "Remember, it's a perishable item," she said gaily. "Like a hotel room. If you don't use it, the time is lost forever."

It seemed a clever way to put it. Although secretly flattered, he was glad he had cleared the air.

"Fabulous," Jan said, looking over his shoulder through the window. "I love it."

"Good for kids and ski resorts," he cracked. "That's all everyone is thinking about." She looked at him, offered a mild glance of rebuke, shrugged, and left the office with exaggerated bounciness. Pressing the intercom button, he waited for a voice at the other end.

"How's the speech?"

"Coming," Harvey Miles grunted.

"He needs it tomorrow."

"I'm not a computer." There was a brief pause. "The sky is falling in."

"That's all everyone is thinking about," he repeated, remembering snows back in the Midwest. In a child's world they were welcomed with great joy. Somewhere deep in the back of his mind he heard sleigh bells. A lost world. He sighed, wondering if that meant he had finally become a realist.

Hanging up, he swiveled again to look through the window. Great clumps of snow fell silently. Cars crawled slowly through the streets. People bent their heads as they struggled forward against the blizzard's onslaught. It was lucky that Lily had a head start on it, he thought.

"It's snowing," Lily had said, opening the draperies earlier that morning. She had fiddled with the dial of the radio until she found a weather report.

"Six to ten inches," he had heard the announcer say, and then he ceased to think about it. His mind groaned under the weight of what he had to do that day, and he was still tired from having worked into the early morning. Her suitcase was already packed and waiting in the bedroom, he noted as he slid in beside her, making sure to keep his cold flesh from making contact with her curled sleeping body—not that they ever slept entwined. Carefully, he had leaned over to plant a kiss in her hair, a ritual with him. Striving time, he had sighed. It was the way both justified their frenetic pace. The object was to cut themselves from the pack, make their mark. It was the way he was taught to tackle life, and, he assumed, it was the same with Lily. Nothing came without sacrifice. She understood completely how hard he had to work on the Hill and how much it meant to him, although she deprecated the political life in her lightly mocking way. Political science had never been her most pressing interest. Nor was the world of fashion his.

"It's not a science," she had said often, especially when he got lofty and overinflated in assessing his work. She also mocked the Congressman as well: "He suffers from galloping egomania."

"You're right there," he told her. "But some stepping stones have got to be utilized." What he wanted was to run himself one day, which was why he continued to keep his official residence in Iowa. He had set that goal for the late eighties. Barring that, his alternate ambition was to move to the Senate or the White House in some decision-making capacity.

His father had been mayor of their little town in Iowa, and although he died when Edward was fourteen, the man had implanted in him the idea of politics as a career. "It's a good life, son," he remembered his father saying, "as long as you keep your real feelings to yourself."

He had not quite understood what that meant at the time. It had taken a couple of years in Washington to drive the message home.

"It's like the retail business," he had often told Lily, who worked for Woodies, the town's largest department store. "You dispense a product to fill a perceived need. If it sells, you profit. If the customer doesn't like what he's bought, he brings it back."

"Problem is, when you elect a politician, you never really know what you're buying. At least with selling clothes, you can try it on first."

"Like getting married."

She blushed lightly. Before their marriage they had lived together for a year, much to the embarrassment of Lily's traditional Italian family in Baltimore. In the end they had yielded to convention, although he, a Protestant and non-Italian, was hardly acceptable to the clannish Corsinis. But at least they were not living in sin.

Her promotion to buyer had altered their tentative plans for children, and the idea simply vanished as an issue between them. The fact was that there was no real issue between them, no contentious nagging theme. They were busy, ambitious people, tolerant of each other's outside job pressures. If there were vague yearnings or dissatisfactions, they never came up. Maybe this is what happiness is, he decided. No big highs. No deep lows. Mutual consideration was the watchword. The emotional thing, he supposed, had mellowed, matured into another phase.

"Be sure you eat right," she had warned. Dressed and shaved, he had come into the kitchen of their apartment on "Q" Street in Georgetown. He had a tendency toward eating quick snacks and junk food, which had thickened his gut. "There are some steaks in the freezer." She had been making a list for him, which she placed on the refrigerator with a magnet. He really enjoyed her concern. He was a bit absentminded and self-absorbed at times.

"I'm perfectly capable—" he began.

"Of not taking care of yourself," she admonished.

"I'll manage," he said, brooding into his coffee. Actually, he hated her trips. Part of the game, he supposed. Life with a wife was a lot different now than in his father's time. He remembered his mother, always bustling about the three of them, his father, his sister, and himself. After Dad died and Sis left the house to get married and he went off to college, that was it for his mother. The Lord took her because of uselessness, people had said. Perhaps it was that memory that had made him so intensely supportive of Lily's career.

"I'll be gone only four days," she said. He felt her eyes watching him as he buttered his toast and read George Will, who occasionally infuriated him.

"Priggish supercilious bastard," he said. As he looked up, she turned her eyes away; her gaze drifted toward the window. The Style section of the *Post* lay on the table next to her coffee. She had not opened it.

"At least it doesn't snow in L.A.," he said.

"What?" Her concentration was elsewhere.

Shrugging, he looked at the weather report in the paper. "Low sixties in L.A. But rain."

"Won't matter," she said, lifting her coffee mug and watching him with her dark eyes peering over the rim. "I'll be inside most of the time."

"What time does the plane leave?"

"Noon."

"Lucky lady."

"I'm not sure where I'll be," she said.

"Will you call?"

"I'll try."

"It will be all right. I'll be so damned busy anyhow. Just come home safe and sound."

He got up from the table and put on his jacket, which was rumpled from having lain in a heap on the floor near the bedroom chair. His collar was open, and the tail of his tie hung unevenly below his belt. He felt her inspection and quickly buttoned his shirt.

"A mess, right?"

"You haven't exactly walked out of *Gentleman's Quarterly*."

She had tried to remake him into a sleek fashionable image. That, after all, was her business. She could get discounts in Woodies on men's clothes, but getting him to shop had been an impossible task.

"A hopeless case," he said cheerfully, bending down to peck her cheek. Not that he was bad-looking. A shock of tight black curly hair which, fearing her disapproval, he kept neatly trimmed. Square jaw with a deep cleft, the blessing of good even teeth, showing whiter against a dark complexion. Actually, he could pass for being athletic, which he wasn't, but it was an image that had given him good marketability.

Only his eyes gave away his innocence and his vulnerability. People said that, but he was never sure why.

"A hangdog look," Lily told him one day after they had met. "Like a spaniel." He had looked in the mirror. "I don't see it," he concluded. "Nobody ever sees themselves," she had laughed.

"But I am lovable." He patted his belly. "And when I get chubbier, I'll be even more endearing." It surprised him that she did not smile at his banter. Preoccupied, he supposed. Pressure of work. Anxiety about the trip. He dismissed the slight ruffle. He did not want her to go, but to tell her that would sound selfish. He was very careful not to provoke guilt about her career. Above all, he wanted her to be happy.

"Anyway, you knock 'em dead. And don't worry about calling. I'll survive."

"You take care," she said wistfully. He stopped on the way out to give her one last appraisal.

"You're one beautiful lady," he said. He was never gratuitous about that. To him, she was beautiful. "Whoever made you knew how to put things together."

"Button up," she called after him. "It's twenty-four degrees."

Leaving, he felt the emptiness of parting. Only four days, he thought. Not a lifetime.

The icy air had jolted him. By the time the car warmed, his mind was on the impending day, which he knew would be difficult. The snow was already thick on the ground as he sloshed through it from the parking lot to his office. As the day wore on it became more and more apparent that his prediction was correct. It's the weather, he decided. It upset the balance. Harvey Mills came in and put a speech draft on his desk.

Looking up he observed the young man, a tangled hirsute mess with tight curly hair grown over his ears and a shaggy mustache that hadn't seen a clipper for months, if ever. With his round-rimmed glasses, he looked a lot like he himself had looked before Lily had done him over. Maybe that was why he had hired the younger man.

Harvey Mills slumped in a chair, his myopic eyes squinting into the whiteness behind Edward, who had begun to read the speech until Harvey's gaze distracted him.

"It's mesmerizing," Harvey said, unable to tear his eyes away.

"It's loused up my day. It's as if you people never saw snow before," Edward muttered.

"It reminds us of what's in short supply around here. Purity."

His telephone rang. He picked it up, scowling at the young man. It was Jan.

"In its wisdom, the U.S. Government is calling off the day."

He groaned and looked up at Harvey, whose eyes continued to focus on the window behind him.

"Odd what a little white stuff will do." He gathered up the papers and went into the outer office where the staff was in various stages of preparation to brave the blizzard. He had it in his mind to persuade them to stay, but even that last shred of optimism was exploded when a white-faced young woman ducked her head into the office.

"Don't go over Fourteenth Street," she cried with a touch of

hysteria in her voice. He recognized her from another congressman's office across the hall. Before anyone could ask for a calmer explanation, she rattled off the details.

"A plane crashed. Out of National Airport. It sheared off the tops of cars on the Fourteenth Street Bridge and crashed into the Potomac!"

Before she had finished, someone turned on the television set, and an announcer confirmed what the woman had said, although there were no pictures from the scene.

"Seven thirty-seven. A big bird," Harvey muttered.

As in all disasters, Edward knew that thinking immediately of loved ones was perfectly natural. A brief panic seized him until he remembered that Lily had left from Dulles.

"Flight ninety. Southair heading for Miami . . ." the announcer said, which was enough to calm his fears and leave him only to face the obvious, which was that there was no way to hold people in tow now. The uncommon event had once and for all ruled out the possibility of any useful labor for the day.

"How many were killed?" one of the girls asked.

"There were eighty-four in all. They think only four survived," someone said. He went back into his own office, slamming the door. Of course it was a terrible tragedy, but it had little to do with him.

4

Before she opened her eyes, at the very moment of consciousness, Vivien knew by the alteration of familiar sounds that the snow was already thick on the ground. It aroused pleasant memories of shivery mornings in her parents' house in Vermont when she had also known instinctively, before she pulled the shades, that a white quilt had settled on the landscape.

Not wanting to disturb Orson, she slipped on a robe and moved swiftly to the kitchen bay window, through which she could see the garden, beautiful and serene under its crystalline white coat. Rubbing his eyes, Ben came in behind her, squinting into the whiteness.

"Snow," she said, embracing him. "Glorious snow."

Hamster, their poodle, stretched and wagged his tail. He had been Orson's Christmas present to Ben two years before.

"Are you in for a surprise, hound!" She laughed, opened the door, and watched a hesitant Hamster sniff at the white flakes. Pushing his rear, she edged him out the door where he was soon thrashing about, leaving paw marks and yellow dribbles in the snow.

"We'll make a snowman later," she said to Ben, filling a bowl with dry Cream of Wheat and mixing it with water from the Instant-Hot.

"No kindergarten, Mommy?" Ben asked, climbing on a chair, the blue of his eyes enlarged by the brightness. No sense fighting the snow today, she decided, feeling a faint flush of anxiety when she remembered Orson's trip.

The snow meant other complications as well. She had planned to shop in town.

"No way," she said, putting the bowl, brimming with honey, on the table in front of Ben.

"A big snowman?"

"As big as we can make it."

One thing about Vermonters, she thought, they knew all about snow. Today's was dry and heavy, perfect for snow sculpture. Vermonters knew how to live with snow, how to cope with it and enjoy it. Not like these prissy southerners. Snow destroyed their equilibrium. She made herself a cup of instant coffee and warmed her hands on the cup.

From the kitchen window, the view could have been a Vermont scene. A thick stand of evergreens edged the large expanse of lawn. The snow had already obliterated the bounds of her vegetable garden and coated the low shrubs into unidentifiable shapes.

Orson came in, wearing a flannel robe. She rose from the table and made him a cup of coffee, then looked out the window.

"Reminds me of our neck of the woods," she said. He nodded, his eyes squinting into the brightness.

"Think they'll fly?" she asked.

"Of course."

Orson had been raised in Newton, a suburb of Boston, but his memories were not as sentimental. His parents had divorced when he was still in his teens, and his mother had shipped him off to boarding schools while she lived most of the time with a new husband in Palm Springs, California.

"We're going to make a snowman," Ben said, dripping Cream of Wheat on his chin.

"If we make it solid enough, maybe it will still be here when Daddy comes home from Paris."

"You can never tell about Washington weather. In one day, all of it could melt," Orson said.

"In Vermont you could build a snowman and be sure it was standing until April."

"They build things to last up there," he mimicked with tight lips and a twang. Compared to his early life, hers had been . . . well, uncomplicated: loving parents, a clapboard house in a town where her dad was the only pharmacist. Doc's daughter, she was. Even now when she visited they called her Doc's daughter.

"Practical solid people," she said, "corny and wonderful." The snow had unleashed memories.

"Like us."

She was not sure how he meant that, but she let it pass. His humor was often wry in the morning.

"Will they take you to Maxim's?" she asked.

"I suppose," he said, but he seemed vague and distracted.

"Give me Paris in the spring," she said. "We had a great time in Paris. Maybe you'll get a chance to go again in the spring. Then you can take me."

"Maybe."

"Me, too?" Ben piped.

"It's not for kids," Vivien said, touching his face. "It's for lovers," she giggled.

"Yuk," Ben said.

When she turned toward the window again, Orson had already gone back to the bedroom. She followed him.

"Did you find the shirts?" she asked, removing her robe and nightgown, and slipping on jeans and a blouse.

"Yes."

One of his Brahmin moods, she decided. She had learned that the best way to deal with them was to ignore them. His mind, when it concentrated on a problem, often made him seem fuzzy and disconcerted to those around him. Coming out of her bedroom she went to Ben's and helped him dress in boots and a snowsuit. For good measure she tied a scarf around his neck and pulled his woolen hat over his forehead. Then she put a shovel in his hands and sent him into the garden.

"You start. When Daddy leaves, I'll be out to help you." She watched as he frolicked in the snow. His first act was to throw a snowball at Hamster. Watching them made her feel lighthearted and joyful.

"God, snow makes me feel good," she said when Orson came out of the shower. She looked at him and smiled. "I wish you could stay home and play with us."

"Duty calls," he muttered, turning away.

"Sure you've got everything you need?" she asked. He had packed himself the night before.

"I'm sure."

She could never fault his self-reliance, and she was proud of him for that, and for his brains and good looks as well. A take-charge man, her mother had called him from the beginning. There was never any doubt that Orson Simpson was going places, although sometimes she did feel slightly subservient. Not that he flaunted his surety. Unlike her, he simply had definite ideas about things. She was more of a muller, more of a Vermonter. It was a trait that mimicked being indecisive, which she did not feel she was.

If she felt on occasion a sense of deficiency, it came strictly from unsuitable comparisons, which she quickly rationalized in her no-nonsense New England manner. Being a wife and mother was a full-time job. She was not one of those women pressured to pursue a career, although she had been doing very nicely as a secretary when Orson was just getting started, an honorable profession with good wages. What jobs were around for English majors? Someday she would go back to school and take her master's, and maybe a Ph.D.

Meanwhile, she would concentrate on being a good wife and mother, like her own mom. Only she would not let Ben be an only child. If there was any serious ripple in her normal tranquillity, it was on that subject.

"Not yet," Orson had told her. "Give Ben a chance to be an entity."

An entity. It seemed a strange word to describe a child. But she did not wish to be a nag about it. Nothing worse than a nag.

She began to make their bed and tidy up.

"I'm leaving three hundred in cash," he said, counting out the money on the bureau, "just in case." He had always handled their finances, although she had her own checking account from which she managed to squirrel away extra money. Actually, she had saved nearly ten thousand dollars—hers to use as she wished.

"It's only four days," she said. "With all this snow, what's there to spend it on?"

"You'll figure something out," he said lightly. When it came to anything but decorating the house, Vivien was not much of a spender. Sometimes such complacency worried her. Perhaps she was too content in the little niche she had carved for herself. Yet, in another age, contentment had been a goal. Surely she should not feel guilty about being content.

"You'll want to call someone in to shovel the snow. Who

knows what they'll charge? Maybe you'll need to get meals delivered. I'd rather anticipate."

At times he had criticized her lack of anticipation—like failing to take her car keys out of her bag until she got into the car. His reaction was always mild admonishment. Sometimes she did it on purpose just to get him to react.

"You needn't worry," she said gently, watching him knot his tie in the mirror and pinch it just under the knot. She also liked the deliberate ways in which he did things.

"And remember to lock the doors at night." That was always his special task, the final lockup, seeing to it that they were safe and snug. He tucked his shirttails into the belt that sheathed his tight slim waist. He took good care of his body, jogging every day.

"I can just see you running down the Champs Elysées."

He laughed.

"Where will you stay?" she asked. "George Cinq?"

"Not sure."

"You have no reservations?"

"I'll know when I get there. The clients will meet me at DeGaulle."

It sounded so exotic, and for a moment as she made the bed, it made her feel dull and dowdy to be doing something so prosaic.

"If you go again in the spring, will you take me?" she asked again.

"Sure," he said.

She came up behind him and put her arms around him. "Paris in the spring. How lovely."

"The perpetual romantic," he mocked lightly.

"I thought I was the practical Vermonter."

"A strange mixture." He laughed and unhooked her arms. She had wanted to cross the space between their beds last night, but he had stayed up late in his study and by the time he had come to bed she had drifted off. And in the morning she hadn't the heart to wake him. It troubled her sometimes that between them there was not much to the physical thing, although when it did occur it was dutiful and gentle. She supposed it was a sign of their maturity and intelligence not to invest it with too much importance. Besides, they were living in an age when sexuality was grossly exaggerated, making it seem that it was the prime factor in a marriage, which was absurd. It was simply not an issue between them.

"If there are any problems, just call Miss Sparks."

"There won't be any."

"Last time I was away, the heating unit went out."

"You know how I am about mechanical things," she said defensively. "I called her only for a suggestion. She was pretty good, actually. Told me to call the gas company. It was only the pilot light."

She admitted to a slight humiliation over that. To counter the possibility of any repetition, he had made a list of service people and stuck it on the wall over the kitchen phone.

"Don't give us a thought," she said. "Just do whatever you have to do and do it successfully."

"The good old New England work ethic."

"You might say that." She wondered if Orson felt the same sense of stability that her mother had given her father. "The old rock will be here when you get back," she said. "Just watch out for those French dames."

"Do you mean look for them or avoid them?" he said, winking at her. He had turned his eyes away when he said it, which confused the idea of the humor.

"Any way you like. Foreign aid is a matter of principle." She wasn't sure what she meant by that, although it sounded rather clever. "Just bring it back safe and sound," she said.

"It?"

She was teasing his prudish streak. In many ways, despite his apparent worldliness, he was a bit of a stuffed shirt. Soon he would reach that stage in life where his pomposity would be earned.

He had come to Washington just out of Harvard Law as one of those hotshots appointed by the Justice Department. They had been married for a year.

"Whither thou goest, I go," she told him then, although she knew she would miss her parents, whom she saw once or twice a month but spoke to frequently. She got a job as a secretary, and they moved to northern Virginia, where the apartments rented for less. When Ben came she quit her job, and they moved to the house in McLean.

By then Orson was making good money. By some standards,

big money. He had become a partner in a Washington law firm, and his income had tripled, although he did work longer hours and began to travel more frequently.

Lately he seemed to work even harder than before, and there were occasional signs of irritability. When she called it to his attention, it only made him more irritable.

"It doesn't come by mirrors," he told her. "You want the good things, you pay the price." Sometimes she felt as if she had all the good things she needed and didn't desire any more.

She did love their house with its comforts and gadgets, and she had lavished a good deal of time on decorating it. Mostly everything in it had her stamp. And since Orson worked so hard, she did want to show her appreciation by providing him with a beautiful setting. A home was not just things, her mother had preached.

When he had finished dressing, she followed him out and put on a coat.

"Where are you going?" he asked.

"Getting the car."

"In this weather? Are you mad?"

"I'm sure the highways will be clear."

"I won't hear of it," he said in a tone that brooked no protest. "I'll call a cab."

"Suppose they're not running?" she asked.

He looked out the kitchen window. "Always looks the worst from here." He frowned. He picked up the kitchen phone and talked briefly. The frown disappeared. "Main roads still clear. They're running." He appeared relieved. "Too important to miss."

Through the window she could see Ben shoveling snow into a large pile. It still came down relentlessly in great white clumps.

"Did you call first to see if they're flying?"

"They are," he said decisively, remembering that their house was not far from the flight pattern, although she had long ceased to pay any attention to the jet sounds. Apparently he had made it a point to let it filter into his consciousness. "Silly to worry," he said. "The airlines know what they're doing, and pilots don't want to die any more than passengers do."

"I wasn't worrying," she said defensively. The fact was that she was a worrywart. For some reason, stoicism alone had not come down through her New England ancestors. As long as she could remember people had told her to stop worrying. Something in her expression, she had finally concluded. Worry was not a trait to be carelessly exhibited. It made people overreact.

Orson went into the study, and Vivien heard him talking on the telephone to his office. "It can wait till Thursday, Miss Sparks." She cleaned the kitchen. Soon she heard the sound of the taxi's horn, muffled by the snow.

Ben came in from the outside, bringing in the fresh scent of the snowy outdoors. His cheeks were bright red. Orson kneeled and hugged the boy.

"Listen to Mommy," Orson said.

"We're going to make a snowman," Ben said. He lifted his arms. "A big one like Daddy." She caught a misty glint in Orson's eyes as he stood up.

"I'm off," he said.

"Think of us," Vivien said.

A frown shadowed his face, for which she felt partly responsible. She had not meant for him to feel guilty. Really, she rebuked herself, it was only for four days.

"How about Saint Thomas in February?" she said as she bent to offer her lips. She kissed him on the cheek.

"We'll talk about it when I get back." He kissed her and went out the door.

With Ben waving beside her, she watched Orson slosh through the snow and get into the cab. It rolled away slowly, the tires following their earlier tracks. As always when she bid him goodbye, she felt brief tremors of loss. This time she felt a bit foolish. It's only for four days!

She spent the day as she had promised, helping Ben build the snowman. They stopped for lunch and finished it soon after. She used chocolate chip cookies for eyes, stuck one of Orson's old bent pipes into a slit of mouth, and put Orson's tweed rain hat on his head.

"Looks like Daddy," Ben said.

"Well, then, we won't miss him so much, will we?"

Alice, their baby-sitter and cleaning woman, called. She was too frightened to drive because of the snow and wouldn't be coming in. Vivien spent the entire day with Ben, which meant isolating herself completely in his child's world. In late afternoon, she made him hot chocolate, sat him on her lap and read to him from *My Bookhouse* until both of them dozed off.

When she awoke, it was dark. The snow continued to fall, and a deep hush descended over the house. She felt serene, satisfied, and content. She hugged Ben to her, breathing in the aroma of his sweet child's body, feeling again the sense of completeness in her motherhood, her home, her husband; a bird secure in her nest. Ben was the image of his father, a fact that made her love him all the more. The pressure of her caresses woke him.

"Mommy loves you," she whispered. Tears brimmed in her eyes. She was overwhelmed with the joy of it. Considering the perils of this world, there was much to be thankful for. The telephone's ring shattered the mood. Her mother's tense voice startled her.

"I saw it on television. Isn't it awful?"

"Awful?" She thought immediately of Orson. Had something happened?

"I mean the plane crash."

"My God." Her heart jumped.

"It went right into the Potomac. Under the ice." There was a long pause. "Vivien!"

Her throat felt constricted. She grunted an answer, and her head began to pound.

Her mother continued, "It was this plane to Miami."

"Miami?"

Relieved, she felt the pounding subside as her mother plunged on with the story: a handful of survivors; they think the rest are dead. She listened patiently, understanding her mother's motive for telling her this terrible news, imagining how many other parents and children were reacting in just that way.

"Orson flew to Paris today," Vivien said. "I've been here with Ben. We're fine. We built a snowman."

In the long silence she felt her mother's embarrassment.

"I'm so sorry, Viv. How stupid of me. I thought everyone knew. I just called to hear your voice, that's all."

"I know, but you did scare the bejesus out of me."

"I'm so sorry, dear."

"It's all right, Mother. You couldn't have known Orson was flying today."

"They shouldn't fly in this weather," her mother said firmly. A public tragedy, Vivien supposed, often triggered anxiety in those whose loved ones were within geographical proximity of the event.

"We're all fine, Mama," she said reassuringly. They talked for a while, and then she put Ben on. But the news, despite its irrelevance to her, had shattered her sense of calm. While Ben talked she turned on the television set. She saw the bridge, the wreckage of automobiles, and the divers going down into the water through a screen of falling snow. A young man's battered body was being extracted from a car.

"Oh, my God," she exclaimed. Ben looked at her, then threw a kiss through the telephone mouthpiece and hung up. Quickly, Vivien turned off the set.

"Nothing that concerns us, baby."

She gathered him into her arms and hugged him. How lucky we are, she thought.

5

Sergeant Lee McCarthy of MPD Homicide could not remember ever having been this cold. They had set up a ribbon bridge that jutted out into the Potomac to make it more convenient for the rescue boats to bring up the bodies. A few yards up the embankment, MPD had set up its Morgue Tent, where the bodies were received, bagged, and their effects inventoried.

On the first day they had set up a heater in the tent, but since the bodies were coming up either frozen solid or semi-frozen, a decision was made to disconnect the heat. It was thawing the bodies.

They hadn't got things efficiently operational until the second day. The Army Engineers brought in their diver teams. Sophisticated radar scanners that could read under water were used to diagram the crash site and divide it into segments so that the divers would be able to organize their rescue efforts.

A ninety-foot crane was brought in to bring up parts of the plane. Police and firefighter boats were summoned, as well as helicopters. In the first hour a helicopter had rescued four people. Nearly eighty still remained in twenty-five feet of water under a partial layer of ice.

On the third day they brought up twenty-six bodies. The objective of the special emergency team that had been assembled, of which McCarthy was a member, was to make a visual examination of the body, dictate the details of observable injuries to a partner, catalogue personal property, label and bag the bodies, and then accompany them to the Medical Examiner's office where the team was to assist in identification and notification of the next of kin.

Identifying the males was a simple process. Men normally carried wallets that contained their IDs. The females were more difficult unless a handbag was recovered in the vicinity of the body. If they had some identifying object on their person, like an engraved ring or a charm with their name or initial, it could be checked against the passenger manifest or, if possible, against the seating assignments. Many females had never been fingerprinted. Visual inspection by the next of kin was the swiftest and surest method of female identification.

By the fourth day the bodies of more than half of the people missing were recovered and fully identified. On that day a white female had been deposited on the ribbon bridge. Nothing on her person gave a clue to her identity, and a handbag had not been brought up with the body. Apparently the woman had not been securely belted, and the impact of the crash had sent her body hurtling through the fuselage. Assessing her, McCarthy dictated the characteristics of her injuries, including physical markings that would be useful. Clutched in her hand, inexplicably, were the remains of what looked like a flower, perhaps a rose. When he looked at it more closely and touched her fingers, it slipped from her grasp. A gust of wind carried it to the river where it sank below the surface. Not important, McCarthy told himself as he continued his dictation.

"Age about thirty. Brunette. About one hundred and twenty pounds. Blunt force trauma. A Casio wristwatch stopped at three-twenty P.M., almost the recorded moment of impact. Front of skull caved in." Kneeling, he had looked up and watched Charlie, his partner, turn away, fighting the temptation to gag.

"Just bag her," he muttered.

"Looks like instant death. Not drowning like some of the others."

"Lucky bitch."

"Lucky?"

At the Medical Examiner's office, partial autopsies were made of every victim, personal property was assembled, and forms and inventories were filled out and filed alphabetically. Polaroids were taken of the face and body, and then the corpses were filed on trays in the Medical Examiner's refrigerator.

Southair, reacting quickly, set up headquarters in a nearby Marriott Hotel and took rooms for the relatives awaiting the news. After a body was processed, the next of kin were brought in to the

Medical Examiner's office for a visual identification, and the body and personal property were released to the relatives.

By the evening of the fourth day the woman's body had not been identified. Her fingerprints had come back negative, which meant that she had never been printed. Two sets of relatives with potential victims of the same age and sex were brought in to view the body, also with negative results. Relatives at the hotel had been questioned.

Since nearly half of the passengers were still to be accounted for, McCarthy was not concerned. The lady would be identified by a process of elimination. She was labeled Jane Doe and placed on a tray in the refrigerator.

On the fifth day the weather was so severe that the divers could not go down safely and operations were suspended, leaving the Homicide division to concentrate on sorting personal property and cleaning up paperwork. By then more than fifty bodies had been accounted for and claimed. Only Jane Doe remained unidentified.

Because of the lull, McCarthy was able to pursue the identity of the young woman. He matched all the known next of kin with the various deceased yet to be recovered. There were a number of women in her age category still on the river bottom, confirmed by relatives either waiting at the Marriott or located in other parts of the country. A small number of the dead still remained without confirmed next of kin.

Among those who appeared on the passenger list but were still not recovered were a Mr. and Mrs. Calvin Marlboro. Jane Doe did wear a marrage ring, the inside of which was unmarked, but there was no way of knowing whether or not she fit the age category of the couple. As yet no next of kin had come forward for the Marlboros. McCarthy checked the telephone companies of all the surrounding jurisdictions. He could not find a single Marlboro listed. He found a number in Florida, but they reported all relatives with that name accounted for.

To make the process more complicated, the tickets purchased by the Marlboros had been paid for in cash at the ticket counter. No telephone number had been given or required. The ticket agent had absolutely no recollection of the purchaser. A return trip had been booked for four days later. In Miami, a rental car had been booked in Mr. Marlboro's name.

For McCarthy, the little mystery offered a welcome diversion from what had become a tiresome and predictable routine. As for death, fifteen years with homicide had desensitized him to most aspects concerning the victims. Once death occurred, there was no more pain in it for the victim. To a professional like himself, a corpse was evidence, nothing else. Pain was for the living. Yet, despite his hard-boiled facade and attitude, he could still feel something at times, especially anger. A child's untimely death reminded him of his own children. Although his divorced wife had them most of the time in Philadelphia and he rarely saw them, he could still feel a parent's loss. Occasionally he did feel pity in varying degrees, but always for the living relatives, friends, and spouses. Most of the time he could easily shrug it off, like the aftermath of a sad movie.

In cases of murder he rarely dwelled on thoughts about man's inhumanity to man. His job was to observe death, identify its victim, define its real cause and, when the means of death went beyond the bounds of legality, to pursue and bring the perpetrator to justice.

He did not speculate on the philosophical aspects of death, especially when it occurred randomly, like the plane crash. Long ago, when he was first exposed to violent death, he had formed his opinions about life and death. People were part good and part evil, part lucky and part unlucky. The poor bastards who were killed crossing the bridge at the exact moment of the crash were unlucky, as were the passengers who went down with the plane. The four survivors were lucky, very lucky. He never called it fate. Just luck. In his life he hadn't had much of that.

As the day wore on, he found himself speculating more and more on Jane Doe's identity. It was a loose end, and loose ends offered challenges. He viewed the remains again with one of the assistant medical examiners, and went over his report.

"From all physical indications, a healthy specimen. Not a scar on her body. A couple of larger birthmarks, one under the left breast and one on a shoulder blade."

He looked at the body, ignoring the smashed face. In contrast with other ways of death, the body flesh looked pink and healthy, an aberration caused by immersion in water of icy temperatures.

The assistant medical examiner, who was very close to the age of the victim, clicked his tongue.

"Can't imagine that a specimen like that wouldn't have people who really cared about her."

"How do you know she didn't?" McCarthy asked.

The assistant medical examiner flicked the tag attached to the body's toe. It read Jane Doe in magic marker.

"Then where the hell are they?" He shrugged.

6

It was not until the middle of the night of the second day after Lily had gone on her trip that Edward Davis began to feel the full impact of the void created by her absence. Cold had replaced snow as the inhibitor of work. Things around the office had become frenetic. Speeches, press releases, new bills, and the usual avalanche of constituent cases were accelerating. Also accelerating were absences and excuses: cars that needed jumps, icy streets, burst pipes, the flu.

Congressman Holmes was a driven man. It was the one quality that had attracted Edward to work for him in the first place. No sense working for a politician who did not want the brass ring. As the Congressman's A.A., it was Edward's job to help create high visibility for the Congressman and manufacture the correct perception of him in the minds of his constituents. It was less a question of merit than manipulation. Edward knew it was a game of mirrors, and although it offended his Iowan instinct for candor and forthrightness, he quickly learned that that was the least effective policy for political success. In politics, appearances were everything. Thank goodness he had his own personal oasis for such deceptions, his Lily.

Without Lily, Edward believed he would have lost all contact with reality. Politics was not reality. Lily was the voice of reason, the therapeutic salve to his sometimes badly bruised moral sensitivity.

"I'm just not used to portraying something that I know is a lie, just for political expediency." If she was sympathetic when he raised this recurrent theme, she would stroke him like a hurt child.

"Sometimes the truth will hurt."

"Hurt whom?"

"Holmes—his chances, his ambitions, his objectives, his votes. What else is a politician after?"

"That sounds cynical," he would protest.

"Honest."

When she was too self-absorbed to be sympathetic, she would say, "Then quit."

"I would, but he's finally getting into a position of power. The timing would be wrong."

"When will it be right?"

"Never, I suppose."

"See. Always tell yourself the truth."

"I try."

"Not hard enough," she would admonish kindly.

"Besides, I have to scramble like hell to keep up. He's got his eye on that Senate seat, and he's got a damned good chance . . . if he doesn't kill me first."

"You'll survive."

"As long as I have you beside me."

"You do. You know that."

"I couldn't face it if I didn't have you to come home to."

Occasionally it was his turn to be supportive, which he was, of course.

"Me and you against the world," he would say. He liked that concept. Everybody needed someone.

That day the Congressman had been irritable. Nothing had suited him, and he had been unusually testy, pressing Edward with impossible deadlines for draft bills, releases, position papers, and correspondence.

That night he felt the need for an injection of wifely support. Picking up the phone, he called a number of hotels in Los Angeles whose names he knew. It was by then 2:00 A.M., but only 11:00 in L.A. Too late to call Woodies or any of her co-workers. He wasn't exactly sure where they lived anyway.

"Just a wee crisis of confidence," he assured himself after he had given up trying to find her. He took half a sleeping pill instead, and by the next morning he was swept into the affairs of the day, which went surprisingly well. People were getting used to the cold and ice, and the Congressman's testy mood had dissipated. He forgot about his anxieties and, therefore, his reasons for wanting to contact Lily.

He went out for a working dinner with the Congressman and

got home too late to call Woodies to check on the hotel where Lily was staying. The fact was that he was so tired by then, he simply fell into bed. He didn't need much help getting to sleep.

In the morning he thought of her, of course, with great anticipation. She would be home that night, although he wasn't sure of the time, and they would have the weekend together. Nothing, absolutely nothing, would interfere with their weekend, he vowed. He was vaguely disappointed that she had not called, but now that the mild ordeal was over, he forgave her. He had, after all, survived.

He spent a couple of hours in the morning cleaning up the house. As always when he was left alone, he had been a slob: Clothes were strewn everywhere, and an empty pizza box lay on the kitchen table along with the remains of a bucket of Southern-fried chicken. Disregarding her admonitions, he had eaten all the wrong foods.

Getting clean sheets and pillowcases, he made the bed, not without difficulty and with mediocre results. But at least Lily would see his valiant effort, and she would remake it anyhow. Then he vacuumed the carpets, tidied up the bathroom, and piled all the rubbish into a plastic bag and put it into the hallway for collection. Making a mental note to buy a good bottle of wine and some pâté for a nice welcome-home gesture, he rushed off to the office. The anticipation of her return made a considerable impact on his attitude. He felt good. Damned good.

The weather had turned a bit warmer, although the forecast called for strong winds and possible snow again by morning. Because he wanted to be home when she arrived, he checked the schedule of the incoming planes from L.A., assuming she would take the one that arrived by 10:00 P.M.—the only sensible one if she was to spend any time at all in L.A. It didn't seem logical that she would take the "red eye." She had never been able to sleep on an airplane.

The day was an extremely busy one. The Congressman wanted changes in a speech he was to deliver on the floor the next day. Edward had to write the speech himself, while Harvey Mills worked on a press release, all of which had to be run off and be ready first thing in the morning.

It was nearly eleven o'clock in the evening when his mind was finally able to focus on anything else.

"Damn."

"What's wrong?" Harvey Mills asked.

"Lily!" He felt awful. How could he have forgotten?

Quickly, he called home and let the phone ring until he was sure no one was here. Then he called the airport and found that the plane from L.A. had arrived on time. If he left now, he might make it home before her. It was then that he discovered he had forgotten all about buying the wine and the pâté. She sure is right about me, he thought, rushing to his car and speeding homeward, feeling waves of guilt and sentiment. He felt unworthy of her.

There were no lights in the windows, which disappointed him. He half expected her to be home, irritable and tired, waiting to rebuke him. Well, he deserved it. Returning home after a long journey to an empty house was always awful. When he confirmed that she wasn't home, he felt a deep sense of disappointment. He missed her then, really missed her. Scrounging in the kitchen, he found a bottle of white wine, put it in the freezer, made some cheese and crackers, and arranged them in a circular design on a plate. At least he would make it warm and cozy for her arrival, he thought.

When she did not come by midnight, he called the airport again and got the same story that the plane from L.A. had already arrived. It occurred to him that she may have taken the "red eye" after all, but since she had not called the office to tell him that, he partially rejected the idea. Then he had second thoughts. She might have called, but someone could have neglected to give him the message. The office was not exactly a model of efficiency. He had often encountered that problem.

He called Jan Peters at home. Her voice was hoarse with sleep, her mind foggy. Ignoring her irritated reaction, he identified himself.

"Well, well . . ." she croaked in a hoarse voice. "Sooner or later they respond . . ."

"Nothing like that, Jan."

"At this hour, what then? My bed is cozy, my instincts sound."

He ignored the coy enticement.

"Did I get any messages from Lily today?"

"Lily!" The enthusiasm went out of her voice. "I didn't see any. Maybe Mary took one." She was referring to the office receptionist.

"She's flaky most of the time."

"That's unkind."

"Forgetting to give me personal messages." He felt a growing sense of unreasonable anger, knowing he was reacting badly.

"I'll check and call you back," Jan said coldly.

Having already assumed irrationally that someone at the office had forgotten to give him Lily's message, he felt his frustration accelerate and started to nibble on the crackers. Most of all he hated uncertainty, and his anger began to focus on Lily. She had been thoughtless not to call, selfish. She probably got so involved she simply forgot. The idea placated him somewhat. He, too, was often forgetful. Still, even if he forgave her, which he would, of course, the matter would have to be aired. In the future they could not leave each other hanging like this. It was too worrisome, and it was not fair. She had no right to destroy his peace of mind. One thing was certain—he would be spending a long anxious night.

He flicked on the television set with his remote gadget, changing stations until he found some news. A commentator was talking about the plane crash that had taken place four days ago. It was no longer the top of the news, although they were still getting bodies out of the river. Old hat now. He had hardly thought about it since that first day. He listened vaguely. Yet, in his present state, the idea triggered his anxiety. Perhaps she had been in a crash? But there were no reports of other plane crashes. Maybe a car crash on the Coast? She would be in some hospital, or worse. He dismissed such thoughts, although he considered them natural. Where the hell was Lily?

Again, his anger focused on Lily, then on himself. They were too independent of each other, too work-oriented. Their priorities were wrong. They would have to make some changes in their lifestyle. The telephone rang again. He picked it up quickly. It was Jan Peters.

"Sorry, Edward. No messages from Lily."

"You're certain?"

"As much as I can be."

"So there is the possibility that she did call?" He was grasping at straws.

"I doubt it."

"Why should you doubt it?"

"Because . . ." He sensed the hesitation. "Because if it was so important, she would have called back."

He mulled it over.

Then Jan said, "Wouldn't she?"

"I suppose," he said lamely, less angry than frightened. It was damned important, he thought. She could at least have spared him a night like this.

"Is there anything I can do, Edward?" Jan asked.

"Nothing," he said abruptly, hanging up.

It was nearly one o'clock by then, and he discovered that he had eaten all of the cheese and crackers. Often, when under stress because of some nagging problem, he would will himself into complete concentration on a single issue requiring resolution, isolating the problem from all others. He could not sit around inactive. His anxiety level was too high. He had to find out where Lily was.

Calling the airlines, he discovered that the "red eye" had not yet left. Then he called the agent at the Los Angeles airport, posing as the Congressman himself, which he had often done, especially when only intimidation would do the job. He literally ordered the clerk to tell him if a Lily Davis had made reservations.

"No Lily Davis, sir," the agent answered, thoroughly intimidated. He probably needn't have been so strong, but he was no longer concerned about other people's feelings.

"Are you sure?"

He had learned never to assume, always demanding certainty from an inquiry. It was too easy for a clerk to say no. Less of a hassle.

"It's a common name," he pressed. "Any Davises?"

"Sorry . . ." There was a pause, and his heart leaped when the agent's voice came on again. "There's a David. Samuel R. David."

"What about tomorrow's flight?"

Another silence. The clerk was obviously punching his computer.

"Sorry. No Davises. No Davids. Nothing even close."

Suddenly, he got an idea.

"Can you check her departure from Washington? She left Monday. It might indicate a return time and date. I might have gotten it confused." He felt himself trying to be ingratiating, as if a better attitude might get a better result. The possibility seemed encouraging. Lily always accused him of listening with half an ear. His anxiety receded. Probably his own fault. She would be coming home tomorrow. Maybe even Saturday. He had flogged himself for nothing.

The agent's voice came on again. "I'm terribly sorry, sir. No Davis on any flight all week."

"That's impossible," he exploded. "It's those damned computers. They drop stuff all the time. I know she was on a flight that left at noon from Dulles to L.A. on Monday."

"I can only relate what the computer tells me," the agent said apologetically. "Are you sure you have the right name?"

"The right name? She's my wife."

"I don't know what to say."

"Say? What's there to say? Your computers are all fucked up!" He slammed down the phone. He felt his throat constrict. Again the brunt of his anger focused on Lily. Why was she putting him through this? Getting up, he began to pace the apartment, trying to remember the names of her co-workers at Woodies. He looked through an index file of telephone numbers trying to recall a name. Halpern, Milly Halpern. He had met her on a number of occasions, a middle-aged woman with frizzy hair. For a moment he hesitated, looking at his watch. It was 1:30. How awful to do this to someone, he sighed, but it did not stop him from dialing her number.

A woman's voice, heavy with fear, croaked at the other end of the connection.

"I'm terribly sorry to call you at this hour, Mrs. Halpern." He tried to be soothing.

"Who is this?"

"Edward Davis, Lily Davis's husband . . ."

"You call me at this hour? Are you crazy?"

He let her agitation recede. "I'm so sorry, Mrs. Halpern. Really I am. Scaring you like this."

"My God, it's one-thirty."

"I hadn't realized," he lied, pausing. In the silence she had obviously regained her composure.

"What's wrong?"

"Nothing's wrong," he said soothingly. "I seem to have forgotten what day Lily's slated to come home."

"Come home?" He caught a note of caution in the woman's tone.

"From L.A.," he added to prompt her.

"L.A.?"

"The L.A. fashion design festival. That's where she went."

"The L.A. fashion festival?" The woman was exasperating him, answering a question with a question. There was a long pause.

"Please, Mrs. Halpern," he pressed into the silence.

"I didn't think they had that until March. But I could be wrong," she added quickly.

"Do you know who would know?"

"Maybe Mr. Parks?" she said.

That would be Howard Parks, the vice-president in charge of her division. He had another vague recollection. It amazed him how little he knew of her business life. Had she simply not told him, or had he not been listening?

"It must be me, Mrs. Halpern," he said apologetically, trying to appear calm, although his palm was sweaty holding the phone.

"I'm sure there's no problem, Mr. Davis. Lily is a very responsible woman. Perhaps she—"

"I'm sure," he interrupted, offering a quick, pleasant good-bye. He didn't, after all, want to subject Lily to questions about her crazy husband. Nor did he want to hear any of Mrs. Halpern's possible scenarios. He had concocted enough of his own by then.

He began to search for Howard Parks's name in the telephone directory. Finding it, he started to dial, then hung up the phone. He was sure to sound paranoid, maybe even hurt Lily's chances for future advancement. Besides, he might have gotten it all wrong. L.A., the fashion festival, the times and dates. He cursed his indifference and lack of attention. Maybe he was suffering from information overrun, when the mind can't take any more input.

Calm down, he told himself. She might have taken a plane to visit people in San Francisco. Perhaps she had mentioned it. He tried to remember. I'm being ridiculous, he decided. He went to the bedroom and lay down, still dressed in his clothes. His heart was pounding, and he felt his pulse throb in his head. Please, Lily, he begged in his heart, come home.

7

On Thursday, Vivien decided to have lunch with her friend Margo Teeters at the Windjammer Club on top of the Rosslyn Marriott. The main roads had been cleared, and the temperature had climbed. There were even patches of sun and blue sky, which was the reason for her choosing the Windjammer since it provided a spectacular view of the river and of Washington from the Virginia side.

Alice had finally been able to get to her house without trouble. The day school buses were back on their regular routine, and Ben was able to get to school.

By then she had reached the child saturation stage and was getting decidedly claustrophobic. She had spent the morning preparing a welcome-home meal for Orson, something he really adored, paella, which required some preparation but could be left on low heat for the rest of the day. She had decided to surprise Orson by picking him up at Dulles. The Concorde sailed in at 3:00 P.M. She figured he would pass through customs by 3:30 at the latest, giving her time for a leisurely two-hour lunch with Margo.

Vivien had met Margo when their husbands were up-and-coming government lawyers. Although they didn't see each other as often since Ben was born, they somehow managed to retain an intimacy which revived mysteriously each time they saw each other. With full-time live-in help and two children already attending elementary school, Margo had considerably more freedom than Vivien allowed herself. More importantly, Margo was Vivien's window to the outside world and all its titillating gossip and activity.

A Southern girl with a Junior League wave that fell softly over one side of her face, Margo drawled out gossip and personal confessions and dispensed Washington wisdom with remarkable authority. She usually got bombed on her first martini, with often shocking results. Vivien liked her, as long as she was able to properly space the visits. Being with Margo sometimes made Vivien feel tacky and dull. It was, she supposed, the price one paid for the entertainment value.

"You look lovely, darlin'," Margo said, lifting her face to receive Vivien's kiss. She had already completed one-half of her martini and played with the olive on its toothpick.

"I hope so. I'm picking Orson up at Dulles. He's coming in on the Concorde."

"Lucky him," Margo said, motioning to the waiter. He came over, and Vivien frowned with indecision. She never could make up her mind about drinks. Margo's eyes drifted toward the window.

"What the hell," she said. "Bring me another." Darker clouds had closed in, muting the promise of a sunnier day. She turned her gaze to Vivien. "You should, too. Warm you up for Orson."

Vivien nodded assent and followed Margo's gaze out the window.

"You can see the crane from here," Margo said.

"What crane?"

"From the crash."

"Wasn't that awful?" Vivien said. On television the crash provided a drumbeat of horror. She had watched the reports for the first two days, then finally shut it out of her life.

"Hard to believe," Margo continued. "All those bodies still under the river—right there—while we sit comfortably watching."

"It's so morbid," Vivien said. "Let's talk about happy things."

"My golf handicap is down to eight."

"Now that's boring."

Margo looked up at Vivien, sipped the dregs of her first martini, and smiled, flashing an envied dimple and good white teeth.

"Most things are boring, Viv."

"Not my life."

"Yours especially."

"I can see that this is not going to be upbeat," Vivien said, laughing and lifting her glass for the first sip.

"You don't play golf, you don't play tennis, you don't play cards, you don't even play around."

Vivien blushed crimson.

"It's a sport, kid. I'm not talking about anything heavy." Margo sighed. "You'd be surprised how soothing it can be. You should try it sometime."

"Don't be ridiculous," Vivien said.

Margo clucked her tongue.

"You are a phenomenon, Viv. The whole scene just passed you by. I'm not talking about breaking up your marriage. Just a little fun, a little romance, a little sex."

"I couldn't," Vivien said with embarrassment.

"Faithful Viv," Margo said. "The good sister." It had happened only once before Orson. Tom Perkins, when she was a junior in college. As in most first times, she supposed, it was a disappointment. But at least it had taken her out of the category of "hopeless virgin."

"Not my style, that's all," Vivien said. "People are different."

"Do you good," Margo said, taking a deep sip of her martini.

"I doubt that."

"Does wonders for sheer boredom."

"But I'm not bored."

"I am. I wish I weren't bored, but I can't help it. Unlike you, I have a very exciting husband. At least everybody tells me he is exciting. Sometimes he really is, but rarely. Lately he has been so damned critical." Again her eyes turned toward the window.

"It's not going to be one of those, is it?" Vivien asked.

Margo shook her head vigorously. The alcohol had already begun to do its work.

"I wish something different would happen in my life," Margo said.

"I don't."

"No, I guess you wouldn't."

"There you go, making me sound boring."

"You're so damned contented. Like a cow."

"I have put on a little weight," Vivien said.

"I didn't mean that. You've got a great figure, Viv. I hope Orson takes full advantage of it."

Vivien blushed again.

Margo shook her head and smiled. "Actually, I shouldn't be bored. Allen will make more and more money. We'll take more elaborate vacations, meet more and more important people. Allen is very into powerful people. He collects them. The kids will grow up and leave school. My golf handicap will improve. I'll go every day to exercise class. Probably drink a bit more. And if I'm lucky, really lucky, I'll find an occasional golf or tennis pro to service the needs of my aging libido."

Vivien looked around to see if someone had heard.

"My God, Margo."

"Well, the fact is that Allen is so damned tired at night. Washington priorities. Ambition before sex. What's a girl to do?" Margo mused.

The waiter came and handed them menus. Margo opened hers and seemed to be reading it.

"Sometimes I think he's got some little chippie stashed away. That's where it must all go. Not much left for us." She winked at Vivien.

"I don't worry about that," Vivien said.

"No, you wouldn't."

Margo pursed her lips and smiled tightly.

"Dammit, Viv. Wouldn't it be great to fall in love with some delicious man? Some uninhibited Adonis? And he with you? All that wonderful anguish, the danger of it."

"Fantasies," Vivien said primly.

"Tell me," Margo exulted. "If I told you what I was thinking, you'd want to wash my mouth out with hard soap. I mean a mad passion where you do everything—everything. Something that takes control of you, something so overpowering that it changes everything inside you."

"I think you're reading too much romance fiction."

"I'm not reading it. I'm longing for it to happen to me."

"Danger stalks," Vivien said. "Better get some food inside."

"It won't happen. You can't will it to happen. It's just that . . . nature is so unfair. Like"—she bent down very low next to Vivien's ear—"every time I think of things like this, I get horny. Sometimes when I feel like that I call Allen and tell him to rush right over. He always refuses."

"Then call one of your—" Vivien could not bring herself to finish the sentence as if it were an obscenity.

Margo chuckled.

"You don't do that with a stranger. What if he rejects your

offer? No. That kind of a suggestion is only for long-term husbands." She lifted her glass.

"It never occurs to me," Vivien said. In admitting it she felt no sense of inadequacy or moral superiority. Her orientation, she assured herself, was tolerance. Also, it was obvious that all of Margo's sexual angst wasn't contributing to her happiness.

"So I'm forced to find another outlet," Margo said, giggling suddenly.

Vivien's laugh reaction did not satisfy Margo's expectation.

"You're definitely not the person to discuss this with," she said, winking as if to take the sting out of her tremor of testiness.

"Once you stop reading *Cosmopolitan*, it all goes away," Vivien said.

"I know you think this is all trivial."

"Not trivial," Vivien said pleasantly. "Irrelevant to me. I've put my faith and hope in one man, body and soul."

"Is that meant to be insulting or to be wise advice?"

"I'm not one to give advice." Vivien paused and laughed. "And I don't insult people I care about."

"That's you. Typical. Goody two-shoes. The great earth mother."

"I've been feeling like that. You should see the snowman I made with Ben."

They ordered. Margo had quiche Lorraine and a salad. Vivien had eggs Benedict and declined a second martini. Margo openly debated but finally declined a third. Would she become, Vivien speculated, one of those sad Washington types, the women who lingered too long over lunch, got sloshed, left only when it became too obvious that they were the last customers in the restaurant? She listened as Margo prattled on. The food seemed to perk up her spirits.

"You must think I'm awful, Viv."

"Maybe you just have too much time on your hands, Margo. Maybe you should get a job."

"Someday," Margo sighed. But her life seemed cast in cement: country clubs, tennis, golf, long lunches, lots of drinks, a roll in the hay with a nubile pro. And under it all, general malaise and vague unhappiness.

To be Margo's friend on any permanent basis required more

intimacy than Vivien was willing to give. For some reason, Margo had dampened her spirits today. Perhaps it was the grizzly view. Or the expressed dissatisfactions. Sometimes Vivien thought that the world deliberately conspired to make many women dissatisfied, and she was determined to resist that conspiracy. Margo had been right. She was content. Margo had made the condition seem like a disease.

Over coffee her gaze drifted again to the river. She saw the crane and turned her eyes away. Considering the pain that life could hand out, Margo and she were quite lucky people.

"You shouldn't let yourself get so down, Margo," Vivien said.

"Well, then, give me the secret of your ups."

"I wish I had an answer."

Margo did not smile, leaving her with the distinct feeling that she had utterly failed as a confidante. They split the check, kissed each other good-bye in the parking lot, and Vivien headed for Dulles. The expectation of surprising Orson restored her cheerfulness.

8

When she arrived at Dulles, the Concorde from Paris had just landed, and she stood patiently in the waiting room, straining her neck to catch the view of the customs area each time the automatic doors slid open. Orson would be totally flabbergasted. She delighted in her little mischievousness, thinking suddenly of what Margo had said: I wish something different would happen in my life. She snickered to herself. It didn't have to be on a grand scale, something dangerous or cataclysmic. What she was doing had its own secret thrill, and Orson would be delighted. Wasn't it always wonderful to see a familiar loving face when one arrived at a destination?

Travelers began to come through the automatic doors, rolling their carts of luggage. The usual ceremony of greeting ensued, and slowly the waiting semicircle around the door thinned. She did not become apprehensive until someone asked a departing passenger whether he was coming from the TWA flight from London. The passenger nodded.

"Has the Concorde from Paris been fully unloaded?" she asked one of the porters, who shrugged.

"Might be some left. They're slow today."

She looked at her watch. It was nearly four. She wondered if she had missed him. Maybe he took an earlier, conventional flight. She waited another twenty minutes, then went to the Pan American counter and asked the agent about the Concorde.

"I'm sure everyone's gone by now," the agent replied.

"My husband must have taken another flight."

"What is his name?" Vivien told her, and she punched the computer keys. "Simpson?"

"Yes."

"I'm sorry. Are you sure he was on that flight?"

She felt a bit embarrassed. "I could have misunderstood."

"Would you like me to check tomorrow's passenger list?"

"No," Vivien said quickly, not knowing why. Perhaps she did not wish to raise the level of her anxiety. She was certain there was a perfectly logical explanation. After all, she hadn't told him she would be there. She slid into a telephone booth and dialed home. "Has Mr. Simpson arrived?" she asked Alice.

"Not yet, Mrs. Simpson. Was he supposed to come straight home?"

It seemed an odd question, but she ignored it, inquired about Ben, and then hung up. She felt disoriented. Surely she had gotten it all wrong. Or his plans had changed. There were any number of possibilities. If she had not come to meet him, she might have been spared the bother. A call or telegram would soon come, announcing a later flight. Finally, she called Orson's office and spoke to his secretary, Jane Sparks.

"What plane was Orson coming in on?" she asked casually. "I must have forgotten." Her relationship with Miss Sparks was strictly business. Secretly, though, she resented her and often felt patronized.

"I assume the Concorde," Miss Sparks said crisply.

"I'm here at Dulles. He's not on it."

"That's strange . . ." There was a long pause. "But then I didn't make the arrangements, so he could be on another flight."

"That's a relief," Vivien said, taking a deep breath. Then she asked pleasantly, "He hasn't called?"

"No. I haven't heard from him since early Monday morning." Vivien remembered that he had called the office before he left.

"He hasn't called any of the other partners?"

"I'm not sure about that. I'll be glad to ask around."

"Thank you." But she didn't hang up. Something nagged at her. Miss Sparks made all his arrangements, especially for travel. "Isn't it unusual that you didn't make the arrangements, Miss Sparks?" That sounded accusatory. She tempered it with a nervous giggle.

"It was unusual, Mrs. Simpson, but . . ." Her hesitation was odd, longer than expected. "Sometimes he does things like that. I might have been busy on a brief or something. Apparently it was a new client. I really don't know much about it."

"A new client?"

"A possible new client, I think."

She had always assumed that Miss Sparks knew everything about Orson's life. It was the very reason she felt patronized.

Her continued hesitation was disturbing.

"Would you switch me to Mr. Martin?" she asked politely.

"Of course," Miss Sparks said crisply.

Dale Martin was one of the partners. Orson and he had both come to the firm together. Surely Dale would know.

"What is it, Viv?"

"I thought maybe you knew what plane Orson was coming in on."

There was another long pause. She felt the backwash of the eggs Benedict in her throat and behind it the sour aftertaste of the martini.

"Gee, I don't know. He said something about a new client in Paris."

"Yes. Miss Sparks said that."

"Well, what hotel was he booked into?" The question seemed directed at someone other than herself, probably Miss Sparks. She heard him say: "You don't know? He made it himself? Now that's strange." The words were spoken away from the mouthpiece, with an odd hesitancy. When he spoke directly into the mouthpiece, his voice was firm. "I'm sure it's no problem. We'll ask around the office. Where will you be?"

The question hung in the air. She was still disoriented, and it took her a few moments to gather her wits.

"Vivien?"

"Home, I guess," she said finally.

It was when she was heading toward McLean on the Dulles Access Highway that she came to grips with her anxiety. Admonishing herself for overreacting, she felt foolish. Nothing more gauche than a hysterical wife, especially one who seemed to be checking up on her husband. Credibility was always an important consideration for Orson, especially in terms of herself. What she had done was embarrass herself before her husband's partner and his secretary; she had made herself less than credible. Any wife worth her salt would know her husband's itinerary, if only to reach him in case of emergencies.

By the time she reached home, she was calmer and her agitation was directed at herself. "Anyone call?" she asked Alice.

"Not Mr. Simpson."

Vivien felt the woman's eyes inspecting her. She felt miserable and foolish. Inadequate. She went through the motions of normality for the rest of the evening, fielding questions from Ben about Orson's coming home. She had told him that Orson would be home by the time he returned from school.

"Will Daddy be home tonight?"

"I'm not sure."

"If he comes home late, will you wake me?"

"Yes, if he comes home late."

"Did he buy me a toy?"

"I'm sure he did."

"Do you know what kind?"

"For God's sake, Ben . . ." She had to get herself under control. No sense going to pieces. She looked out the window and saw the outline of the large snowman that she and Ben had built. It reminded her of the day Orson had left, and she tried to remember all he had said. Had she missed something? She tried to reconstruct the conversation. Paris? The Concorde? Thursday? She hadn't used much of the three hundred dollars he had given her. "It's only for four days," she had told him. Well, the four days were past.

After dinner she planted Ben in front of the television set and went into Orson's study to search through papers for clues as to his whereabouts. Nothing seemed related to the trip. She felt utterly baffled and dialed Margo's number.

"He wasn't on the flight." These were the first words she blurted out.

"Probably stayed in Paris," Margo said lightly. "A casual affair."

"I'm serious, Margo, and a little frightened. Orson's not a person who wouldn't call if his plans changed."

Margo became instantly serious.

"What about his hotel?"

"I don't know it."

"Well, then, call the office, Viv. It slays me. You seem to get more helpless every time I see you. Surely his secretary knows. They always know everything."

"She doesn't."

"That's impossible."

"She just doesn't, and neither does his partner," Vivien said, her heart sinking. She was simply ashamed that she hadn't the faintest idea about what to do.

"Maybe he just missed the flight. Simple as that."

"Then why hasn't he called?" Vivien cried, pausing to resist the oncoming waves of hysteria. "I'm sorry to have upset you," Vivien said, detesting the apology. She heard a sudden click. She had one of those phones that signaled when an incoming call was coming in. "I'll call you later. That may be Orson."

The brief burst of relief quickly dissipated. It was Miss Sparks. "Any word from Mr. Simpson?" she asked.

"Not yet." Vivien tried to say it calmly. From her tone, it seemed that Miss Sparks had anticipated the answer.

"I did check the Concorde flights for tomorrow. Also the regular jets . . ."

It annoyed Vivien at first that Miss Sparks had duplicated the effort with the Concorde people. She herself had forgotten, or been too timid, to check the regular jets. She could tell from Miss Sparks's tone that she had met with little success.

". . . and a number of likely hotels in Paris."

She heard the emission of a strange sigh. So Miss Sparks, too, was becoming anxious, she thought, not at all heartened by the knowledge. "I'm sure I'll hear from him before the night is over," Vivien said as if she were trying to soothe Miss Sparks.

"Oh, I'm sure of it," Miss Sparks responded with an optimistic lilt that seemed forced and artificial. "I know your husband. I'm sure there is a logical explanation."

"I just don't understand why you didn't make the arrangements," Vivien said. It was a compulsive reaction, so out of character that it left a long pause on the line.

"It's a mystery to me," Miss Sparks said. "But I'm sure everything is all right," she added quickly.

"I just don't understand it," she said. "It's just not like him."

"No, it isn't, Mrs. Simpson," Miss Sparks said. She could no longer hide her deep concern behind the crisp facade. For a moment Vivien felt as though she were a genuine ally.

"If I hear tonight, I'll call," Vivien said.

"Will you? I'd appreciate that."

After hanging up, she paced the study. Mostly she hated the feeling of total helplessness. Her emotions drifted from fear to panic to anger. Anger seemed the most productive, holding at bay any debilitating anxiety. How dare he do this to her! It was callous, unthinking. Then she directed her anger against herself. She had been stupid, a typical brainless do-nothing wife who left everything to her husband. She was a dimwit, the ultimate traditional woman, the quintessential nonassertive wife. She deserved to be in this state. She should have known where he was going, how and when, instead of expecting others to know for her. That would change, she vowed. Maybe she *had* become too contented. Bovine.

She put Ben to bed, after enduring another bout of questioning about Daddy, which only unnerved her further. To take her mind off her fear, she turned on the television set to the news, and the first image that assailed her was the crash, evoking the immediate horror of accident. She quickly turned off the television set and thought about that. If he *was* in an accident, he carried identification. Shuddering, she pushed that thought from her mind and debated whether or not to call her parents in Vermont. She rejected that idea. No sense in getting others upset.

For a long time she sat in the silence of the hushed house and looked out into the backyard at the stoic visage of their snowman, calm and serene in the chill night, staring out at the alien world with his cookie eyes. Then she opened a bottle of brandy, poured a glass, and sipped it slowly. The warmth felt good as it trailed through her chest, soothing her.

Soon, she was certain, she would discover a perfectly logical explanation. That thought reassured her, but only for a little while.

9

On the fifth day the weather eased, and work began again on the rescue operation in the river. Early in the morning the crane brought up the tail section. As it rose from the semi-frozen river, two bodies slipped from it and fell back into the water, sinking beneath the surface. The spot where they fell was quickly marked, and divers were sent down to recover them.

Later in the day the big crane brought up the fuselage, which, as it rose, looked like some giant beast emerging from the deep. A number of bodies were found there, still strapped in their seats. Because of the proximity of the baggage racks to the victims, they were identified quickly. The rescuers were also able to match the seating plan to the overhead racks and determine the ownership of various personal belongings.

The extreme cold did not bother Sergeant McCarthy as it had during the first days. He came to the temporary tent fully prepared with heavy gloves, long underwear, and earmuffs. The body bagging and identification went smoothly. There were no more Jane Does. The only odd thing was a group of mysterious divers who went down along with the divers from the Army Engineers.

"Some big classified thing," someone said. "Defense stuff."

There were military men aboard, and the sudden injection of intrigue gave the day an uncommon feeling. It had begun to seem like routine.

By the end of the day another twenty-three bodies had been recovered, leaving less than twenty still on the bottom of the river, including the pilot and the co-pilot who were obviously in the front part of the plane which had not yet been raised. Everyone was happy with the progress of the operation. The official departments involved took pains to commend their personnel and to backslap themselves with the media, representatives of which continued to haunt the site with their cameras and equipment although with less enthusiasm than at the beginning. They did, however, continue to press officials with questions that hinted at the possibility of sabotage or foul play. These suggestions were quickly and firmly denied.

Back at the Medical Examiner's office, McCarthy sifted through the victims' personal belongings, assigning them to the names that appeared on his list. The objective was to return both the body and the property to proven relatives as quickly as possible. There were occasional altercations between the police and distraught relatives regarding property. Some complained of jewelry being missing. Another insisted that a briefcase belonging to one of the victims had been rifled of ten thousand dollars in cash. Still another, the husband of a woman whose arm was severed, swore that it had been done deliberately to mask the theft of a three-carat ring. The relatives blamed the police. The police blamed the divers or the Army Engineers. Human nature was like that, McCarthy knew. He had little faith in the inherent goodness of human beings.

He and his partner, Wally Forbes, took turns bringing in the relatives. It was impossible to fully steel oneself against the surge of emotion. Even the most hardened professional could not fail to be moved by this unending saga of human agony. Many of the relatives had to be held up as they were led to the refrigerator where the trays were opened to reveal their grizzly contents. The event was so stupefying that the police had to change shifts often. It was just too much to bear.

By the end of the fifth day there was still no clue as to the identity of Jane Doe. And the Marlboro couple still did not attract any relatives to the now dwindling numbers staying at the Marriott. McCarthy was being pressed for a solution by his chief, who, in turn, was being leaned on by the member of the Southair management team assigned to the crash—the young vice-president Jack Farnsworth. His eyes were badly hollowed out by exhaustion and fatigue, his face was pale, and his clothes were wrinkled.

"We do not want any mysteries," Farnsworth told McCarthy. "That's the object of my business. No mysteries."

"Mysteries mean undue media attention long after the event," Farnsworth explained.

McCarthy agreed. He hated the media and did all he could to thwart them.

"I'm glad we see eye to eye," Farnsworth told him. It wouldn't have mattered. There was a lot of information that remained deliberately hidden from the media: the ring on the severed hand, mysterious divers, gory details about the condition of the bodies, facts pertaining to the pilots and stewardesses. In one of the stewardess's tote bags, a twenty-two-caliber revolver had been discovered.

"I hope that doesn't get out," the vice-president sighed to McCarthy, who had found the pistol.

"What I'd like to know was how it got in."

"So would I."

"Any clues as to why the crash occurred?" McCarthy asked.

"Not yet. The whole world seems to be investigating it."

"What do you think?"

"It would be nice to find out it wasn't our fault," he responded gloomily.

As usual, McCarthy thought, everybody wanted to shift blame. That did not matter to him. He had only one mystery on his plate. The bigger picture was out of his hands. He needed only to discover the identity of Jane Doe and the Marlboro couple to finish his official work.

10

When Edward awoke it seemed as if he had not slept at all. His skin felt dry, his mouth sour. He had slept in his clothes. Opening his eyes, his anxieties came to life. Where was Lily? He turned on the TV, listening while he puttered around and looked for Mr. Parks's number. News about the weather and the Russians floated into his consciousness, and they were still working on recovering the bodies in the plane crash. No other crashes had been reported. Finding Mr. Parks's home number, he looked at his watch. It was seven-thirty. To hell with him, he whispered as he dialed the number.

A woman answered.

"Mr. Parks, please."

"He's in the shower."

"Please, it's very important."

The woman seemed to have just awakened and was in no mood to be accommodating, forcing him to go through a long harangue of identification. His urgency seemed to shake her awake, and she dropped the phone to get Mr. Parks, who presumably came dripping in from the shower.

"Sorry to disturb you."

"No problem." The man was obviously used to dealing with recalcitrant or hysterical clients.

"I'm worried about my wife. She was supposed to be home yesterday evening from L.A."

"Maybe she'll come in this morning."

"She's not booked on any of the flights."

"May I ask you a question?" Mr. Parks asked politely.

"Of course."

"Why are you calling me?"

The question did not seem mean-spirited, but it did take Edward by surprise.

"She was on business for you," he said, annoyed by the man's indifference. He hoped Mr. Parks would not see it as a flash of temper.

"For me?"

"The fashion festival in L.A. Doesn't that classify as store business?"

The hesitation at Mr. Parks's end was nerve-wracking but eloquent, confirming the message that Edward was about to hear.

"There wasn't any fashion festival in L.A.," Mr. Parks said with surprising gentleness.

"Are you sure?"

"It's my business to know."

Edward hesitated again, as if waiting for a response. He couldn't think of a thing to say.

"Besides, I would have had to approve the trip. I'm sorry, but I don't understand."

"I don't either," Edward said. His stomach was knotting, and his hands began to shake.

"How long has she been gone?"

"Today is the fifth day."

"My God!" Mr. Parks exclaimed. Obviously disturbed by his impulsive outburst, he tried to reassure Edward. "I'm sure it's nothing. Sometimes the pressures of our business are just too much. Maybe she had to get away by herself." He must have realized that he was getting deeper and deeper into an anxiety-provoking explanation. He paused, then changed his tack. "I'll tell you what. Let me check around when I get into the office. Maybe I'm wrong. You never know in this damned business. Sure. Maybe I did approve a trip."

Edward hung up, feeling worse than ever. Yet he could not focus on any specific feeling. His emotions seemed to vacillate among anger at Lily, self-pity for himself, frustration at his lack of knowledge, and a growing, engulfing wave of despair.

He called Congressman Holmes at his apartment and explained his predicament.

"That's a bitch," the Congressman said.

"I don't know what the hell to do," Edward said gloomily. "Who checks on things like this?"

"I don't know. The police, I guess. Missing persons. Listen, I'm just a congressman. I don't know everything."

Edward wasn't sure whether or not it was an attempt at humor. He hoped it wasn't. Callous bastard, he thought.

"I can't think about anything else," he said, foreclosing on what was sure to come next.

"Then you won't be in?"

Of course not, you asshole, Edward thought. "I'll keep in touch with things, though," he lied. "I'm sure I'm overreacting."

"Hope you're right," the Congressman said. The remark had an ominous tone.

When he hung up he did not know what to do. He took a hot shower, then turned the taps to cold, hoping it might shock him into conceiving some course of useful action. As he dressed he looked around the apartment. Somehow he felt Lily's presence there. A sob bubbled up from his chest, and he fell on his knees, leaning his elbows on a kitchen chair. He was not a religious man and had not done that for a long time.

"Please, God, make Lily come home to me. She is my life. Please, God, bring Lily home."

He soon realized that he was sobbing hysterically. He let it happen. Had he ever done that before? Once! He remembered his grandfather, whom he adored. One summer the man lay between life and death, and Edward had gone into the woods and prayed, sobbing like this. His grandfather had lived. He had forgotten all about it until this moment.

He knew he could not stay in the apartment. But he had to do something, something constructive. Standing by the telephone was like watching grass grow. When he pulled himself together he called the office again and spoke to Jan. There were still no messages from Lily.

"Pretty rough, Edward?" Jan asked. Her so-called mother instinct seemed to grasp him by the throat. He did not respond.

"Is he rampaging because I'm not there?" he asked instead.

"Listen, you've got other things on your mind," she responded evasively.

"That doesn't answer the question."

There was a long pause.

"Well, he's not in the best of moods."

"Pissed off?"

"You might say that."

"Can't blame him, I suppose."

"Everyone's trying to keep up, Edward." She lowered her voice. "Look, not everyone understands."

"Thinks it's some domestic difficulty?" Edward said with disgust.

"What do you care what he thinks?" Jan asked belligerently. He agreed with her and told her so.

"Just keep it together, Edward. It'll work out."

Before he left the apartment he called Lily's sister in Baltimore. He deliberately did not call Lily's widowed mother, a very emotional woman who barely lived in the modern world. She would detect his anguish immediately. Lily had two sisters and a brother but was closest to Anna, who was two years older than she. Anna was not bright like Lily but was devoted and worshipful about her sister's success. Edward was very cautious, not wanting to alarm her.

"No, she didn't call," Anna said after he had asked in the most circumspect way he could devise.

"I was just wondering."

"You didn't have a fight?"

"Nothing serious." He was glad to be offered the excuse.

"She'll call. Lily never stays angry long."

He hoped he had not caused a problem. They were the kind of family, typically Italian, that seemed to revel in confrontations, big emotional incidents, loud talk, too much food, and lots of touching. Lily seemed totally out of character with them, an alien being.

"Someone has to be the voice of reason in all this hullaballoo," Lily told him after his first visit with her family. They treated him as though he were on an operating table, probing every organ, cutting him apart—particularly her brother Vinnie, a large crude man who ran the family's wholesale fruit business. He had been especially insulting.

"What did I do to him?"

"You fell in love with his little sister."

"What's wrong with that?"

"You're not an Italian or a Catholic or from Baltimore. You're a foreigner."

"I'm an American," he had responded with sarcasm.

"American doesn't count."

"Bet he tried to talk you out of me."

"He did. Until I told him I was pregnant."

"You didn't."

"No." She laughed. "I didn't want you murdered before the wedding day."

The memory floated past him, and he clutched at it, then tried to fling it from him. That kind of nostalgia would only reduce him to tears. Stop this at once, he ordered himself. It will all turn out fine. You'll see, he promised lamely.

But all the lies he told himself were to no avail. Unknown powers were simply toying with him, he was convinced. It was some sort of game. He decided to go to Woodies and confront Mr. Parks directly. The man was in his office, and Edward was ushered in immediately. Parks was a bald man with a thin face, thick lips, and heavy eyelids that drooped over large, sad eyes.

"I've checked everywhere, Mr. Davis. Lily just wasn't on official business."

"Maybe she took the trip on her own. You know, to learn more."

"Who knows? She was very dedicated"—he was suddenly embarrassed—"very dedicated." He cleared his throat, swallowing with effort. "I don't know what to say." He paused. "She's never done this before?"

"Never."

"Did you have an argument?" He knew he was probing, and it made him uncomfortable.

"Not a blip," Edward said.

"Have you explored every possibility?"

"Like what?"

"I don't know."

Did he mean she had deliberately run away, disappeared? Or worse? He kept his temper. After all, he didn't want to hurt Lily's business chances any more than he already had.

"We are a very devoted couple, Mr. Parks."

"I didn't mean . . ."

"I know."

He left Mr. Parks's office with a heavy heart. Maybe she had simply run away, lost her memory, disappeared. Outside, he stood in front of the entrance, cold, sad, utterly helpless.

Lily, please, he begged in his heart. Where are you?

11

"You look tired, Mrs. Simpson," Alice said when she came in the next morning. Vivien, by an act of massive will, had managed to get Ben off to school, desperately trying to hide her anguish and her tears.

"Do you hurt, Mommy?" Ben asked as she dressed him in his outer clothing.

"A tummyache," she mumbled.

"See," he said, "you ate bad things." She hugged him to her with uncommon ferocity.

"Now you're hurting me, Mommy."

"Sorry, love," she said, releasing him.

She could not confide in Alice, who always expressed an unfavorable view of the male gender. A grandmother in her sixties, Alice had been married three times and had come up from West Virginia to escape what she referred to as "a brutal life." She was paid quite well.

"I had an awful night, Alice," Vivien said when she noted that Alice was inspecting her suspiciously.

"Mr. Simpson get home?" she drawled.

"Not yet." She was forcing cheerfulness and making a botch of it. "He decided to stay a bit longer."

"Happened to me once," Alice said. "Husband didn't come home when he said he was."

God! Don't answer her, Vivien begged herself. Had she been that transparent?

"Zack. He was my second. One day he went out hunting, and I ain't seen hide nor hair of him since."

"Maybe he was shot. Killed?" Vivien said maliciously.

"Maybe. Only he never came home. Police looked. Everybody looked. Just upped and never came home."

"It must have been terrible," Vivien said. She wanted to get away but was rooted to the spot.

"He was no good as a husband. No good as a man. I looked some at the beginning. Then I stopped. I figured he went off and left me. We didn't get on much."

With disgust, Vivien felt compelled to speak.

"And you never heard from him again?"

"Nope. Never even called in to check up on our three kids."

"Do you think he's dead?"

"I think he just run off. Men are weak. They do that. I was no angel to live with neither."

Surely Alice's remarks bore no relevance whatsoever to her situation. Yet they did release a whole spectrum of new emotions. She had known Orson nearly eight years, and not once in all that time did she detect the kind of brooding dissatisfaction that had obviously infected Alice's second husband. The idea of Orson just taking off and leaving them was impossible. But panic opened up some very bizarre possibilities. She quickly rejected them.

She could not wait to get Alice out of her sight. She went up to the bathroom and looked at her face in the mirror. It seemed ravaged. Her skin had a pasty, unhealthy look, purple rings had begun to form below her eyes, and an ominous sprinkle of pimples had begun to appear on her lower chin.

When the telephone rang she dashed to it. Her hands were clumsy with tremors, and she dropped the instrument. Retrieving it, she took a deep breath before responding. Please let it be Orson. It was Dale Martin, Orson's law partner.

"Any word?" he asked.

"None." A sob leaped to her throat.

"Vivien?"

"Uh-huh."

"I'm coming over."

She nodded and hung up; she fell across the bed, her shoulders shaking convulsively and tears pouring out of her eyes. She felt utterly abandoned and alone, totally empty and vulnerable. To muffle her sobs, she pressed a pillow over her head, fearing that Alice would walk into the bedroom. She did not want comfort. She wanted information. She wanted her husband.

She managed to pull herself together before Dale came and put on a thin coat of makeup, slightly botched by shaking fingers. Dale looked at her warily, obviously trying to decipher the extent of her composure. He was a tall man with blond hair fading to gray, ice-blue eyes, and a long, jutting chin.

"This is definitely not like Orson," he said gently.

"Definitely."

Alice brought in coffee, and he sipped it in between pacing up and down in the kitchen.

"That's a great snowman," he said suddenly, stopping to admire it. Then he turned away, frowning.

"Am I upsetting you?"

"Too late for that."

"I had Miss Sparks check all of Orson's correspondence, all his notes, all his doodles. Our existing Paris clients had no knowledge at all of an impending visit. He never called them in Paris, which is unusual in itself. We have no idea whom he went to see. It was never even brought up at our weekly new business meeting, although there is some vague recollection of his saying that something new was in the works. The point is it wasn't . . . well, official."

Vivien felt a shudder run through her, but she said nothing.

"Was there anything different about him, Vivien?"

"Different?"

"In his attitude, his demeanor . . ." He looked at her long and hard. "In his relationship with you."

"I don't understand."

"Was he secretive, guarded? Unusual in any way?"

"I didn't notice. He is a very reserved man, as you know. He is a good father, a loving husband—" She paused abruptly. "Was there something *you* noticed, something at the office?"

"I think I really irritated Miss Sparks. I think she was insulted that he made the arrangements himself. She characterized him as guarded lately. But it was only a subjective judgment. It doesn't tell us much."

"Dale," Vivien said, firmly, "what are you thinking?"

"I don't know what to think."

"Dale, I know lawyers. What do you think?"

"It's not what I think. They'd only be speculations."

"I might as well hear them out in the open." She hesitated. Her own speculations, she knew, had been ruthlessly edited.

He stopped his pacing and held up his hand, using his fingers to illustrate the possibilities.

"Accident? Crack-up? A form of amnesia? Perhaps a nervous breakdown? Embezzlement? We went through the firm's books. I'm sorry, but we're still a business. Anyway, it was all negative. Nothing unusual. We even looked through his billing file. Nothing. Malfeasance of some sort? A bad mistake that we didn't know about? Nothing. Not yet. Fed up? Maybe he just ran away from some pressure."

"He had no pressure. Not from me."

"Another woman?"

"Ridiculous."

"We thought so, too."

"We?"

"The other partners."

It distressed her to think of them chewing over their personal life. Orson would be appalled.

"Discount all of that. It's not like my Orson at all. Not my Orson." She felt indignant. Her voice had risen.

"I'm sorry, Viv."

She felt a wave of panic coming on, a weakness that might bring on more tears. She stood up and turned away, fighting it.

"Should I call the police?" she asked.

"Not yet. Wait another day. We might all have overreacted."

How can I possibly get through another day? she thought. But she nodded, knowing he was thinking of the firm. He was being practical, protecting their interests. Hers as well.

"Nobody vanishes into thin air," Dale said.

She thought of her earlier conversation with Alice. "Zack did," she said.

He looked at her oddly, but she did not explain it.

12

On the sixth day the first body to be recovered was that of a one-year-old baby. One of the divers found it half-sunk in the muddy river bottom. It was still muddy when it came up, but those parts of it that were clean showed ruddy pink, healthy-looking flesh.

Seeing it lying on the floor of the temporary morgue, it became for McCarthy and his colleagues the truly tragic image of the entire affair, an image that they would surely never forget. The weather had warmed, and a fine mist caused by the river's melting ice steamed upward from the surface. They had opened both lanes of the Fourteenth Street Bridge to traffic again and had reduced the number of personnel needed for the operation.

The crane had brought up the front end of the plane, including the cockpit with the bodies of the pilot and co-pilot. A blowtorch had to be used to extract the co-pilot. By the end of the day there were still five bodies to be recovered, as well as some additional personal property stuck in what had been the overhead racks. The entire load of baggage in the hold had been recovered and painstakingly assembled in a room outside the Medical Examiner's office. Most of it had been identified and released to relatives. Nothing in the baggage offered the slightest clue as to the identity of Jane Doe, and no one had stepped forward to inquire. Her body still lay on a tray in the refrigerator of the Medical Examiner's office.

McCarthy checked the passenger list for the remaining names of the bodies. In addition to Mr. and Mrs. Marlboro, there was an elderly couple in their seventies, whose children still waited for word at the Marriott, and a teenager, whose parents were also on hand. But no one had stepped forward to claim the Marlboros.

With only five bodies still to be recovered, the emergency homicide team was broken up the next morning. Most of the group was reassigned. Because of the open nature of the Jane Doe ident, McCarthy and his partner Forbes were assigned to remain with the operation. They were both bachelors and therefore natural candidates for the job. The past week had been hell on family life, and the captain of Homicide, satisfied that his staff had done a superb job, had a fit of magnanimity. Besides, it was Sunday.

McCarthy arrived at daybreak at the ribbon bridge, as he had done for the past six days. Wally Forbes brought a jug of coffee and a bag of sticky buns, which they drank and ate while the divers went down for what they all hoped would be the last time.

The first body to be brought up was that of the teenager, which they quickly bagged and identified. Then came the older woman, followed by two males—one about seventy, the other in his mid-thirties. Both bodies had lodged behind a small section of fuselage that had inexplicably broken off from the main body of the aircraft. They quickly identified the older man. After his body was bagged and labeled, they tackled the younger man. McCarthy went through the man's pockets and extracted his wallet.

"Marlboro?"

"New face in the crowd. Man by the name of Simpson. Lives in McLean."

"Then where's Marlboro?" Forbes asked.

"Could be an alias," McCarthy said. "It says on the sheet Mr. and Mrs."

"That's it," one of the divers said, scrambling onto the ribbon bridge. "Nothing else down there but some stray baggage." He slid off the bridge back into the murky water.

"Leaves Jane Doe," McCarthy said.

"The missus," Forbes snickered.

"Maybe."

People travel under aliases, McCarthy thought. He always rejected the obvious first, leaving that for last. There were numerous possibilities. If they were genuine cheaters, why not single aliases? Why travel married? They might be a team of some sort, working a scam, establishing married credentials from the beginning, just in case. Maybe they were traveling on someone else's ticket? Maybe they didn't know each other at all and were merely taking advantage of a stray ticket? And maybe they really were married?

He mentally thumbed through the possibilities without conviction. He was too familiar with marital betrayal. Six years later it still burned in his gut and resurrected the old helpless feelings, the ugly images. He had caught them, his wife and best friend, the centerpiece of all that was sacred in his life. It was a violation that he could not live with, and even now the fires of the old hatred burned as hot and bright as ever.

What had been an oasis suddenly became a mirage. Even the most work-hardened homicide detective needed one soft place to keep his humanity alive. Billie had been that place. Sweetheart, mother, and friend. Three months earlier they had had Timmy, light of his life, named for the dad he loved, the old Cap. "Couldn't be mine!" he had shouted, beating his fists into her face. "I swear. I swear!" she had cried. Even when she had begged him to understand, on her knees on the floor of the motel room, hands clasped in prayer, face distorted in tearful agony, he had turned away, the soft part forever hardened to impenetrable rock.

When trust dies, everything, the whole system, goes down the drain. No explanations needed. No apologies required.

The betrayal had badly damaged his faith in his own instincts. How was it possible that he could not see through the elaborate subterfuge of his wife's betrayal? It had happened directly in his field of vision. Jim, his friend, his neighbor, his drinking buddy. How long had it gone on? Would he ever know?

The wound, he knew, would never heal. It distorted his entire life, his self-image, his relationship with his children. Could he vouch for the two oldest? Nothing was ever the same again. No! Mr. and Mrs. Calvin Marlboro were no mystery. None at all.

They zipped up the bag covering the body of Orson Simpson. As they did so, one of the divers came up and dropped some tote bags and a woman's leather pocketbook on the deck of the ribbon bridge. He fingered the damp leather skin of the bag. Certain it was Jane Doe's handbag, he put it in a small plastic bag. He sent the other baggage and the four bodies back to the Medical Examiner's office.

Because this was the last of it, he stayed with the others as they dismantled their equipment, including the temporary morgue. When everything had been loaded, one of the divers opened a bottle of Scotch and passed it around as a kind of farewell toast. There wasn't much talk.

It was already dark when he and Forbes got back to the Medical Examiner's office.

"Wanna knock it off for the day?" Forbes asked.

"You go," McCarthy said. "I'll hang out here for a while."

Forbes watched him for a moment, then shrugged a good-bye. They were partners but not intimates. McCarthy had seen to that. Everyone around him knew how high McCarthy had built his wall. He grunted a good-bye as Forbes sauntered off.

When he had gone, McCarthy spilled the moist contents of Jane Doe's handbag onto one of the metal tables. There were the usual personal objects of a woman's life: makeup, wallet, key ring, money, perfume, a half-filled tube of mints, scattered small change. The woman's name was Lily Corsini Davis. It was all there on the various identification cards: her driver's license, an American Express card, her medical plan card from Woodies. On some of the IDs she was Mrs. Edward Nelson Davis. Her address was on "Q" Street in Georgetown. Five feet three, 120 pounds, hair black, eyes brown. The small driver's license photo showed a dark prettiness, perhaps beauty. He checked the details on the license against the height, weight, and body description provided by the Medical Examiner's report. There was no doubt about her identity.

But there was nothing in the contents to suggest any connection with the man. On another part of the metal table he spread out what had been removed from the pockets of the man's clothing: a wallet, a pile of bills in a money clip, some coins, a leather key case, seven different credit cards, a driver's license, a photograph of a young boy. The license told him that the man's name was Orson Oscar Simpson, age thirty-five, 180 pounds, six foot three, brown hair, brown eyes—facts already partly deduced from a visual inspection of the body. There was an address in McLean.

A fragile, waterlogged ticket confirmed that the man was indeed the Calvin Marlboro of the passenger list, which meant by a process of elimination that the woman was most likely, although not completely confirmed, Mrs. Marlboro. Unless there was another body around, this just had to be the missing woman. The unused remaining ticket indicated a Miami return four days from the date of takeoff, three days previous. He felt an odd twinge of psychic pain but let it pass. Somebody out there must be sick with worry.

With painstaking thoroughness he went through the contents of the recovered tote bags. In each tote bag were summer clothes and the usual toiletries, each defining a gender. Still there was no obvious connection. In the woman's small toiletry duffel bag, he found what he assumed were the usual toiletries. Nothing unusual, even to his trained detective's eye. He fingered the waterlogged bills in the man's money clip, extracted them and counted nine hundred and thirty dollars, including eight hundred-dollar bills. It seemed like a great deal of cash for a four-day trip, considering the number of credit cards. A bit of circumstantial deduction, he thought. A cheater would not use the cards. Cash only. No records. In theory, there was little doubt in his mind that the two were connected.

Somewhere, perhaps among the objects spread on the table, was hard evidence of the connection. Why search for it, he wondered? Unless it led to a conclusion of foul play in terms of the crash itself. Others were pursuing that end of the investigation. So far they had recovered the little black box of pre-crash tapes, and he had heard that the salvaged pieces of the plane were being assembled in a heavily guarded hangar. It would, nevertheless, disturb him if something were overlooked—murder for insurance or revenge or political advantage. The stuff of thrillers, to be sure, but possible, quite possible. In this case the devastation to the living was profound. The bastards, he thought, feeling the anger well up inside him, his suspicion concentrated impotently in a dark void.

"All wrapped up?"

From behind him he heard the familiar voice of Southair's young vice-president, Jack Farnsworth. The man looked pale and haggard, worse than he had ever seen him.

"Seems to be."

"The Marlboros?"

"A facsimile thereof."

McCarthy provided the terse information on the identification.

"How do you read it?" Farnsworth asked. He lit a cigarette and inhaled deeply.

"Except for conjecture, there is no conclusive connection." McCarthy paused. "Not yet. Is it possible that there are two bodies still not accounted for?"

"We've been assured that there are no more bodies on the bottom, and the numbers check out."

"Then it has to be them," McCarthy said. Unconsciously, he put the woman's key ring around one of his fingers and twirled it.

"Doesn't matter," Farnsworth sighed.

"It does to their spouses."

"Maybe they know all about it. Maybe they don't really care."

"They care," McCarthy said with some embarrassment.

"Wouldn't they have called Missing Persons?"

"Maybe. It's a drastic step, and most people don't call until desperation, which should be just about setting in."

Farnsworth sighed.

"Nasty business," he said. "Are you sure?"

"In my gut," McCarthy admitted. "Now comes the worst part. The telling."

"Damn," Farnsworth said, growing more ashen. "Complications. My job is to tie up all loose ends as fast as possible." He lifted sad eyes that locked into McCarthy's. "Does the media have to know—I mean, if there's no foul play, no real negligence, nothing relevant? Death is final. Scandal goes on."

"You're right there," McCarthy said, showing Farnsworth a policeman's hearty distaste for the media.

"Besides, there might not be a connection after all. Why make assumptions without absolute proof?"

McCarthy snickered. He liked the young man.

"Not absolute," he said.

"And we still have nothing definite on the cause of the crash."

"So why sprinkle skunk juice on the roses?"

"Right."

It was then that the keys he had been twirling gave him an idea, and he opened the man's leather key case and compared keys.

"Bingo," he said, holding up two Yale keys. Pressed together, they were perfectly matched.

"You're a helluva detective," Farnsworth said. "I wish you weren't." Again he looked directly into McCarthy's eyes. "Do we have to tell them that?"

"I hope not."

"Why hope? Let's just not do it."

McCarthy thought about it for a moment. If there had been no foul play, it might not be relevant, but if there had, the dead couple could be exhibit A. On the other hand, if human error was deduced as a cause of the crash, the dead couple would only serve to impress the story further in the public mind. It was little bits of dirt like this that people remembered.

"Why bring their families more misery?" Farnsworth pressed. "Why inflict more pain? I've seen enough of it since Monday to last me a lifetime."

"You're young yet."

"Can it wait until tomorrow?" McCarthy looked at his watch. "Just a few more hours," Farnsworth implored.

There was no escaping what they both knew had to be done. All next of kin had to be notified in person by a policeman and a representative of the airline. Those were the rules they had set. Most of the relatives who had stayed at the Marriott had been notified in that fashion.

"I suppose." McCarthy shrugged. It was nearly 2:00 A.M. He wondered which would be more cruel, a few hours' delay or bringing bad news in the middle of the night. McCarthy relented. "Just until the sun comes up," he agreed.

"Thanks. Maybe I'll get lucky and not live through the night," Farnsworth replied.

13

They knocked on Edward Davis's door first. It was seven o'clock in the morning. The day had broken bright with sun, and the air was crisp with a cool, clean bite.

The man who opened the door showed the effects of his ordeal. He looked as if he had slept in his clothes, and his eyes were red and puffy. Sprouts of beard were coming out of his facial skin in uneven tufts. God, will this hurt, McCarthy thought. Poor bastard.

"Are you Edward Davis?" he asked politely, flashing his badge.

The man nodded, and McCarthy could tell from his eyes that he already knew what was coming. Davis backed away, leaving the door open for them to come in. He collapsed heavily on the couch. Farnsworth and McCarthy sat opposite on upholstered chairs.

"It's about Lily?" the man asked lamely. He looked weak. Panic and anxiety had already beaten him. "She's been gone since Thursday," the man said. "I was about to call."

"Sure," McCarthy whispered. He glanced at Farnsworth, whose hands clutched his thighs, knuckles white.

"I'm sorry to inform you that your wife Lily went down with Southair flight ninety."

Flight ninety?" the man repeated, not comprehending.

"The plane that went down last week in the Potomac," McCarthy said.

Davis's face seemed to cave in upon his skull.

"That's crazy!" he cried. "It's a mistake. Why would she be on that plane? It was going to Florida. For a minute there you had me really frightened. She went to L.A. I think you've got something confused. Maybe the computers . . ."

He would have gone on had McCarthy not interrupted him.

"We have her handbag, her possessions and, I'm afraid, her body."

"That is absolutely impossible."

"I hope you're right, Mr. Davis," Mr. Farnsworth intruded sympathetically. He was obviously suffering through it. "You're going to have to come down to the Medical Examiner's office and identify the body. There's a cruiser outside waiting to take you there."

"I'm telling you it's a waste of time."

His lips were trembling, and his chest began to heave as he gasped for breath.

"You can't just leave her there, Mr. Davis," Farnsworth said gently. For a moment McCarthy thought he, too, might be breaking down.

"Leave her where?" Davis said. He was completely disoriented.

"Downtown. At the Medical Examiner's office."

"Oh, God." Reality began to seep into his consciousness. He rose and put on his coat, which had been thrown clumsily over the dining room table. He didn't bother to put on a jacket underneath it.

"All right," he said, "Just to convince you how wrong you must be."

They let him walk out first.

McCarthy hadn't expected Mrs. Simpson to be so attractive. She was wearing a turtleneck sweater and beige slacks that showed off the rounded firmness of her figure. She wore no makeup, but her skin was clear and pale, and her chestnut hair, although cut short, fell neatly in soft waves. To McCarthy, the woman had an air of cleanliness about her, a kind of brightness that even this terrible predicament could not quite obliterate. But the puffiness beneath her brown eyes and the frown etched on her forehead betrayed sleeplessness and anxiety.

A little boy of five, whom McCarthy had recognized instantly from the picture in the dead man's wallet, leaned against his mother's thigh as she stroked his hair. As they followed her into the house, Farnsworth glanced at him, then looked up at the ceiling, hiding moist eyes. It was the child, McCarthy knew. He complicated everything, melted their resolve. They would have to dig deeper into themselves to find a second line of emotional defense.

She led the boy into another room and turned on the television set, then returned. She was desperately trying to regain her composure.

They were exceedingly gentle, although McCarthy's stumbling hesitance seemed to acknowledge her comprehension even before he stated the raw and disastrous fact. When he did, finally, she did not deny the possibility but sat, stunned.

"It can't be," she whispered.

McCarthy noted the odd similarity of her reaction to that of the Davis man, deliberately suspending his judgment. He was relieved that she had weathered the first shock wave without collapsing. Her demeanor was more of disorientation. The problem here, McCarthy knew, was acceptance. It had to sink in at its own pace, nor could he deny her the futile hope that would soften the shock.

"Without a visual identification, I could be wrong," he said. He wondered if his face reflected his professionalism. The boy came back into the room and scrambled onto his mother's lap. Making no move to return him to the other room, she hugged him and rhythmically rocked her body from side to side. McCarthy exchanged glances with Farnsworth, who flicked away an errant tear. It surprised McCarthy that after all the man had been through in the past week, he still had the capacity for tears.

"It can't be," the woman said. "He went to Paris."

"He didn't, Mrs. Simpson," McCarthy said, admonishing himself. The contradiction was uncalled-for. She would learn the truth soon enough.

"It's been awful," she whispered, continuing to hug the boy, who looked at them curiously.

"You know my daddy?" the boy asked suddenly.

McCarthy smiled and tousled the boy's hair.

"My housekeeper is not here yet." She put the boy aside and stood up, her hands fluttering to her hair. "But I thought he was in Paris." She seemed to have trouble deciding what to do next.

"Have you someone to leave the boy with?" Farnsworth asked.

"The boy?" She was trying desperately to anchor herself in reality. McCarthy was thankful she had not collapsed. Women like that were a slow burn, their reaction delayed. He would have to watch her closely. As she moved around the room of the well-kept, luxurious house, he could not help comparing her with the dead girl. They were both about the same age and both attractive, although the condition of the victim's face did not suggest that image. What did this man Simpson want? He thought of his wife, and the old acid burn came back. What had Billie wanted?

"May I call my husband's partner?" she asked, childlike, as if she were begging permission.

"Of course."

She went out of the room, but the boy stayed. Taking McCarthy's hand, he pulled him toward the window.

"See my snowman?"

"What's his name?" McCarthy asked, thinking of his own children and all that he had missed.

"He looks like Daddy," the boy said.

When the woman came back into the room, her eyes were glistening.

"He wants to speak with you." She hesitated, not having remembered his name. He did not remind her. It didn't matter.

"Sergeant McCarthy, MPD Homicide," he announced into the phone.

"Are you certain?" a man's voice said.

"Yes. But we need the visual identification to wrap it up."

"My God."

"Tough break," McCarthy said. He heard the man's breathing.

"I'll meet you. My wife will take the boy."

McCarthy came back into the room. The woman was staring out the window, holding the boy's hand, looking at the snowman. Her back was straight and stiff, and he knew she was making a valiant effort to hold herself together.

"I'll dress Ben," she whispered. She took the boy out of the room.

"Nothing satisfies people," McCarthy said when she left the room. "The son of a bitch had everything." Again he thought of Billie.

"Some people are hogs," Farnsworth said. "They never have enough."

"Poor lady."

"Poor kid."

They remained silent, ignoring each other until she came back into the room.

"Where are we going, Mommy?" the boy asked when she began to put on his outer clothing.

"For a ride."

"Will we see Daddy?"

The woman turned and looked helplessly at them both, her lips quivering. A sob rattled in her throat, and her eyes filled with tears. Hiding her grief, she busied herself, buckling her quilted coat.

"Are you all right?" McCarthy asked.

After a few moments she nodded, took the boy's hand, and went outside. They opened the rear car door, and the woman and the boy got in.

The traffic was fairly heavy, and the bright sun made the city's white monuments sparkle in the dazzling light. Considering their mission, McCarthy thought, the weather was a cruel irony.

The woman did not speak. She clutched a handkerchief and from time to time blotted her eyes. She made a great effort to hide her grief from the boy, who chattered away. Farnsworth kept up a patter to deflect the boy's interest and keep his mind on other things.

"I've got a little boy," Farnsworth said. "One year old."

"That's not a boy. That's a baby."

At the entrance to the Medical Examiner's office, a couple was waiting. The man gathered Mrs. Simpson in his arms and patted her back. Still she held herself tightly, unwilling to give in to her grief.

"I don't understand," was all she could say.

The man introduced himself to the detectives as Mr. Dale Martin, Mr. Simpson's law partner. He exchanged intense glances with Farnsworth, and after the boy had gone off with Mrs. Martin, he led them through the door of the office.

"Can you do it?" Martin asked. One of his arms was wrapped around Vivien's shoulder.

"I'm not sure," she replied. "I'm not sure about anything."

McCarthy was surprised to find the Davis man still sitting there, listlessly, in a corner of the office. Beside him was a plastic bag, containing his dead wife's possessions. Forbes, sitting nearby, waved two fingers as an acknowledgment that Davis had identified his wife's body. Apparently his shock was so great that he had not found the energy to move. It was a common occurrence, and the police rarely forced people to leave immediately. Forbes was merely "baby-sitting."

They followed one of the technicians into the refrigerator. McCarthy deliberately kept his eyes averted from Mrs. Simpson's face. How many times had he been through this ritual? He had no pity for the man on the tray. Yet he was not indifferent. He detested the man for creating this unnecessary horror.

The group stopped midway in the refrigerator, and the technician opened a drawer. With fluttering lids, Mrs. Simpson forced her eyes downward, her body sagging as a sheet was peeled away from her husband's corpse. Martin caught her, preventing her from hitting the floor. Surprisingly, not a sound issued from her throat. She had not fainted. Recovering somewhat, she nodded recognition.

"It's him," Martin muttered, flashing McCarthy an angry look. They led the woman back into the Medical Examiner's office where she collapsed into a chair. Farnsworth brought her a drink of water in a paper cup.

"Don't think you won't hear from me on this," Martin said angrily.

McCarthy looked at him, confused.

"There will definitely be legal repercussions."

"I'm sure of that," Farnsworth said.

"Malfeasance. Inefficiency. Neglect. Police stupidity."

McCarthy's eyes probed the man's face.

"Police stupidity?"

Martin's lips tightened. He moved away, motioning sharply with his head for the men to follow, obviously not wishing to be overheard by Mrs. Simpson.

"Why did you put her through this? You knew he was down there. You had the passenger list. Why didn't you notify her immediately? She's been through two . . . no, three days of hell. You haven't heard the end of this."

McCarthy looked at Farnsworth, remembering their earlier discussion. See, he thought. Somebody is always fucking things up.

Understanding, Farnsworth returned McCarthy's gaze with raised eyebrows.

"I wouldn't make a big thing about it if I were you."

"Why the hell not? You were cruel, heartless." He looked at Farnsworth. "Your company should be destroyed."

"We didn't know," Farnsworth muttered. If he were more in control of himself, more rested, if he hadn't been through the last week, he might have said it differently. Apparently the ordeal had shortened his fuse.

"How could you not know?" Martin asked. Under other circumstances he, too, might have acted differently.

"Because," Farnsworth said, "he didn't give his right name."

"He didn't? What name did he give?"

"I think you'd better let me—" McCarthy said, not holding back now.

"What's going on here?" Martin asked, looking at them with suspicion and with unmistakable superiority and contempt. McCarthy had seen it often: The Ivy League patrician lording it over the red-necked cop. Like the swelling of a pus-filled boil, he felt the pain of it, felt the absolute necessity of the psychic lancing that had to be done to make the pain go away. Ignoring Martin, he walked over to where Mrs. Simpson sat and put a hand on her shoulder.

"How do you feel?" he whispered gently. When she did not respond, he said, "What I mean is are you able to hear the explanation? You'll be asking for it soon enough." She slowly lifted her head and nodded. He could see that it was already beginning to gnaw at her. Sometimes, he had learned, it was easier to lay on the pain all at once, instead of paying it out with agonizing slowness. Besides, even the most cursory investigation would establish the facts, especially with this son of a bitch Martin wanting to make a federal case out of it.

Returning to Martin, he said politely, "Could you wait in the outer office please, Mr. Martin?"

"I demand—" Martin began.

"You'll have ample opportunity," McCarthy said. Martin fumed.

"I'm her lawyer."

"Of course. That's her prerogative. After we talk to her, she can do what she wishes."

Martin, confused, looked toward Mrs. Simpson.

"It's all right, Dale."

"Are you sure?"

She nodded, and he walked, sulking, into the outer office.

"It will only be a little while," McCarthy called after him with exaggerated politeness, often a weapon of intimidation.

Across the room he could see Davis rising in his chair and lifting the plastic bag. He motioned toward Forbes.

"Wally, please ask Mr. Davis to stay on for a moment," he said with formal seriousness.

Davis turned, confused, frowning at McCarthy.

"I hope you know what you're doing," Farnsworth said.

"They have to be told. The rest is up to them."

"Are you sure?" Farnsworth asked.

"It's their lives. And it affects them both." He paused. "They have a right to know. But only them. What they do with the information is their business."

Farnsworth nodded his consent.

He led them into a small private office and closed the door, leaving Farnsworth to deal with the fuming Martin.

To McCarthy, the man and the woman together looked like bewildered children. He introduced them to each other, and they nodded indifferently. From their reaction he was certain that neither of them had seen the other until that moment. Others might judge it differently, he thought. So much of police work was purely instinctive.

Sliding behind a little metal desk, he directed them to two chairs placed in front of it. He did not like the configuration, but there was little choice. His eyes darted from face to face. Pain and shock had obliterated any signs of alertness. Both of them would have preferred to be alone, invisible.

"Mr. Davis," McCarthy asked, his voice steady, businesslike, "is the name Orson Oscar Simpson familiar to you?"

At the mention of her husband's name, the woman's jaw twitched. Am I really doing the right thing? McCarthy wondered. No, he decided. Only that which is necessary. He knew exactly the pain he was about to inflict.

Davis frowned, looked at the woman, and shook his head negatively.

"Mrs. Simpson, is the name Lily Corsini Davis familiar to you?"

Davis wrinkled his forehead. He turned his head toward the woman.

McCarthy resisted telling them that any loose end could be exploited by insurance investigators, the airlines, law enforcement people, anyone looking for a cause other than an accident. People were known to go to great lengths to knock off a faithless spouse. In his gut, watching these two living victims, he was certain of their innocence, although he was trained to distrust such hunches. He had been wrong before.

"I don't . . ." Mrs. Simpson began, then sighed.

"Lily Corsini Davis," McCarthy repeated, watching the woman struggling to respond. Had there been a tremor of recognition? The woman lifted her head; her eyes drifted to Davis, then to McCarthy as she struggled to comprehend.

"You knew Lily?" Davis asked, clearing his throat.

"Lily?"

"My wife."

Mrs. Simpson frowned with uncertainty, her eyes squinting in confusion.

"Mrs. Davis was also killed in the crash," McCarthy explained gently. They're in the dark, he decided, the old pain rising sharply.

"I'm sorry," the woman said in a barely audible whisper. Sorry for Mrs. Davis or sorry for not knowing, McCarthy wondered. Or just sorry. Sorry for living. If the names were not familiar, then perhaps the faces would be. No, he decided firmly, I will not put them through that. Tell it straight, he directed himself. Like a professional.

"They were traveling on a ticket"—McCarthy cleared his throat—"that purported them to be man and wife."

"Man and wife," Davis repeated, suddenly alert as if struck by a sharp blow. The woman shook her head.

"They were traveling under fictitious names," McCarthy continued, "Mr. and Mrs. Calvin Marlboro." He waited for a response.

"Something is wrong," Davis said, rising to his feet. "Maybe . . ." He drew in his breath in a long pause.

"It wasn't my wife," McCarthy completed the sentence, adding for himself: "Would you like to see the body again?"

Instantly deflated, Davis shook his head and sat down again.

"No mistaking her?" McCarthy asked gently. "There was a great deal of trauma."

The reminder turned Davis dead white. McCarthy wondered if he would faint. Slowly, what little color could be mustered returned to his face.

"It was she," he whispered.

McCarthy turned to the woman. "No doubts, Mrs. Simpson?"

The woman shook her head and tried to speak, then gave up.

"It can't be," Davis said, with little resolve left.

"I have the ticket," McCarthy said. "It could only be them." He watched their reactions. It was a cruel business. "The reason you were not notified earlier," McCarthy said crisply, "was that we didn't know." He directed his next remarks to the man. "Mrs. Davis's body has been here for four days, but she simply could not be identified. It was only when we found her handbag. . . ." Swallowing hard, he felt himself faltering. "Mr. Simpson's body was one of the last to be recovered. Only the names of Mrs. and Mrs. Marlboro were left on the passenger list."

"Are you saying . . ." Davis began. He tried to rise from his chair, then collapsed back into it.

"I'm sorry," McCarthy said.

The woman was shaking her head, as if she were denying the truth to herself alone. He felt compelled to put it to them again.

"You had no knowledge of this, either of you?" He was certain of that, but he pressed on. "No hint, no clue, no knowledge of why . . ."

"There must be some mistake," Davis said with little conviction left. He looked at the woman, whose glance had drifted toward him. "Could have been a company thing," he said, grasping at obviously flimsy possibilities. "A way to save expenses. Something like that. Besides"—the man waved his hand in the air—"it's only a ticket. Just a ticket." McCarthy let the man talk. "You just don't know Lily. It's not like her . . ." He wound down.

"No," the woman said, her hands held tightly in her lap, the knuckles white.

McCarthy allowed them a long silence, letting reality sink in. "There's more," he finally said, sighing. He was about to explode the last shred of hope. He reached into his pocket and brought out the man's key case and the woman's key ring. Both sets of eyes flickered with recognition. And fear. "Actually, there is nothing other than the ticket to connect them to each other. Just these." With a deliberate sense of spectacle, he removed one key from the man's set and one from the woman's. Then he held them together, placing them both between thumb and index finger. "A perfect fit." There was no reaction from either of them, as if the new blow were incapable of stunning them. "More than likely the keys to some place in which . . . I doubt very much that they are the keys to your respective homes."

The man and the woman looked at each other and turned away. I know exactly how you feel, McCarthy thought, feeling a stab in his bowels.

"Look," he said gently, "Everything here is circumstantial. I really don't want to pry into your personal lives. Frankly, I'm just trying to head off any problems for both of you." He looked at the woman. "Your husband's law partner was opening up a can of worms that would be better off left in the can. If he wants to be helpful, let him concentrate on the insurance claims." He checked himself. He had suddenly grown angry. "I'm sorry to be so blunt, but I believe any decisions to carry this further should be left entirely in your hands." I'm on your side, guys, he wanted to say. An ally.

"Sergeant . . ." Mrs. Simpson began. She was obviously calling on all her reserves.

"McCarthy."

"Must I deal with this now?"

"No. There's really nothing to be dealt with. I just felt that anything further must be left to you." Was it really magnanimity on his part? he wondered. Or a desire for others to suffer what he had suffered—to know the horror of betrayal? He stood up. "Have you understood what I have been saying?" he said gratuitously, officially.

The woman nodded.

"I suppose," the man sighed.

"There was just no way to ignore it," McCarthy said quietly, deliberately trying to create an emotional distance.

He replaced one of the keys on the woman's key ring and handed it to the man. Then he replaced the other key in the dead man's leather key case and gave it to the woman.

"That's all I wanted to say," he said.

"That's all?" Davis asked with forced sarcasm.

The woman said nothing.

14

The bright afternoon sun bled through the closed blinds. Fully clothed, Edward lay on his bed, their bed. His eyes were open. He was afraid to close them, afraid of the nightmares he would encounter in his dreams. He had tried to drink, upending the Scotch bottle and swallowing half of the burning liquid in the bottle as quickly as he could. Not being used to it, he had vomited it over the side of the bed.

A police cruiser had returned him to his apartment, along with Lily's possessions in their plastic bags. Almost immediately on entering the apartment, the telephone had rung, and he had picked it up by rote. It was Lily's sister.

"Edward."

He cleared his throat, the sound of which must have passed for acknowledgment. Until then the dread of informing her family had not surfaced in his mind.

"No word?"

No need to soften the blow. Hadn't he seen her remains? "Lily's dead," he said abruptly. He was surprised that the words did not come out with a sob. Blinking, tears fell onto his cheeks, and he wondered who they were for, Lily or himself. His sister-in-law had screamed in response, a primitive female shriek of mourning, he supposed. Looking blankly at the telephone receiver, he waited until the odd sound abated, while tangled thoughts rolled around in his mind. Was the Lily he had seen really Lily? Was the Lily they had talked about really Lily? Could he have been mistaken? Could that policeman be mistaken? He felt compelled to explain.

"She went down in the plane crash last week. I didn't know." He was deliberately evasive. Had he resolved not to tell them the truth, not to tell anyone? The truth? Was there a real truth? Then, suddenly, the screaming ceased, and his sister-in-law's voice was clear and stern.

"How come you didn't know?" she snapped. Her tone was sharp, accusatory. "You said she was going to L.A."

"She must have changed her mind at the last minute."

"How could you not know that? You're her husband."

"I was." He felt foolish, defensive.

"How could a husband not know where his wife was going? How is that possible? What kind of a man are you?"

That fact had been challenged as well. Indeed, he thought, what kind of a man am I? Obviously a stupid one. And worse.

"I didn't know," he said, feeling the full impact of his impotence.

"How am I going to tell Mama?"

"I don't know."

"Lily was her favorite." He heard the familiar hint of sibling rivalry. "You'd better bring her home. She wasn't married Catholic, but she'd better be buried Catholic." A threat was clearly implied, summoning an image of Vinnie, their brother.

"Of course," he said, relieved in a way by the sense of direction being offered. Up to then a paralysis of action had set in. "I'll make arrangements."

"How am I going to tell Mama?"

"I suppose I should." He felt the sheer terror of it.

"No." There was a long pause. "I wish she had never met you. How could you not know where your wife was going?"

He felt a tiny urge toward maliciousness. I'll tell them what she did, he thought. Then he rejected it. Out of shame? he wondered. He could not deny his humiliation. What did it matter? To Lily's family he had always been the enemy. "I'll make the arrangements," he repeated. "What is the name of that church?" Saint something, he thought.

She told him, and he scrawled it on a notepad.

"How am I going to tell Mama?"

"Let Vinnie."

"Vinnie! Vinnie will bust your balls."

He heard the click and shrugged. They've already been, he thought.

Through some miracle of concentration, he managed with the

aid of telephone information to find a funeral parlor near the family home in Baltimore. The man on the phone instructed him on costs and details. Then Edward gave him his sister-in-law's number. He was sure the family had cemetery plots. They had lived in the area for two generations. The man from the funeral parlor asked for a deposit, and he promised to send it immediately. He wanted the whole matter to be disposed of as quickly as possible. He went to his desk, took out their joint checkbook, wrote a check, addressed the envelope, and pasted the stamp on it. All so banal, so ordinary, he thought.

When the telephone rang again, he let it ring until he could not bear the sound. It was the *Washington Post*. They wanted a picture of Lily.

"I don't have one," he lied. He couldn't bear the idea of it in the paper, visualizing it next to—what was his name?—Simpson?

"Surely you have a picture."

"Bug off," he said, slamming down the phone.

He had never experienced this kind of emotion. When each of his parents had died, he had known terrible grief. The loss seemed overwhelming at the time, unbearable. For a while in the Medical Examiner's office, before the sergeant had brought them into that little room and told them about Lily and that man, he had felt a familiar sense of grief, a recognizable and understandable emotion. Now it had become confused with anger, which created other feelings, feelings with no frame of reference.

Yet what the sergeant implied was incredible. A fantasy. An absurd concoction. Perhaps his own hysterical mind had conceived it. He had absolutely no perception of Lily as other than what she was, the loyal, devoted, loving wife. But this new perception, despite a conscious effort to deny it, forced its way into his consciousness. Still, logic challenged memory. Not Lily. How could it be? When the sharp knife of reason had done its work, a single lie blocked his path, one among what was surely many. It loomed, a giant presence, too overwhelming to escape: Lily had embellished the L.A. trip with such a wealth of detail—the design festival, the time the plane would leave, the time of return. He had barely listened. Now it gurgled up at him with the stench of stale lies like a backed-up drain. He had trusted her. He had believed in her. To doubt her then would have been inconceivable.

"You dirty lousy bitch," he muttered aloud, his body stiffening. Then the image of her mutilated face intruded. "God punished you," he cried. "How could you?"

Where was his compassion? he wondered. Forgiveness? So far he had found only anger, bitterness. Humiliation gnawed at him. What had happened to love? When he looked further inward, he found only a heart that raged with hate.

He wondered if there were those among her colleagues who knew: Mr. Parks, Milly Halpern, others? Surely someone had to know. It was one thing for them, the spouses, not to know, but could they have fooled the entire world? He remembered the identical keys. Suddenly he began to cry, losing all control.

"It can't be. It simply cannot be," he moaned.

Stripping away his soiled clothing, he got into the shower and stood under the spray until the hot water had cooled. Still wet and dripping, he stretched out on the couch, soaking the pillows, feeling the chill; he was utterly bereft of self-worth, of dignity. Along with Lily, his own persona had surely died. Finally, he took a Valium and drifted into semiconsciousness. Sometime in the middle of the night he awoke. His skin felt icy. His teeth chattered, but it was not from the physical cold. He had no doubt about its source. He was alone, brutally, cruelly alone. To survive, to be saved, he needed to touch someone, someone who would understand the heart of his anguish. A woman's face, ashen but whole, surfaced in his memory. She would understand.

He had forgotten the man's first name, but a search through the various area directories had triggered his memory. Orson Oscar Simpson. He had no idea what the woman's first name was, nor could he recall her features distinctly, only her pale face. For a brief moment their eyes had met. Had they both seen the similarity in their mutual pain? They had turned away simultaneously. With a shaking finger, he dialed the numbers on his telephone.

"Yes?"

A woman's voice made an urgent effort to respond. He heard her breathing, hesitant, quivering.

"Mrs. Simpson?" he asked tentatively.

"Yes."

"Forgive me. I'm terribly sorry. I'm Edward Davis."

He felt her tension in the long pause. Had she remembered?

"I wasn't sleeping," she said hoarsely.

"I . . ." he began, suddenly forgetting what he might have said. No sense larding it with politeness. "Had you any idea, Mrs. Simpson?"

"Idea?"

"About them."

"Them?"

He felt a flash of anger. "This is Davis. The woman's husband."

"I know."

"Do you understand what I'm saying?"

"Of course."

"I must ask it. Please don't be offended." He swallowed. The bitter taste of phlegm rose in his throat. "Did you really not know?"

There was another long pause, then a sigh. Her breathing seemed troubled.

"How could I know?" she asked, struggling to control her indignation.

"I didn't know either. It came as a complete shock. I'm stunned."

"Only that?"

"Do you believe it?"

"I don't know what to believe. About anything."

He wanted to hear more, to say more, to break the barrier of suspicion. We have common enemies, he wanted to say. Instead he asked: "Have you . . . made arrangements?"

"Please," she began, "is this necessary?"

"I'm sorry. Please don't misunderstand. There is simply no one else to discuss this with."

"Why must it be discussed?"

"I don't know."

He started to drop the receiver into its cradle but then put it to his ear again.

"Mrs. Simpson?"

She did not respond, but she had not broken the connection.

"Maybe some day we can talk about this," he said into the silence. "I don't mean now. Now is not the time." He felt the words racing on under their own power. "It's bothering the hell out of me. The person . . . the woman they referred to, the woman I identified." The memory of her broken face intruded, and he suppressed a sob. "The woman they talked about wasn't her at all." The words choked him finally. "I can see that this is not the time. Look, I live in Georgetown. Edward Davis. If you feel like calling . . . Please forgive me."

He hung up. Was it an irrational act? He had, of course, lost his moorings. Looking toward the window, he searched for dawn breaking. No sign. He got up and looked out, shivering. His teeth continued to chatter. Daybreak would soon arrive gray and gloomy. There seemed to be a hint of more snow in the black sky.

When the telephone rang again, the sound seemed different, ethereal. Lily, he thought, his logic totally disoriented. She's calling to apologize. He picked up the phone.

"All right," Mrs. Simpson said, as if the previous conversation had not ended, "I'm willing to discuss it."

"I'm really grateful."

"I can't imagine why."

"Who else is there?"

"There's something in that," she said gloomily.

"I'm not sure it will do either of us any good."

"We won't know until we do it." Was it sarcasm or aggression in her tone? He wasn't certain.

"Not on the phone. I can't bear the phone," she said.

"I'll meet you anywhere you say."

"What time is it?"

He looked at the digital clock.

"Five-thirty. You mean now?"

"Well, neither of us is sleeping." Now it seemed to be she who was pressing. "And my maid's here for Ben."

"Ben?"

"The boy."

It sounded odd, and he wondered if the "boy" was her child.

"There's an all-night coffee shop on Lee Highway." There was no mistaking her resolve now. She was leading him. "Say . . ." She hesitated. "Where did you say you lived?"

"Georgetown."

"Forty minutes, then."

He made her repeat the location of the coffee shop, then hung up. Compulsion, he decided, was writing its own scenario. It frightened him.

She was wearing jeans and a beige turtleneck sweater, which emphasized the fullness of her breasts. He felt slightly ashamed that such a detail should arrest him at that moment. In his mind she had seemed neutered, like him. Her skin was as white as alabaster, as smooth as polished marble. The air of vulnerability which he had observed about her at the Medical Examiner's office was gone. Instead, a tightness in her pursed lips hinted of resolve. It made him curious. Where had she found the strength?

They sat in a booth at the rear of the coffee shop. A steady stream of customers came in and out, people of the night and early morning. They seemed much different from humans who lived by day, an alien breed.

"I've never been to an all-night anything before," she said after the waitress had poured them coffee, automatically. "I remembered the sign." Her fingers fluttered nervously until she finally steadied them around the coffee cup. "It seemed a logical choice. Only ten minutes from the house."

She looked at him briefly, then turned her eyes away.

"Convenient." He shrugged.

"It's awful. Absolutely awful," she said abruptly. "Like the ground opened up under my feet."

"Our feet, Mrs. Simpson."

She tried to lift her coffee cup, but her hands shook too much. She let it clatter back into the saucer, spilling drops.

"I feel so stupid and foolish," she said, shaking her head. "Even being here is . . . well, bizarre. I can't imagine why I came." She lowered her eyes. "As you said, who else is there?"

"Not another soul, I'm afraid. Just you and me."

"Stuck in the same cell. You'd think we'd want to escape."

"I wish I knew how."

He wondered if she was having regrets about coming.

"Perhaps it wasn't such a good idea," he said.

"As good as any. What will I do back there? Toss and turn. Besides, I'm cried out."

"Me, too."

"I can't believe it's possible for us not to have known," she said. "I just can't grasp that." She looked at him, accusing.

"I swear to you, Mrs. Simpson. It comes as a total shock."

"But she was your wife. How can she have hidden it from you?" She looked into the coffee cup. "Now that's a stupid question. Where was I, you might ask."

"All right. I'll ask it. Where were you? They say a woman can sense those things."

"We'll just have to stop these generalizations," she said irritably.

"I'm sorry," he said. It had started badly. Perhaps this was not really a good idea after all.

"Did it happen before?" she asked, ignoring his apology.

"Did what?"

"Her being, you know, unfaithful."

"She wasn't a whore," he said between clenched teeth, instantly defensive. "What about him?" Was he trying to assign blame?

She shook her head.

"Never?" he asked cautiously.

"Who can say that now? I'll never say never again."

He rubbed his chin, feeling the rough stubble.

"Neither will I," he mumbled facetiously. "Maybe she *was* a whore. She certainly was a liar on a grand scale."

"Both of them were, Mr. Davis. Both of them were." She lifted her cup again. Coffee spills gathered in the saucer, but she managed a sip.

"But how? Why?"

"I don't know. That's why we're here, I suppose."

"Where did she say she was going, for God's sake?"

"To L.A. She's a—she was—a fashion buyer for Woodies. I thought nothing of her traveling. She did it periodically. She was, after all, a responsible executive." The old pride in her surfaced. Recognizing it again, he cursed her in his heart.

"A buyer for Woodies? Where would she have crossed Orson's path? He was a lawyer. Corporations. Lobbying. Far afield."

"They could have met anywhere, I suppose." Then, after a pause, "It doesn't matter now."

"That's what I keep saying to myself. But I can't get it out of my mind. All the speculation. I saw nothing. Nothing. I keep asking myself: Am I so insensitive, so thick and stupid?"

"The pronoun, Mrs. Simpson. Use the plural." It seemed a misplaced stab of humor. "We!"

"What is even worse"—she lowered her voice—"is that I feel more anger than grief."

"I know what you mean."

Her brown eyes inspected him, and he felt drawn to meet them.

"I wish I didn't feel that. I've never felt it before. And I keep saying to myself that a stranger was killed, not my Orson."

He nodded. Nor my Lily.

"I had no reason to assume that we had anything but a good marriage. I can't even envision Orson in this role. At first I thought there must be some other explanation—a dual personality. I'm sure it's possible. But then, in your case . . . Two dual personalities? What are the odds against that?"

"Staggering, I suppose."

"And you?" Their eyes had not drifted. Now his turned away, and he looked at his fingers.

"The same. As you said, I had no reason to assume otherwise. I felt good about our marriage. I didn't pretend to be the greatest husband. I've got faults." He checked himself. His instinct was to be self-effacing, but something held him back. He did not want this woman to see his imperfections, although he was not quite certain why.

"There could be some other explanation." It sounded almost like a wish. "Like a CIA thing, something like that. A secret mission, like on TV." Her eyes widened. "You think I'm crazy?"

"Not crazy."

"Grasping at straws?"

"More like that," he said gently.

"Anything to explain it away, I suppose. To absolve them and us."

"Us?"

He did not wish to pursue that line. Next, they would be blaming themselves.

"We'll never know for sure," he sighed.

"That policeman said the only connection was that key." She

fished out the key case from her pocketbook. Then she opened it and upended the keys. "I don't even know which one it was."

"I left the key ring at the house."

"I've thought a great deal about that key. What did it open? Just another unbearable question to live with. God, I hate thinking about it." She raised her eyes to his and locked them there again. "I hate discussing it."

"I'm sorry."

"So am I. Sorry for everything. You know something?" He felt the intimacy of her tone, and it disturbed him. "I don't think I'll ever be able to trust anyone again," she said. "I don't even trust myself. If I couldn't see what was happening right under my nose, how could I ever again trust my own instincts or judgment?"

Bending low over the table, she began to raise the cup again. Her hands trembled, and she put it down, placing her hands on the table's edge. Edward looked at her fingers. They struck him as being delicate, gentle. He felt an urge to be touched by them, as if somehow they would soothe, assuage pain.

"How long do you suppose it was going on?" she asked.

"I was afraid to ask myself," he murmured.

"A long time? Months? Years?"

Her alabaster skin seemed to whiten as she spoke.

"Are you all right?" he asked, reaching out but not touching her.

"I'll never be all right."

Outside, it was getting light, and more recognizable daytime types, white collar workers, began arriving. Vivien and Edward sat in silence for a long time. Edward felt enervated, emptied of all vitality. Vivien nodded her head as if she were contemplating the oil slick on the surface of her tepid coffee.

"I'm just taking it one day at a time," he said finally, clearing his throat of a sudden hoarseness. "The worst thing will be facing my wife's family. They'll think I murdered Lily. . . ."

"Lily?" She shot him a quick angry glance, as if to repeat the name was somehow an obscenity.

"A bit old-fashioned, naming kids after flowers. Her parents were old-fashioned Italians."

"Corny. Like Orson. His mother is dead, but his sister is still alive." Her throat emitted an odd bubbling sound. "She objects to my decision to cremate Orson, so she won't come to the service."

He searched her face for some sign of irony, but her features were impenetrable.

"She called it a burning."

"It's a perfectly proper way to dispose of the body," he said, as if suddenly compelled to come to her defense.

"Perfectly proper." She looked at him, offering an unmistakable flash of belligerence. Their eyes locked.

In hers he imagined he could see the battle between fury and resignation, a mirror of his own.

"What an odd way to put it," she said. In his heart, he agreed with her choice, sensing it was deliberate. But he did not explore it further, fearing that his own choice for Lily's disposal was somehow an act of cowardice.

"It was all so strange. The way he looked. All pink and healthy. Lying there so quiet and innocent." Her lips pursed.

His last image of Lily intruded suddenly. The upper part of her head was caved in: Retribution? The question posed itself as though it were independent of his will. His stomach lurched, and a chill shot through him. Such ideas were alien and terrible, part of the distorted perceptions of a nightmare.

He looked about him, fixing his sense of place and reality. He was, he told himself, completely awake, living the immediacy of the moment.

"Anyway, that part will be over by tomorrow afternoon." She took a deep breath.

"I'll have to go up to Baltimore and face it with her family. Clannish, emotional Italians. It will be a ghastly experience. In a way they have a point. If I hadn't married her, she'd still be alive."

"I doubt that. Women like that always create some kind of mischief." She checked herself quickly, but it was too late to retrieve.

"Like what?" Incredibly, he was still defending. As he watched her, she seemed to be debating what she might say next. Her tense expression gave away her response. Oddly, he seemed to be girding himself.

"You're not going to deny it. The woman must consent. It's not exactly like rape." Her features distorted in anger.

"And the man? Isn't he supposed to be the pursuer?"

"Orson was not like that," she stammered.

"Takes two to tango," he said. Was she actually trying to affix blame? "Maybe three," he muttered. "Or four."

"Four?"

The idea transformed the issue. Up until then she had seemed poised for combat.

"Us. Something lacking in us," he said. "Something that drove them away from us, toward each other. Maybe we're cold, indifferent, unloving."

He watched her facial muscles go slack.

"I was a devoted, loving, dedicated wife, an old-fashioned hausfrau and mother. I tended the home. I was a good little lamb."

"Who never strayed?"

"Never." She sucked in a gasp of indignation.

"Me, too," he sighed. Suckers, he thought. Unless she lied.

"Maybe we *are* to blame," she said after another long silence. She lifted her hands from the table, clasping her fingers to keep them from trembling.

"Maybe."

"Well, they're not here to explain it." Her voice rose. People in the next booth turned.

"That's for sure," he said bitterly.

"And even if they were . . ." Her lips clamped shut as she fought for control.

"Did you tell anyone?" he asked, surprised at the direction of his thoughts. Public shame was another alien idea. Now, for some reason, it filled him with dread. He could not deny the challenge to his manhood. He thought suddenly of Jan Peters mocking his faithfulness.

"Absolutely not. Never." The vehemence of her tone startled him, but it, too, merely articulated his own reaction. "Not even Dale, my husband's partner. It's not his business. He pressed me. Wanted to sue the airline for withholding the names so long. I said absolutely not. It won't bring Orson back. Thank God. I wouldn't want him." She looked determined. "I told no one. My parents are coming down tomorrow. I usually tell them most things. But not this."

"Do you suppose it will be in the papers? The *Post* called for a picture. I gave them nothing."

"I didn't either." She paused. "I couldn't bear to see it in the papers."

"Do you trust the cop? I mean, not to spread it everywhere. It would make a juicy story."

"I told you, I will never trust anyone again."

"I'll vote yea on that."

"Never."

He nodded, further underlining the resolution. Her fingers unclasped and formed themselves into balled fists. Without realizing, his own had done the same. They seemed to be feeling each other's anger.

"The bottom line is that neither of us knew a damned thing. Nothing."

"Where do you suppose they were going?" She looked at him, her lashes fluttering nervously.

"Does it matter?"

"No, I suppose not."

"Four days, she told me."

"Paris by Concorde and back."

"That's where he said he was going?"

She nodded.

"What lies. What horrible lies." This time his voice rose and a number of customers turned around.

"Maybe we should leave it alone," she said, pushing the coffee cup toward the center of the table. "If we go over and over it like this, it can't be good for us. I have a child to worry about. His child," she added, her eyes narrowing. "You?"

"No children."

He supposed he should be thankful for that. With the thought came another realization. He would not have a living memory to remind him always of her. His stomach tightened. Her betrayal!

"Someday my son will ask me exactly how his daddy died," she said.

"What have you told him?" The question seemed an intrusion.

"That he went to heaven." She flashed an empty smile.

"Heaven. That's a gas."

"When he's old enough he'll find out the truth; then he'll probably blame me for being inadequate."

"So don't tell him. Keep the secret." It struck him that the "secret" had become a kind of bond between them, like two independent witnesses to a murder.

"Maybe. It's too early to think about that," she sighed.

Too early to think about anything, he supposed, confronting the tangle of his own thoughts and emotions.

"Dammit," he said sharply, compelled to describe his state. "My mind is repelled by what I feel."

Her eyes suddenly widened.

"Yes. That's exactly it." She paused and nodded her head. "Yes. Are we supposed to be demolished by grief? I feel nothing like that. Shouldn't we be forgiving, tolerant, understanding? After all, hasn't the punishment fit the crime? Where is our compassion? I don't know about you, but all I feel is . . ." Her voice quivered, and the muscles of her neck worked to hold back hysteria.

"Anger?" he offered.

"More than that. I feel so much . . ."

He waited, sure she would say what he himself felt.

"Hatred," she gasped. "And I hate myself for feeling it. But I just can't help it. They had no right . . ."

"I know," he said gently. He moved one hand and put it over her still-balled fist. "Who the hell but us would understand that?"

She nodded, then removed her hand from his and brushed away a tear.

His mind drifted. Again he thought of the impending ordeal in Baltimore.

"I hope I don't blast it out to my in-laws. They think of Lily like her name—white and pure." A low chuckle rose from his throat.

It was the one weapon against her family that he was holding in reserve. If they pressed him too hard, he would take that arrow from his quiver.

"I hope you will resist that," she said with sudden panic, as though he had taken an oath of secrecy.

"I'll try," he said sincerely, knowing it was not going to be easy.

"It's that other fellow that worries me. Not the cop. The man from the airlines," she said. "Do you think he knows?"

"Probably. I thought about that. I don't think the airlines would let it out deliberately. If he says something, it will probably be later. A cocktail party joke."

"I'll never forgive them for that as well. Making our lives a filthy joke."

"Some joke." He shrugged.

"Mr. and Mrs. Calvin Marlboro."

"Very funny."

"What a mockery it makes of us."

"People will split their sides."

"I couldn't bear it," she said.

"Let's hope we don't have to."

"According to Dale, we'll be getting lots of compensation."

"I hadn't thought about that."

"I have. I won't touch a cent of it. Not a cent of that dirty money." Flush spots suddenly appeared on her cheeks.

"Maybe it's still too early to make that kind of decision," he said cautiously.

"Not for me," she muttered. She seemed to be fading. Her brief animation dissipated. "I'd better go," she said.

She stretched out her arm, and he took her hand, cautiously offering the pressure of common purpose. When she returned it, he clasped harder. Somehow it felt like a ritual, the sealing of a lifelong promise.

"I'm glad we talked," he stammered. "It's as though we're in it together. Like conspirators."

A frown of confusion shadowed her face.

She got up, yet some vague idea was germinating in his mind, and he delayed releasing her.

"Do you suppose . . ."

She waited, standing at the table's edge.

"Suppose we found that place where they . . . where they met. Now it's hanging in limbo, but if we found it, saw it, confirmed it, might it somehow put things in perspective?" He wasn't quite sure what he meant.

"I doubt it," she said. Releasing his hand, she began to move away. Then she stopped. "What would it prove?"

"I don't know. Just a thought." Still, he did not want her to leave.

"Maybe." She shrugged and began to walk away. He rose after her, fishing in his wallet. At the door he caught her attention. As she turned, he thrust a business card in her hand. Then he watched her walk out into the cold gray morning, leaving him feeling empty.

15

At first she was not certain as to why she had come. Going home, she knew. She had come to compare agonies, and she had gone away satisfied. His pain was no less than hers. It was as if they shared a semi-private room in the same hospital. Someone had decided that two people with the same condition would be more comfortable together.

This odd conversation with the husband of her husband's mistress actually raised her spirits. In the car she emitted a trill of ironic laughter. Misery does like company, she thought.

All day she had felt like a participant in a scavenger hunt in which she was the only hunter. Each step presented a strange new obstacle, each of which she felt ill-prepared to confront.

"I'll make all the arrangements, Viv," Dale assured her after he had brought her home from the Medical Examiner's office. Her husband's partner had barely been in her field of vision in the old life. She was already referring to all events before the crash as the old life. Perhaps they had happened to someone else.

With lawyerly tenacity he had persisted in probing her. He was not a fool. Certainly he surmised why the policeman had called them both into his office at the same time. The point was that he did not know for certain. But she had declined to press charges, as he suggested, which surely titillated his already keen curiosity. Also, even if the implication was clear, he would resist, in every way possible, exposing the law firm and its clients to scandal. Even without the stigma of infidelity, it was enough to contemplate how his ordered universe would react to a partner who had gone off secretly without telling either his office or his wife of his destination.

It was not for nothing that Dale Martin had been made managing partner; he was the perfect Ivy League prig down to his old-fashioned garters, which he proudly exhibited on occasion to prove that he was a devotee of the tried and true ways of old money and class, and, therefore, not subject to contemporary fads. In deference to her husband, Vivien had always resisted detesting him.

"He's high Episcopalian," Orson had said once.

"That explains it?"

Now he reminded her of Orson, the Orson she had just learned about, the Orson who had lived behind his facade of lies. The cheating Orson. The real Orson.

"I'm executor of your husband's estate," Dale told her, settling into a chair in her living room. He had poured himself a drink and sat cross-legged, exhibiting preppy navy socks and their striped garters. "I've forgotten the details of the will, but I'll know tomorrow when I look at it again. I wrote it. I'm sure you'll have no immediate financial problems."

She let him go on without comment. It was an area of complete ignorance for her. What did she know about death and its details? Even Orson's body, pink and remarkably healthy looking, hadn't looked dead. Often she had seen him sleeping like that, in just that position, on his back.

"I suspect you'll want to bury him up in Boston. I'm sure there's cemetery space up there. New Englanders usually make provisions. Unless he's made arrangements here. Would you know about that, Viv?"

She shrugged indifferently, although it reminded her that she had to call his sister. She had never been really close with her, a bloodless woman who had always thought of Vivien as beneath her brother in both forebears and intellect. A picture of the woman sprang into her mind. Like Orson, she possessed the same sharp-edged features—handsome in a man, cronish in a woman. The idea of seeing her again made her feel nauseated. Was it at that moment the idea of cremation was confirmed in her mind?

"Would you like us to keep Ben for the night?" Dale asked.

"No," she replied after a moment's thought. She'd call Alice. Her reaction to Orson's sister frightened her now. It had never occurred to her before to actually hate the woman; in fact, she had never really allowed herself to hate anyone. Not until now.

"We never hate," her father had lectured. "We always try to understand." Well, that was one lesson that would need some relearning. She wondered suddenly if she would grow to hate Ben as well because he was a part of Orson. She shrank from the horror of that possibility.

"I think I'd like to be alone now, Dale," she told him, ashamed of her thoughts about her son. It was all right to hate Dale and Orson's sister because they reminded her of Orson, but surely not Ben, not little Ben.

A tiny scratching noise intruded suddenly. Hamster scratching at the door. She had put him out this morning.

"What is that?" Dale asked.

"The dog. He wants to come in."

But she remained seated. Hamster was another reminder of Orson, his gift. Let him stay out, she decided, conscious of this new sense of malicious assertiveness.

Before Dale left he pecked her on the cheek. Her skin twitched where he touched it.

When he had gone, she called her parents. Her mother answered, and she poured out an altered version of the tragedy, exhibiting proper grief.

"I'm so sorry, Viv. Oh, how awful." The woman dissolved in tears.

Her father got on the phone. "Are you all right, darling?" he asked firmly. "And Ben?"

"Well make it, Dad."

"Poor Orson."

"Yes, Dad. Poor Orson." She gritted her teeth in anger. She felt total indifference, and when her father began to probe further, even in his gentle understanding way, she cut him off.

"When you get here, we'll talk about it." She vowed then never to tell them the real story. They would, of course, be appalled. Such things happened only to other people.

Telling Orson's sister was the worst of it.

"I don't believe it," his sister said.

"He was in the wreck all week," Vivien explained. "I just found out this morning."

"How horrible." Control was a Simpson trait, his sister had once told her. "Poor Orson. Oh, how ghastly."

She let his sister gather her wits. She had always been proud and worshipful when it came to Orson.

"I suppose you've made arrangements to bury him near father

in the Simpson plot in Boston. Perhaps we can have a service there as well. I'll notify our cousins—"

"I'm having him cremated," Vivien said abruptly.

"Cremated?" His sister cleared her throat. "The Simpsons don't cremate," she said.

"It's my choice."

"Was it Orson's?"

"He's dead."

She heard her draw in a deep breath.

"I won't come then."

"Suit yourself."

"You can't do this."

"Yes, I can."

His sister began to speak, but Vivien hung up, cutting her off. I'll send you the beloved ashes, she vowed.

16

Orson was cremated the next day. A respectable crowd of colleagues attended, as well as her friend Margo Teeters and her husband, her parents, and others they had met along the way. The service was brief. At her request, very brief. Even Dale was urged by her to keep his remarks short. "It's my wish," she told him, unwilling to explain further. There was a small story in the papers, recounting only that the last survivors of the air crash had been brought up. Names were given. Nothing more.

Wearing a black veil and trying to play the role of the aggrieved widow, she sat appropriately in the front row with her parents. She held a bunched handkerchief in her hand, but it was not moist. The minister's abbreviated eulogy was glowing but inane. Dale offered his own condensed testimonial of Orson's achievements, which seemed utterly ludicrous. Be a good soldier, she begged herself, suffering through the charade, her thoughts running in a different direction. Must she passively accept this violation of her self-respect? She felt degraded, abused. By dying, Orson had escaped her scrutiny. Burning his corpse, while symbolically dramatic, brought little satisfaction. He had no right to leave her without explanation, with all his secrets intact. The Davis fellow had hit upon something. Putting things in perspective, he had called it. Why? How? Where? These had become important questions. She had been violated, betrayed, her illusions shattered. How would she be able to confront the future without knowing these answers? The rest of her life was at stake.

"I must know," she whispered while Dale was speaking.

"What is it, dear?" her mother asked.

"Nothing."

No, she thought, she would not let them have their perfect crime. Everyone left clues.

"What about the ashes?" her father asked as they made their way to the parking lot after the service.

"They'll be along," she lied. Actually, she had made arrangements to have them sent directly to Orson's sister.

Before she got in the car, she tossed her black veil into a trash can.

"I hope I never need this again," she said, placating her parents who had looked at her strangely.

"What a positive attitude," her mother exclaimed, offering a thin smile of reluctant approval.

"Life must go on," her father said.

"Yes," she agreed. Not quite yet, she thought.

Her parents consented to take Ben to Vermont. She did not set any time limits. If only the child were not the living image of his father. To be conscious of such an idea seemed wrong. Her own child! Yet when she had looked at him that morning, Orson's eyes had looked back at her, Orson's once innocent eyes. Now they glared at her with imagined cunning and ridicule. And she had turned away in anger from her own flesh and blood. And Orson's. Her insides seemed to flare up in revolt.

"There are so many details to attend to. I appreciate this, Mom."

"Nonsense. But will you be all right?"

"I'll be fine."

Her parents watched her, unsure, assessing her state of mind. She knew that they suspected something was not quite as it should be. The balance of their relationship was slightly awry. They had probed her in oblique ways. Yet she could not bring herself to lie to them outright. Her explanation had been selective but truthful. No, she had not known he was on that plane. To avoid further probing, she told them that she was simply not ready to talk about it. That, they were willing to accept.

"When you finish those details, will you come up to Vermont?" her mother asked.

"It would be good therapy," her father encouraged.

"We'll see," she answered. But first she had other things to do.

She said good-bye to Ben with fervent kisses and promises that seemed hollow and weak, as if they came from someone other than herself.

"Mommy will come up soon. You just listen to Grandma and Grandpa."

"And will we make another snowman?"

"Of course we will."

She felt her son's beating heart next to her own. A wrenching sob made her tremble, but no tears came. Something inside her was hardening. In her arms, in the living creature that was her child, she again felt Orson's presence. Her grip tightened as she crushed him against her.

"You're hurting me, Mommy," Ben grunted.

She unlocked her elbows and held him at arm's length.

"I would never hurt my baby. Never."

She was protesting to herself, and it frightened her. This is my child, she thought, determined to ward off the horror of this aberrant feeling.

"I love you very much," she said. The words were expelled rather than spoken.

"And I love you, Mommy."

Was hate more powerful than love? She had kneeled to embrace Ben. Now she stood up. Her knees felt weak.

"Come on, Hamster," Ben called. The little dog barked at hearing his name and nuzzled up to Ben.

"You can't bring Hamster, Ben." Her words seemed shockingly stern.

"It's perfectly all right," her mother said.

"I'm sorry. I simply will not add to your burdens."

"But it's no—"

"Please, Mother."

Her mother nodded and turned to Ben. "Your mother is right," she said.

Ben brushed away a tear with the edge of his jacket. She felt like someone had cut her into two distinct parts, each warring with the other.

"He'll keep me company," one part of her said. The other part detested the idea and had other plans for Hamster.

"Now you're sure you're all right, darling?" her father whispered, lingering behind as her mother and Ben got into the car. She let him hug her and kiss her cheek, but she did not answer the question. Sure? she wondered. Would she ever be sure of anything again?

When they had gone she felt an enormous sense of relief, a pleasurable sense of forbidden freedom. She could now search the house in peace, probe the last vestiges of Orson Oscar Simpson, without the strictures of showing a false face to others.

Beginning with the closets, she removed every article of his clothing, carefully going through the pockets for stray notes, signs, clues, anything that might lead her to what, in her mind, had become her prey. She felt the full lust of the predator as she worked with single-minded dedication. Soon there was a giant pile of discarded clothing on the floor of the bedroom. Pickings had been slim as far as pocket contents were concerned. She found nothing to lead her in any direction. He had, obviously, been very cautious.

By late afternoon she had gone through every stitch of Orson's clothing, which she packed into large plastic garbage bags and placed outside the door. After she inspected and discarded every article that could be designated as "his," she would call the Salvation Army and rid herself of them, get them out of her life once and for all. Testing her resolve, she was satisfied that she felt neither a single tremor of conscience nor a bit of remorse.

Working late into the evening, she went through papers, books, checkbooks, packets of cancelled checks, piles of old law briefs. Nowhere, as far as she could ascertain, did she find a single clue to his other life. She pored over old telephone bills and whatever she could find of credit card receipts. When she became satisfied that it had nothing to do with his other life, she flung the paper or article into a plastic bag. She wanted no part of them.

What she was seeking was something tangible, although it was not identified in her mind as anything specific. She believed only that she would know when she found it. When something familiar recalled a feeling of sentiment, she threw it aside, earmarking it for the rubbish heap. With these sentimental objects she was flinging away the old life—the life of hypocrisy, the life in which she was cast as victim. Never again, she vowed.

Somewhere there had to be a clue. At times she clung briefly to the idea that what Orson had done could not possibly be real or true. When such an idea struck, there was an interlude of memory that was difficult to control. Hadn't there been good moments between them? But the sentiment would dissipate quickly.

At the coffee shop Edward Davis had said: "It's like we're in it together. Like conspirators." It seemed to be an indisputable truth. All relationships now seemed conspiratorial. Orson and the Davis woman. Perhaps Dale and Mrs. Sparks. McCarthy and the man from the airlines. Margo conspiring against her husband. She conspiring against her parents. Against Ben. My God! Guilt rose inside her, burning her insides.

Confronting her frustration, she recalled the Davis man again. His image was etched sharply in her mind, his voice was imprinted in her memory. "What lies! What horrible lies!" he had shouted in the coffee shop, another perfect reflection of her anguish. Reflection. He was her mirror now. In him she could see herself, the twisted, tortured image of her abandoned and betrayed self. She needed to confront it again, needed it now.

She rummaged in her pocketbook and found his card, noting for the first time that he was an administrative assistant to a congressman. Also on the card was his home number, which she called. As it rang persistently, she remembered him saying that he was going to bury his wife in Baltimore. When he answered, she was surprised.

"I thought you would be gone," she said without identifying herself. There was not the slightest hesitation in his voice. He had recognized her instantly.

"Tomorrow," he said. "I had her shipped. I couldn't bear to sit around with them. I'll show up at the church at the last possible moment," he explained. "I'm the outsider. Just a gesture. Why not?"

"It's over for me," she said. "He was cremated today."

"So it's behind you," he said with an air of sympathy.

"You think so?"

"Not really. It'll never be behind us."

"Can we talk?" she asked, not bothering to hide her urgency.

"Of course. Same place?"

"No."

"Then where?"

"Someplace not public. But not here." She looked around the house. "Your place?"

There was a brief pause. "It's an absolute horror. I'm a terrible housekeeper."

"You should see mine." She looked about her, surveying the wreckage from her search.

She wrote down the directions to his place, then brushed back her hair and washed her face. Earlier she had let Hamster out again. Vaguely, she remembered, he had scratched on the door. She put out his dog food. Orson's gift. Even her relationship with Hamster would never be the same again. She tried to chuckle away the idea but failed to savor the humor of it.

She drove quickly over the Key Bridge. At that hour there was hardly any traffic, and she arrived in a surprisingly short time.

He opened the door, tired and disheveled, more ravaged than he had looked at their meeting in the coffee shop. She could see that he had made a halfhearted effort to tidy up but had not been completely successful.

"I told you, it's a shithouse. Lily was as neat as a pin."

Towels, articles of clothing, empty pizza boxes were strewn about. Pictures were awry, pillows mashed. Crumbs were everywhere. A hint of pine-scented deodorizer seemed incongruous in the disjointed atmosphere. In his haste he had probably oversprayed the room.

He was wearing jeans, a torn sweater, down-at-the-heel loafers, and no socks. On his haggard face was a day's growth of beard. Her inspection lingered a trifle too long, making him uncomfortable.

"I just sat here all day," he said, stroking his face, clearing a place on a chair thick with cast-off shirts and socks. "Tomorrow I'll drive up to Baltimore. It's going to be awful."

She removed her coat and sat down. "Mine was surprisingly routine. A crackling fire. Over and done with." She patted her knee. Then, standing abruptly, she walked to the window, parted the curtains with her fingers, and looked out over the darkened city. She felt him watching her. To tell him why she had come she had to turn and face him. He looked forlorn.

"I want to know what really went on between them."

"You do? Isn't that masochistic?" His change in attitude surprised her.

"Why give it a name? I just have to know."

He locked his fingers together and rubbed the palm of one with the thumb of the other.

"I've spent the day trying to reject the idea. But it's all I could think about." His eyes swept the room. "As you can see, I'm not coping very well."

"I think that if we really found more—the truth—it would help us cope with the future. Maybe find out what went wrong with both of us. Why they did it." Was it herself talking?

"You do really want to know?"

She nodded.

"I have that need. Yes." Was it the real reason? Catching her reflection in a wall mirror, she saw an image of determination: jaw jutting upward, eyes narrowed with intensity, and head held high. Who was this creature? she wondered, turning again to face him. He had sagged onto the couch.

"I'd rather forget it," he muttered. He looked up at her like a helpless puppy. "But I can't."

"You see?"

"What's the point?" He shook his head. A burst of mocking laughter hissed out of his throat. "It's like asking someone: How are you? And he tells you the absolute truth. Who wants to know?"

"I want to know. I spent eight years with a man I believed in, someone to whom I was committed for a lifetime, the father of my son. That man betrayed me, and I want to know why."

"No, you don't," Davis said. "You want to know how. You'll never find out why. My dilemma is more of a who. Who the hell was Lily? The person I knew and loved and married and lived with? Or the broken woman on the tray? That's my problem. If I couldn't recognize the person with whom I've had what I thought was the closest possible relationship, then how can I ever judge anything again?"

He appeared surprised at his own outburst. A flush appeared on his cheeks, little round dabs of red that gave his face a doll's look. A shock of hair fell over his eyes, and she resisted the urge to set it right. Yet she could not deny that their common predicament drew them together, nor deny that in his presence she felt attractive again.

"May I call you . . ." She hesitated, having forgotten his first name.

"Edward. Sure, why not?"

She found herself being deliberately ingratiating. Of course, she told herself, she needed his help. "And I'm Vivien."

"Viv."

"Okay with me. Any way will do. I'm still the same person, not like them. . . ." If they were sharing these intimacies, she reasoned, exchanging first names would make them less like strangers.

"All right, Viv, but I'm still sorry. I admit I might see the point of knowing, but they're both gone and they haven't left us much to investigate."

"We have these keys," she said, watching him react. "All we need is an address."

"And then?"

"We use the keys . . ." She hadn't speculated that far ahead. At that point the search seemed an end in itself.

"Pandora's box," he muttered. "God, I don't even want to think about it."

She felt a flash of impatience with his reluctance.

"I don't want to force you to do anything," she said testily.

"It's just that it's too much to think about at the moment."

"You did call me first."

"That may have been stupid. Sometimes when you've been hit in the gut like this, you do strange things." He stood up and came toward her. "Look. I'm sorry. I hadn't intended for this to go beyond our meeting. I just want to forget, to wipe it all out of my mind."

"I have that same hope."

"Then why . . ."

"Dammit," she cried. "It was you who put the idea in my mind. Last night as I left. You said finding out might . . . might put things in perspective."

"It was just an idea that popped into my mind. . . . I can't explain it."

She had, she remembered, felt the unmistakable magnetism of

his urgency and perhaps something else that she could not yet define. Whatever it was, it had lingered and had found ready tinder within her.

"Then you didn't mean it?" she challenged.

"I did," he shot back vehemently. "I did mean it at that time. Then I thought about it. Maybe we should let go now." He paused, obviously confused and uncertain. "Why dwell on it? I have my job. It's very demanding. I just want to clear my mind of it and get back to work. I'm willing to accept the facts. Over and done with. Lily was unfaithful. She lied and cheated. The hell with it."

She saw his anguish. His eyes smoldered with pain and confusion.

"I just don't want to have to relive it."

"You think you can just be reborn again? Without memory?"

"I'd like to try."

"Time won't cure it," she said. "It will always be there."

"We'll see." Despite his outward resolve, he seemed somehow tentative and unsure.

"So you're saying you won't help," she said regretfully.

"I don't know how I can."

"By pooling resources. Finding out."

She resented his planting the idea and then abandoning it. It seemed pointless to argue. She stood up and put on her coat. He had sat down again and seemed lost in thought.

"Even if you won't help, I'm still going ahead. Sooner or later I'll find what I'm looking for."

When he didn't answer, she shrugged and let herself out. In the end you only have yourself, she thought bitterly, trying to force him out of her mind. Unfortunately, like the legacy of Orson, it was taking on a power of its own.

17

Edward sat on the jump seat of the lead limousine. Ahead was the hearse, polished to a bright sheen, carrying Lily's body. A long line of cars followed, all of which contained longtime friends and acquaintances of the Corsini family.

It had not surprised him to see the church completely filled. The Corsini family had deep roots in this part of Baltimore. From a pushcart, Lily's great-grandfather had founded Corsini Produce, a wholesale firm that supplied fruits and vegetables to supermarkets.

Lily's brother Vinnie, a burly, crude bull of a man, ran the business that supported various brothers-in-law, cousins, nieces, nephews, and the sons and daughters of old family friends. Only a handful of Corsini offspring ever left the fold, geographically. Lily was one of them. They never forgave Edward for that. It hardly mattered that he met her after she had left home. They always felt that her sojourn in Washington was only temporary. So they were right after all, he thought.

How he had once envied them their closeness! A fortress, he had called them. Compared to his blood relations, they were a kind of miracle. A long time ago he had had an older brother, Harold, who died in a car crash. All he had left now was a maiden aunt who lived in Seattle, from whom he received a Christmas card once a year.

Vinnie sat in the center of the back seat between his mother and his sister Rose. Beside Edward on the other jump seat was Anna, sniffling, in deep mourning. In the church he had sat beside Lily's mother, barely coherent with grief; her face was hidden behind a black veil, and her arthritic fingers were entwined with rosary beads. Deepening the grief was the fact that Lily had been the baby of the family.

As much as he had prepared himself for the icy reception, it was difficult to endure. He was the ultimate alien, and he felt it.

"You didn't know where she was?" Vinnie had barked at him, refusing to accept his proffered hand. Jowly, chunky, with thick curly hair tumbling over a low forehead, Vinnie's eyes glowed with menacing hatred. "You fuck."

Vinnie's reaction set the tone for the rest of them, imbuing the family with a Mafiosa mentality. Once he had chuckled at the reference. Now his thoughts about it turned morbid. He wondered if they would seek revenge on him for Lily's death.

During the service he perspired profusely. His ears felt stuffed, and he could not understand the priest's eulogy. It was, he decided, the biggest trial of his life. Worse than the death of his brother Harold, worse than the death of each of his parents. In those instances there was no secret to keep, nothing to hold back, nothing for him to test other than the endurance of his own grief. Hell, he thought, he had seen so much of death, it had become nothing more than a natural phenomenon. What he faced now was unnatural. In this company, Lily had been raised to sainthood, and he had become the devil incarnate.

They had let him sit in the lead car for appearance's sake; they had also put him in the front row beside his mother-in-law, who had not even nodded in his direction. Ignore this, he begged himself, and keep your cool. Say nothing. Leave them with their illusions.

"The priest said a nice Mass," Rose whispered, dabbing her eyes.

"Didn't have to be," Vinnie said.

"Leave it alone, Vinnie," Anna said with a sidelong glance at Edward.

"How can I leave it alone? Look at what he did to Mama."

"It wasn't his fault," Anna pleaded.

"Whose then?" Vinnie said. "A man who doesn't know where his wife is is a scumbag. He has a wife, he takes care of her."

"You couldn't expect anything better," Rose said. Of all the clan she had always been the most vehement about him. Once he had asked her, "Why don't you like me?" And she had answered, "You smell funny." Lily had said Rose had a mean streak.

"If he didn't work for that prick congressman, she would have come back to Baltimore. We could have fixed her up good."

I love them, but I can't stand them, Lily had told him. On his part he wished that they had loved him. Now he suspected they could be right about him. Maybe he had not loved Lily enough. If he had, wouldn't he be forgiving in his heart? Instead, he felt only anger, humiliation, and hatred.

"What are you giving him a hard time for, Vinnie?" Anna asked when Vinnie continued his diatribe in the car as if Edward were invisible. "Not like us. Look at Mama," Rose said.

Edward said nothing. It was important to hold everything in, to control himself. He might drop the kind of information that they would take as vindictiveness and lies. The image of his mutilated body thrown into an open grave floated through his mind, and he shivered with fear. He wished he could cry, show them the kind of grief they needed to see. He couldn't.

"You marry outside," Vinnie hissed, "you get this. My kids marry outside, I'll cut their hearts out. He didn't even become a Catholic. From the beginning no priest blessed them. He completely turned her around."

He was stoking his anger, and Edward expected a blow to land at the back of his head at any moment. If Vinnie touched him, he vowed, he would spit it out at them: Your sister was a cunt, a whore. He would tell them the truth.

"Lucky they didn't have kids," Vinnie said as the cortege drove through the gates of the cemetery.

He stood shivering beside the open grave as they lowered Lily's coffin into the ground, accompanied by the loud wailing of the women. That can't be Lily in there, he told himself, remembering the sight of her broken face. He had been the only one of the crowd to see it. Where had the real Lily gone? he wondered. For a fleeting moment he recalled the words of Mrs. Simpson. Viv. Couldn't be the Orson I knew, she had said. She had had his body burned into ashes, dismissed. Lily was being put underground. Memorialized. Boxed for a slower disintegration. They would bring flowers on her birthday. As he watched the graveside service, he slipped off his marriage ring. When it came time to fling handfuls of dirt into the open grave, he mixed his with the marriage ring and heaved, imagining he could hear the ping on her metal casket.

They got back into the car, and the cars broke ranks as the procession headed home. Life, after all, went on. On a residential street not far from the cemetery, Vinnie asked the driver to stop.

"You can get out now, scumbag," he shouted.

"Vinnie," Anna protested. Mrs. Corsini paid little attention. She rested her head against the side of the car, lost in grief for her dead baby.

"It's all right," Edward whispered. "I understand."

"You understand shit," Vinnie said.

"Let him go," Rose said.

"Come on, Vinnie," Anna pleaded.

"I don't want to see any more of him. As far as I'm concerned, he killed Lily."

"Now that is stupid, really stupid," Anna shouted between convulsive sobs. She started to open the door on her side. "He goes, I go."

Edward turned to her. "It's all right, Anna," he said, opening the door. He put one leg out, then turned to Vinnie. He wanted to say it, but instead he said, "I loved her, the girl I married, your sister. I loved her once. I . . ." He felt the words jumble in his mind, then lose their meaning.

"You are a bastard, Vinnie," Anna cried, but she did not get out.

Panicked, fearful that he might blurt it out, Edward slammed the door shut and ran from the car, darting into a drugstore. He heard the car drive off.

"Can I help you?" the clerk asked from behind the counter.

He shook his head. No one can help me, he thought. Except . . . the image of Vivien surfaced.

He went into the phone booth and called Virginia information, got Vivien's number, and dialed. Her voice sounded familiar, warming after the frosty reception of the day.

"I've thought about what you said, what you wanted to do," he stammered. "Maybe it does make sense."

"It was your idea."

"All I could think of," he said, grateful for her warm response, for her being there at the other end of the connection.

"It's like"—he paused, wanting to express the way he felt—"being alone on a mountain."

"Something like that," she agreed. He could sense her caution.

"She's buried," he blurted. "I'm calling from Baltimore."

"Was it what you expected?"

"Worse," he said. "You can't imagine."

He wanted to tell her more. Who else could possibly understand?

"I'll be back in a few hours. We could meet at Nathan's. Say seven o'clock?" It was a restaurant in Georgetown. The idea sounded ludicrous. Was it to be a kind of celebration?

"I'll be there," Vivien said. She hung up.

"Thank you," he whispered into the dead mouthpiece.

18

They sat at a table in the rear. It was a small restaurant, and business was slow.

"Do you feel funny about this?" he asked. He had ordered duck à l'orange, and she had ordered broiled rockfish. The waiter poured out cold Chablis from a carafe.

"It's fine," he said, tasting it. He repeated the question.

"Funny?"

"I mean inappropriate."

"No. I don't feel inappropriate."

He sipped the wine. It felt tart on his tongue but smooth going down. In the soft light he noted the angles of her face—deepset eyes that peered over high cheekbones. Her nostrils flared, making her nose seem flatter from a frontal view. Her lips were full with a wide angel's bow, which she had darkened with lipstick, giving her a different appearance than before. More confident, perhaps. He wasn't sure.

Her small, pale, tapered fingers played with the stem of her wineglass. Although he had observed them yesterday, he was surprised that her hands were so small. Lily's hands were long and thin, the fingers delicate but bony, the wrists thin with a large nob rising on the outside.

"I'm glad that's over," he said, pulling his gaze away from her, looking instead into the bowl of the wineglass. "Her brother accused me of being Lily's killer."

"Nice people."

"Just sick at heart," he said gently, although it belied what he really felt. They had been cruel. He told her other details about the funeral.

"I wanted to look grief-stricken," he said. "I guess I wasn't as good an actor as I thought."

"I know what you mean."

He felt no compulsion to press the point. Instead, he fished in his pocket and brought out the key.

"I brought it," he said, holding it up. Her eyes widened as she looked at it.

"Now we need to find the lock. I checked a locksmith. If it's a Medeco, it's registered and numbered. Ours is a Yale. Very common."

Ours. The possessive pronoun was disconcerting. But she did not correct herself, and he let it pass.

"I tore the house apart looking for an address. I didn't even know what to look for." She took a deep drink of the wine. "I tossed out everything that belonged to Orson, the physical things. I kept the pictures, though. They're for Ben. Mementoes of a father. Just for him." Her eyes glazed, as if masking some inner anguish. After a moment they cleared.

"I haven't yet been able to summon the courage to go through her things."

"But you must," she said. "Somewhere there is a clue. Somewhere . . ."

Her entreaty had not lost any of its urgency.

"Yes. I'll try tonight."

He had deliberately avoided opening her closets, looking through her drawers, touching her makeup and toiletries. Too painful? Too overwhelming? He was not sure.

"If you'd like, I'll help," she said haltingly, lowering her eyes.

"It didn't bother you . . . to go through his things?"

She looked up at him.

"It bothered me not to find what I was looking for."

"You didn't feel . . ." He groped for the word. "Funny?"

"I felt like a searcher. Nothing more."

"His things . . ." Again he hesitated. Was the image he sought sentimental or unclean?

Her eyes narrowed as she inspected him. No mistaking her purpose, he thought. She knew what she wanted.

"I told you, Edward." Her tongue lingered over his name. "You don't have to go along."

"But I want to," he said quickly. Her eyelids flickered, and she turned away. "I'm really committed," he said. "It was my idea, remember?"

"I remember."

He had used the word committed, and he was, he told himself, but he was frankly frightened by what it suggested. Commitment carried the implication of entanglement. He felt sticky-handed, caught in an increasingly intricate web; he wondered who was spinning the strands. To mask his bewilderment he poured more wine into their glasses. Lifting his, his hand shook.

"Look at me," he said. "That damned funeral. It unnerved me." He felt compelled suddenly to dredge up his reactions as though she had been a lifelong friend.

"When Vinnie, Lily's brother, accused me of being her killer, I half-believed it, as if something I did flung her into the arms of another man." Looking up, their eyes met.

"That's what they want. For us to feel guilty."

Us! There it was again. This time it referred to him. Was she confusing him with Orson?

"For a moment I actually did feel that way."

"That's why we've got to find the holy grail," she whispered.

The waiter came with their food. They ate little and without relish. Silent for a long while, they occasionally gazed at each other warily, their eyes locking momentarily.

"Why?" he asked boldly. "He didn't seem the least bit short-changed." His gaze washed over her face briefly, then lowered. Her body suggested a completeness Lily's had lacked.

"I could ask you the same question," she said gently, showing some embarrassment.

He felt a hot blush rise on his cheeks.

"I'm no bargain," he muttered. He was not being modest or self-effacing; after all, his self-esteem had taken a terrible blow. "I've always been a realist about myself. Actually, I felt lucky to have her. Some luck." He sighed.

"Margo"—she showed good teeth in a half-smile—"a friend of mine—only the other day at lunch she said I was dull."

"Some friend."

"Actually, I agreed with her. Maybe that was it. Maybe Orson did find me dull."

"Well, it's not apparent to me."

"Now you're being kind."

"What's wrong with kindness?"

It worried him that she might think he was patronizing her, a perception that he felt needed correcting.

"I've often thought I was too, well, self-absorbed," he said. "Maybe it made me unexciting. Not to myself, mind you. To her. We were so busy, so involved in work, in its demands. Often I would get these twinges, a kind of guilt, as if I were being neglectful." He grew thoughtful for a moment. "But she was busy, too. We both had careers. She was doing very well."

"I was just a housewife and mother, the lowest form of womanhood in today's world . . . for my generation. The keeper of the nest." She sighed. "Maybe *Cosmo* is right."

"Talk about broken egos."

"I'm sorry," she said, lost in her own thoughts. "The fact is, I used to defend the concept. You know, a growing family needs a woman in the home. Like my mom. The rock." She shrugged. "I deluded myself. A rock is inanimate, stationary, immobile." She released a low, joyless chuckle. "While he was a rolling stone."

"That's all beside the point." He hadn't meant it to be a dismissal of her point, and before she could respond, he continued: "What I mean is that however we define ourselves, or them, is irrelevant. The fact is that they concocted a modus operandi for deliberately, maliciously, and systematically betraying us . . . as though they were moles in some crazy intelligence setup, pretending to be other people. Right under our noses." Feelings of anger and humiliation rose again, stirring rage. "How did they get away with it?"

"And why didn't we see it? Are we so . . . so thickheaded and unperceptive? So blind? How could we not know?" She tapped her forehead with her knuckles. "It pulls the rug out from under all our perceptions about ourselves, about who we are, what we see, how we feel." She leaned over the table, drawing herself closer until he actually felt her proximity, as if she had taken possession of the space around him.

"Two sides of the same coin," he said.

"Unless we know about them, how can we know about us?"

They exchanged glances of silent confirmation, and he felt the stirrings of—was it alliance, camaraderie?

"At least we've got a purpose, a point of view and"—he felt a sudden wave of embarrassment—"a team effort," he said stupidly. She nodded.

"Although finding the place where they met will be like looking for a needle in a haystack," he said.

"At least we have a starting point. That's something."

"It has to tell us something. Provide some sort of clue."

"More than I learned from investigating my own home. It told me nothing, as if that other life didn't exist."

"They were crafty bastards."

"That's the way we'll have to be ourselves. Think like them. Get into their heads."

"But we didn't know them," he said. "As we have discovered." His mind was beginning to lock into the problem. "We'll have to make assumptions about them. Re-create them. Come up with theories."

"All right. Toss one out."

He watched her as she stroked her chin and sucked briefly on her lower lip. The waiter came and took away their plates. They hadn't eaten much.

"Not good?" the waiter asked.

"Us. Not the food," Edward said. The waiter shrugged. "Not that we're not good," he said foolishly, looking at her. "We're not hungry."

"We're good." She nodded, and he saw her nostrils flare.

"Let's hold on to that."

"Damned straight," he agreed, feeling the strength of her support. He could tell she was feeling the strength of his.

"Let's start with this theory: simple boredom. They were bored with us, for whatever reasons," Vivien began.

"But that implies we were a party to it."

"Maybe we were."

"Can anyone be responsible for another person's boredom? Were we supposed to be entertainers?"

"Maybe."

"Perhaps Orson wasn't even conscious of his boredom." She looked at him. "I can only re-create him from previous observations. His life had a certain sameness—the way he dressed, the way he spoke and acted. He was a very controlled man. Almost rigid. Our lives together were on a track. Tranquil. I thought he wanted it that way."

"A fair assumption," Edward said.

"Before Ben came, things were different."

"How so?"

"We had only each other to think about." She thought for a moment. "No. I had only him to think about. He had his work."

"What kind of a man was he?" Edward asked, knowing the question was impossible to answer, especially now.

She stared into space, looking at the ceiling, a gesture of her concentration. He, too, had a special gesture. He looked at his fingernails, palms up, joints of four fingers bent. When Lily mentioned it, he realized that it was a good excuse not to confront a person's eyes. Finding the memory in the ceiling, her eyes drifted downward.

"He was interested in moral issues. The right and wrong of things. It bothered him sometimes to take cases just for money. I liked that in him. It reminded me of my father."

"So there you were, living with a moral man." He had not intended the heavy sarcasm, but when it emerged, he felt good about it. Damned hypocrite, he thought, remembering Lily who detested the mask of politics. "Holmes is full of shit," she had told him more than once.

"He wallowed in integrity," Vivien continued. "I liked that, too. It gave our relationship a cerebral quality. I was always proud of Orson's intelligence. He graduated magna cum laude from Harvard. I was impressed by that. I also liked the way he spoke about things; he was articulate, balanced, never emotional." She tapped the table, then took another sip of her wine. "I was always afraid I would marry a man that wasn't smart. Not that I'm an intellectual or anything like that, but I liked it in him."

As she talked he tried to imagine their relationship, forming his own picture. Orson was a clever bastard, shrewd, a bamboozling Ivy League son of a bitch. He knew the type: superior, arrogant, self-confident. He thought for a moment. Was he jumping to conclusions? Hell, he hated the bastard for his own reasons and dreaded the moment when the focus would shift to himself and Lily.

"We bought this beautiful house in McLean," Vivien continued. "I spent lots of time putting it together just right. He wasn't overly interested in decorating, but I knew he liked the setting. He was very conservative. The house had a New England feel. He was such a reticent man. I assumed he loved it, loved our life, loved his work. A happy man. He seemed like a happy man. Shows you how much insight I have."

"You say he was reticent. Do you mean shy?"

"Oh, he was very shy. I was always the one that had to break the ice with people."

"That would be Lily," he murmured. A frown indicated her confusion. "That could be how they met," he explained. "She could have been the aggressor. I mean in the initial introduction. That's the way she met me." He did not want to tell her the story of their meeting. It seemed so prosaic. They had shared a cab going down Sixteenth Street on a rainy day. He would never have started the conversation. "It was one of the things I admired most about her. She wasn't afraid. She was easy with people. It came from that big Italian family, I suppose. Everybody used their mouths at once."

"So you think she made the first move?"

"From what you told me about him, I'd have to say yes."

"But where? They were from different circles. Wasn't she in fashion?"

"At Woodies. She was a buyer of better dresses."

"He wasn't remotely interested in fashion. I could have worn a burlap sack for all he would notice. And he never went shopping, except for his own clothes. Brooks Brothers."

"Random selection then—a train, a bus, a plane. Something like that. Even a cocktail party."

"Orson hated cocktail parties, although he often went for his business. He detested them. He never used trains or buses."

"Lily went mostly to fashion shows and retail cocktail parties."

"Far afield for Orson."

His mind was racing now.

"All right, a plane. Lily was always shuttling up to New York."

"So was Orson."

"Score one," Edward said. "They sat next to each other on a plane. She probably asked him for half his newspaper. Then they spoke."

"She did this before, then?"

"Spoke to people? Strangers? Yes. I told you."

Her tone had been accusatory.

"Picked up men, I mean," Vivien said.

He was irritated, oddly defensive, and protective. He watched Vivien's face; she seemed pugnacious.

"I hope you're not implying that Orson was an innocent victim of a predator. I said Lily was friendly, open. I can't conceive of her picking up men, as you put it. She wasn't promiscuous."

"Are you sure?"

"Some things you know about people instinctively."

He began to perspire, and moisture appeared on his upper lip. He had to blot it with the napkin. He wished he could retract his last remark about instinct. It had struck a false note. If his instincts had been accurate, he would have known what was happening. He felt compelled to explain himself.

"It would be out of character," he said, clearing his throat. "She liked people. She liked to find out about them." He wanted to say that she wasn't overly sexual. She liked to be cuddled and hugged, but the sex part had always seemed obligatory. In college, she told him, she had gone steady with a guy who was her first. Maybe there were others in her single days. Except for the first one, they never discussed it, as if the subject were a little embarrassing for both of them. It seemed so intimate, even now. Especially now. He realized he was editing, but he could not bring himself to be more explicit.

"So you think they met on a plane?" Vivien said, nodding. "Now there's a powerful irony."

"Live by the sword, die by the sword," he blurted. The remark made him feel strange, as if he could not quite reconcile the idea of Lily's death with this revelation. "Fits with random selection."

"Also a sop to us. It means they weren't actively seeking."

"Not consciously," he corrected. "They had to be throwing out vibrations."

"Let's accept it, then," she said testily. Her discomfort was obvious, and she lengthened the physical distance between them.

He was aware of it instantly. "Maybe we should get out of here," he said.

The restaurant was crowded now, spoiling the intimacy.

"I'm ready," she said, getting up.

"We'll go to my place." The suggestion had a connotation he had not meant. "You said you'd help go through her things."

"Yes, and I will."

He paid the check and helped her on with her coat. As she struggled into it, he caught the scent of her, savoring it. In the process he had also felt her shoulders and the weight of her as she leaned against him inadvertently. It surprised him how sensitive he had become to her physical proximity.

They walked back to his apartment. The streets were slick from a light drizzle. It was still quite cold, and vapor poured from their mouths. He turned up the collar of his coat and nestled his chin against the fur lining. There were still pockets of ice and snow on the ground, and she slipped an arm under one of his for balance. He said nothing, although he was intensely aware of her.

19

He emptied the contents of her drawers and scanned papers, mostly paycheck stubs and tear sheets from *Vogue* and *Harper's Bazaar*. He saw the large checkbook of their joint account. When he found the time he did the balancing, but mostly he relied on her. He thumbed through the stubs. There were other items: her passport, stationery, pencils, cast-off bits of string, broken sunglasses, bric-a-brac of a past life. He felt no sentiment. They were merely things, inanimate, now worthless.

Vivien looked through Lily's bedroom closet.

"Nothing of consequence in the pockets. Just the usual female things." She grew contemplative. "She had a terrific wardrobe. Size eight."

"She got the clothes at a discount."

"So she was quite good-looking," Vivien mused vaguely.

He pointed to her passport.

"See for yourself."

She picked it up and studied it.

"A dark beauty."

"You can't really tell from that picture. She had the family nose, which you can't see from that full view. Aquiline, I think you're supposed to call it. But on her it looked good. Went with her eyes." Still proud, he thought, baffled.

Vivien studied the picture for a long time, then put the passport down, stole a glance at herself in the mirror, shifted, posed for a side view.

"Opposites. Maybe that was it," she said.

Vivien was fairer, taller, larger-boned, with a bigger bosom. In the mirror she saw him inspecting her and flushed. He came and stood beside her, offering the physical comparison.

"Orson was six foot three," she said to his reflection.

"Beat me by five inches. Probably in better shape, too." He

patted his paunch, which had gone down in the past few days. "I used to be thinner."

"Orson was a jogger. Burned the calories off. He also watched himself at the table. More than I did."

So he was taller and surely better looking, certainly smarter.

"Sounds like I wasn't much competition."

"Nor I."

"You were different. She was more . . ."

"Delicate."

"She was quite strong. With lots of energy. I'd sag first."

"Me, too. I used to blame it on Ben. He really wore me out. Maybe that was part of it."

He did not answer, not wanting to go down that road again, but he continued to look at her in the mirror. She had a full-bodied, substantial attractiveness, a type that normally did not interest him. His gaze seemed to make her uncomfortable, and she turned away.

"I don't think I found anything," he said. It had felt eerie, both of them going through Lily's things, a violation of her privacy. Couldn't be helped, he thought. She had brought it on herself.

"There just has to be something," Vivien said, stroking her chin and looking about the room.

"There probably is. We just don't know what to look for. If they were being secretive and clever, the last thing they would leave lying around would be an address." Suddenly, Vivien's attention was arrested by a little digital clock that read out the time in green characters. She was totally lost in thought, and he watched her silently, noting the intensity of her absorption.

"Time," she said finally, as she swung to face him. "They had to allocate time"—the muscles in her neck pumped as she swallowed with difficulty, gulping the words—"for each other."

A flash of irritation intruded. The anger flared again. He pondered the disguises Lily had had to assume, the concoction of a false identity, false words. Lies! The growing rage jogged his memory. His mind reached back for clues in their routine, in their habits, and sorted through the confusion of old images. He knew he was searching for abrupt changes, uncommon actions, strange moments. An affair required physical interaction. When did they meet? How?

Edward always left the house early, before seven. It gave him a chance to get into the office and plan the day. It had become a habit. Lily was always still in bed, fogged with sleep. He had even developed a superstition about it, as if the day might be a disaster if he had not kissed her. Since she was asleep, she never reacted, and he had been very gentle, not wanting to wake her. How thoughtful, he mocked himself.

Lily's working day began, when she wasn't traveling, at ten. She often told him how frenetic her day was. The retail business—it sucked you in. He worked late most nights. She did not. She, therefore, had ample opportunity to meet Orson while Edward worked. Except that the routine was not consistent, and their relationship implied consistency.

"Orson was an early bird," Vivien said.

"Not Lily."

"He used to jog in the mornings." She brushed a hand over her chin, again making the now familiar gesture of looking at the ceiling. "Then he stopped and began to jog in the evenings." She became animated, turning to face him. "But he continued to rise at six and leave for the office before seven. He claimed he could always get more done before people started to come in."

"He was right about that."

"He rarely stayed late at the office. He nearly always came home for dinner. First he'd jog for half an hour, then he'd shower. Then we'd eat together in the dining room. After dinner he'd go into his den and work."

"So they couldn't have met in the evenings."

"Considering Orson's routine, not on a regular basis."

"Lunchtime, then?" A frequent hour for meetings of this sort, he thought. Common knowledge.

"The law firm had a company dining room. Clients would come in."

"Days, then? Afternoons?"

Had they been so self-absorbed, so unobservant, so stupid?

"You don't know about lawyers. They keep accurate time books."

"He could have lied, written false data. Remember, we're dealing with shrewd, calculating people."

"Miss Sparks, his secretary, would have noticed. It was a discipline of the firm."

"Maybe she did but said nothing. Kept her mouth shut."

"Maybe."

"Weekends?" He stood up and began pacing the floor. "Saturday was a working day for both of us. Sundays we slept in. We were together on Sundays."

"Orson spent lots of time with Ben on weekends. You might say he was a devoted father."

"Aren't we only assuming that they met frequently? Maybe they met only sporadically. Once a week. Maybe once a month."

"But when? And where? And how frequently?"

"The keys imply very frequently, I'm afraid."

"Why afraid?"

"Just a figure of speech," he stammered.

"Of course. To validate our own ignorance." She looked at him archly until she noted the thin humor.

"Mysteries within enigmas," she sighed. "Keys! Mr. and Mrs. Calvin Marlboro! Like . . ." She paused. "If I could cry, I wonder who it would be for. Them, or us."

"And if the crash had not happened, would we ever have found out?"

"Probably not. We were too myopic and unaware. All we would have gotten was a pink slip. That's another reason why we owe it to ourselves," she said.

A great weight of sadness suddenly descended on him. He felt acutely foolish, embarrassed, violated. He began to shiver, and his lips trembled.

"Are you cold?" she asked gently.

She extended her arm across the gap between them, and his hand reached out to meet hers. He grabbed it, like a drowning man might grab a lifeline.

"You are cold," she said, rubbing his hand between hers.

"Cold hands, warm heart," he said.

They held each other's hands for a long time. It was she who disengaged first, standing up. But her touch had been physically warming. Something more, as well, but too incongruous to define, he decided.

"We'll sleep on it," she said. "I'm tired now. I'd better go home. Home?" A rattling sound escaped her lips, as if she were trying to laugh. He stood up and faced her. There was little space between them. He found himself looking deeply into her eyes. He did not want her to go, but he said nothing to delay her. He helped her put on her coat.

"You think we're getting any closer to the heart of this?" she asked.

"Yes. Yes, I do."

"At least we're doing something—not being passive." She shook her head. "Never again," she said firmly.

"Never," he replied.

For a long moment their eyes locked. Wounded survivors, he thought. Ambulatory, but barely. And still full of pain. When she left he listened until her footsteps faded. Then he felt cold again. And empty.

20

When she was alone, tossing and turning in the bed in the guest room, Vivien's mind reeled with speculations. Now that she had a detailed image of Orson's paramour, her imaginings became more frenetic. Periodically, Edward's face surfaced in her mind. Remembering the touch of his hand gave her goose bumps. Yes, she decided, they were smart to be involved in this together. After all, it affected them equally.

The idea did not present itself until the morning light filled the cracks of the blind. "Of course," she said, sitting up with a start. But soon the satisfactions of logic gave way to the old rage, which rushed at her with renewed fury.

"Of course," she cried.

She was dressed by six, surprisingly energized. It had always been like this when her purpose was single-minded, clearly defined. What she needed now was confirmation. Then she would tell Edward.

At seven she was in front of the polished double doors of Orson's law offices. Still on the door was "and Simpson" in brass lettering. Bradley, Martin, Conte, Barnes and Simpson. Bradley, who had founded the firm during Roosevelt's time, died years ago. The door was open, and she went in.

"Mrs. Simpson," Miss Sparks said with surprise. She had glasses attached to a chain around her neck, which she removed as she talked. Prim and graying, a cashmere sweater worn casually on her shoulders over a white blouse, she looked the quintessential executive secretary. A cup of coffee was steaming in front of her on her desk, along with a half-eaten doughnut. Yet her presence implied that Orson did, indeed, work during those early morning hours. With effort, Vivien remained calm.

"Would you like some coffee?" Miss Sparks asked.

"No, thank you."

Beyond Miss Sparks's desk she could see Orson's office. The morning sun glinted on the polished desk top, devoid of papers. So they had not lost any time, she thought, feeling a stab of anger. Miss Sparks had attended the service at the crematorium. Vivien had caught a brief glimpse of her.

"I'm so sorry," Miss Sparks said.

"I thought I'd come by and pick up my husband's personal things."

"I've packed them in a carton," she said apologetically. "We were going to messenger them over." Miss Sparks's shrewd eyes observed her. Her visit seemed awkward now; her confidence was swiftly eroding. She wished Edward were here with her.

"Is there something I can help you with?" Miss Sparks said. A great deal, Vivien thought. This, too, was part of Orson's other life. Here, she had always been the stranger, the wife, the intruder. In this other world, Miss Sparks held the reins of power. She, Vivien, was always the supplicant—a presence to be deflected. How good she had been, how obedient.

"Do you always come in so early, Miss Sparks?" Vivien asked. It occurred to her at that moment that she no longer had to observe the amenities. Miss Sparks appeared to be considering a reaction.

"It's the best time of the day for me," she answered sensibly, looking at her watch. "Two hours before most of them arrive. Then things get hectic."

She had said "for me," Vivien noted. "Not "for us."

"I'm organizing his pending cases." She put on her glasses. "He had a great deal on his plate." She paused and removed the glasses again. "We all miss him, Mrs. Simpson. What an awful tragedy."

Vivien could sense Miss Sparks's extreme caution. The wagons had already closed the circle as far as the firm was concerned.

"I suppose you both got a great deal of work done at this hour?" Vivien asked, determined to be casual.

"He liked highly detailed preparation. That's why I came in so early. Got into the habit. I wanted to be ready for him when he came in." Her response was crisply informative, without any hint of suspicion.

Vivien was pleased with her own pose of detachment. She

nodded and turned away, hiding her expression, her heart pounding.

"It left him more time for his morning jog," Miss Sparks said. "We were a good team. He was the kind of man who made every minute count. Wasted absolutely no time. By ten, when he came in, everything would be set." Her pride was talking now.

In a perverse way, Vivien felt her own sense of pride in her deductive instincts. It gave her the courage to expand her inquiry. Ten in the morning. There it was. Spots exploded in her vision, and she felt faint.

"Are you all right, Mrs. Simpson?"

"Fine," Vivien said, clearing her throat to mask her sudden weakness. "Still shell-shocked a bit." She made an effort to smile. She gulped deep breaths, summoning her strength, which miraculously rose to the occasion.

"Miss Sparks," Vivien said sharply, "I thought you knew everything."

Miss Sparks's lower lip flapped open. Then she put on her glasses and looked at Vivien.

"I swear to you, Mrs. Simpson . . ." She lowered her voice. "I swear to you. I had no idea. I can't imagine what he was doing on that plane. I did think I knew everything about his working life. I know how terribly awkward this must be for you, but I assure you . . ."

Vivien let her drone on. She had gotten what she had come for.

"I do believe you, Miss Sparks." So she, too, had felt the sting of betrayal.

"I can't understand it. I always made his travel arrangements. Always."

She could see that the partners, certainly Dale, had given her a hard time and that her days at the firm were numbered. Still, she felt no pity.

The confirmation carried more impact than the revelation and, in the street again, she felt the full impact of her rage. The clarity of her logic made her dizzy, and she had to lean against a lamppost for support.

More than a year. Orson had given up his morning jogging

more than a year ago. She remembered that it was winter, like now. He had stopped abruptly. She had been mildly curious. Better to do it in the evening, he had explained. She fought down a wave of nausea and dashed into the lobby of an office building. Finding a phone, she called Edward's number. There was no answer. Then she looked at her watch. Only eight o'clock. She remembered, with some irony, that he went to his office early. But she forgot the name of the congressman he worked for. She called Capitol information and found him.

"I'm sorry," she began.

"Don't be, Viv," he said. "I'm glad to hear your voice."

"There's something I want you to know"—her voice wavered—"but not on the phone." Somehow to say it publicly seemed obscene, a dirty little secret. It was something to be imparted privately. "Dammit, Edward, it gets worse and worse."

"I called you first thing this morning," he said. "I was worried." He sounded embarrassed by the concern.

"I went to Orson's office. I think I have some answers."

A half hour later she picked him up in her car in front of the Rayburn Building.

"Let's just park somewhere," he told her. She headed down Independence Avenue and turned left toward the Fourteenth Street Bridge, planning to reach the Virginia side where things were more familiar.

"Must we cross that?"

"How stupid of me."

But there was no way to turn around. Instead, she headed the car into the curving road that led to the Jefferson Memorial.

"It's okay here," he said. She parked the car in the deserted parking lot, cutting the motor. They did not get out. From where they were they could see the frozen pond glistening in the sun and across it the barren cherry trees, waiting for spring. Above them loomed the graceful giant statue of Jefferson, surrounded by a circle of Greek pillars.

"If it gets too cold, I'll turn on the heater."

"It's okay," he said.

"I don't quite know how to put this," she began, facing him. "Mornings," she blurted. "They met in the morning. Every weekday morning."

"But she was sleeping . . ." he began. Then understanding filtered into his mind. "So it seemed," he said sadly.

"He never got to the office before ten."

"My God." She saw his fists clench.

"He left the house at seven. That left three hours."

"As soon as I was gone," he said angrily. "She must have jumped out of bed. Our bed. Then went to his. How revolting. How utterly revolting."

"There's more."

He evaded her eyes.

"Remember I said he used to jog every morning? Then he switched to evenings?"

"Yes."

"That was a year ago."

"A whole year!"

"I'm afraid so."

"I'd bend over her, kiss her. It was an unfailing ritual of my life. I always left the house with this good feeling. . . ."

"They were very clever," Vivien said. "Choosing the morning. The innocent hours."

"The lousy lying bitch. How could she?"

"And he?"

"And for more than a year."

"Degrading, isn't it?"

He did not respond. The unthinkable seemed remarkably rational. Inadvertently, they had moved closer together in the car. One of his arms was stretched across the back of the seat, his hand touching her shoulder. She felt its pressure but made no move to extricate herself.

"Nobody knows anybody," he said after a long silence. "There's the lesson of it."

"A whole year," she mused. Just to contemplate the idea of their own ignorance was an embarrassment. No! She was not going to insult her self-worth. "Just imagine what they had to do to keep us from knowing. It wasn't just a single lie. They had to create another person to go through the routine with us."

As she talked she became aware of the pressure of his hand on her shoulder. While it felt comforting, it made her uneasy, as if it were *she* who was being unfaithful. She looked around her. The situation had all the trappings of a clandestine tryst, a midday affair: the deserted parking lot, the male stranger beside her, the odd sense of sensual anticipation. She imagined she could hear Margo's knowing giggle.

Then another thought intruded. When she turned, would it be Orson beside her, the handsome craggy face, the watchful eyes—hiding the Machiavellian intelligence, all the mechanisms of Byzantine plotting, behind an accusing gaze—as if she were the guilty party, and he had arranged the entrapment? Suddenly she moved away, beyond his reach.

"What is it?"

Edward's voice recalled the reality. She looked across the pond at the barren cherry trees, dormant and waiting like herself.

"What is it?" he repeated. His elbow still rested on the seat's rim, but his arm was up, like a teenager frightened on a first date.

Somehow the image softened her, and she moved back toward him, waiting for the arm to come down. Yes, she decided, she could understand his need to touch another human being. And hers, as well. She wondered if she was receiving more than simple comfort, whether she needed more than that. It was irrelevant, she decided. And, considering the circumstances, a bit odd.

He lay his head back against the headrest and closed his eyes. His hand caressed her shoulder. Despite her sensitivity, the uneasiness passed.

"Maybe it was we who invented them," he said.

He breathed deeply and sighed.

"More like they invented themselves."

"A whole year." He shook his head in disbelief. "There must have been something. Something! Surely you must have picked up vibes, felt something intuitively."

"So much for woman's intuition. Mine must have been in mothballs."

"I was too self-absorbed. Working my ass off. It wasn't even in my frame of reference. You were a housewife. Your world revolved around him. . . ."

"Makes me the dumbest, I guess."

"I didn't mean it that way."

"What way?"

"The way it sounded. Like it was an accusation against your . . . gender."

Enough, she cried within herself. She was too exhausted to defend the role. Besides, she now hated what she had been, the trusting wife with the lamp always lit in the window. It hurt to think about it.

"Theirs was a crime against, well, against the concept, the bond of marriage," he said, "against commitment. Like"—he paused—"embezzlement. Stealing without the owner's knowledge. An inside job." The idea seemed to excite him, and he went on. "Think of how devious they had to be. They had to know our every quirk and habit, our routine, our way of living. They had to cover their tracks in advance, take advantage of our trust, and conspire against us. God, how well they played us."

"Like musical instruments."

"A regular quartet."

"Everything had to be precise, in perfect harmony. One sour note, and we'd both suspect." He paused. "Or would we? How thickheaded they must have thought we were. Two naive pinheads."

"No denying that. They were right, of course."

A muffled sound escaped from his throat, a kind of sardonic chuckle.

"What is it?"

He shook his head.

"Too crude to say," he muttered.

"We can't have secrets," she said lightly. Her hand had brushed almost playfully against his chest.

"All right. We shared bacteria. The four of us."

"How gross." She suppressed a giggle. The idea was ludicrous.

"Like herpes." He began to laugh full throated. His body shook. "I'm sorry," he said when he had settled down, wiping his eyes. "It's not happy laughter. More like hysterics." He seemed apologetic.

"I can see," she said. "Black humor." An idea suddenly imposed itself. "But why did they choose Florida at precisely that moment?" She answered her own question. "Maybe to make a decision. Maybe they needed a place to think. A place away from us. Orson was like that. The lawyer's mind."

"But they had a place," Edward said.

She felt a sudden cramp.

"Are you all right?" he asked.

"I'm afraid not."

He reached over and opened the window, letting in the cold air. She breathed deeply until she felt better.

Another car rolled into the lot, passed them, then moved to the other side of the monument. Looking through the mirror she saw two heads move toward each other, silhouetted against the white background. He raised his eyes to the mirror.

"Cheating spouses," Edward said. "Last week I might have said lovers."

"Last week I wouldn't have noticed. Or cared."

She saw the heads disengage and turn toward the rear of their car to watch them.

"They must think we're doing the same thing," she said.

"Why else would a couple come to this place"—he held his wrist up—"at eleven A.M. on a weekday in winter?"

Through the rearview mirror they could see the people still watching them. Finally the couple turned again, locking together.

"Obviously a common occurrence. We just weren't tuned in," she said, still looking through the mirror. "Imagine the pressure of going through life worrying about getting caught."

"It didn't seem to worry them."

Resetting the mirror, she turned to face him. In the stark whiteness, his face was pale and his cheeks a trifle hollower than they had been when she had first met him. Underneath his eyes were dark rings. She wondered if he, too, saw signs like that in her. A sudden cramp gripped her again, then passed.

"Edward," she said after a long pause.

"Yes?" A nerve palpitated in his jaw as he looked out at the frozen Tidal Basin.

"I'm glad they died."

"Me, too."

She said nothing more, gunning the motor.

21

When Edward returned to the office, the Congressman and most of the staff were out to lunch. Jan Peters sat at her desk reading a newspaper and eating a sandwich.

"You okay?" she asked. There was no avoiding her desk. From the moment he had arrived her scrutiny had been merciless.

"You should have taken more time," she had told him that morning. That was before he and Congressman Holmes had had their little chat. To the Congressman, time away from the office constituted a mortal sin, whatever the circumstances. Not that Edward expected compassion, but the Congressman could have dispensed with the syrupy sentiment, which was laughably transparent. As they say, it went with the territory. Besides, what would he have done with his day? He was not mourning Lily. If anything, he should be mourning his own lost life, the end of his innocence. Even self-pity seemed shallow. At least there was Vivien. Viv.

"The work will do you good, Eddie," the Congressman had said, wearing the appropriate expression for such an occasion, a look of earnest concern.

"Yes, I believe it will," Edward had agreed.

"I know it's rough."

How the hell would he know? Edward wondered. Before, it had been easy to deal with hypocrisy, the little public lies and dissimulations that were the idiom of the political trade. But now that they had spilled over into his inner life, his real life, he could not bear it. A lie was a lie. There were no little lies.

"If there's anything I can do . . ." the Congressman had said, winding up the obligatory hearts and flowers and getting back to business. He rattled off a string of suggestions for press releases and bills, ideas to make public impact—his only real objective. Dutifully, Edward took notes, illegible scrawls, but the activity gave him the look of sincere interest.

"Exposure, Edward. That's the name of the game. A steady drumbeat. Statewide exposure. Get the name out. As long as we've got the frank, let's use it. It's a tenfold advantage over any challenger. Do you read me?"

"Of course," Edward answered, offering a smile with, he hoped, the light of devotion in his eyes. Lily would have done it better, he thought bitterly. She had certainly proved her prowess on that score.

Vivien's deduction offered a stunning revelation. Mornings! Perhaps every morning. It was humiliating. Yet it was odd how these crushing events had sharpened the power of their deductive instincts. Too bad he would have to forgo the pleasures of revenge. He could not imagine how he might have reacted to the revelation if Lily were alive. Was he capable of murder? And how could she have lived with him under the same roof and gone through the motions of intimacy, while living in a cocoon of hypocrisy and leading him through a maze of falsehoods and contrivances?

He wondered if all this discovery would have the desired effect on their lives, their future. Was it like cauterizing a wound? It burned, but it did kill the unwholesome bacteria. The cure is in the knowledge. This was essentially their purpose—to know more. There was no way to stop now.

But acquiring knowledge demanded ingenuity, resourcefulness, and the kind of guile and cleverness that Orson and Lily had displayed. Think like them! Be them. If the trail cooled, what then? He remembered the keys. What did they unlock? Above all, they needed to know that, needed to find their filthy rat's nest.

How did one begin? He remembered the police detective and forced his memory to recall his name. Then he picked up the phone and dialed police headquarters. Hadn't McCarthy found the key connection in the first place?

"You'll have to speak up." The voice at the other end was gruff, impatient, remarkably like Vinnie's.

"Sergeant McCarthy."

The voice became muffled, fading, inquiring elsewhere. "Mac here?"

The pause was short, and the voice returned in force.

"He's off duty. Want to leave a message?"

He gave his name and number by rote, regretting it instantly, then rationalizing. It was not as if he would be talking to a stranger.

He sat in his office and stared at a blank page in his typewriter. His thoughts were disjointed, like flashing lights. He felt light-headed, slightly foolish. All this is beyond my range of understanding, he decided.

"Tell me how you feel," Vivien had demanded earlier, just before he got out of the car. The shame of it had released a blush of hot blood, blotching his skin with little red hives.

"Like a damned fool."

"Me, too," she had said, as if she knew how much he needed her reassuring echo.

Jan Peters came in and she sat down.

"I think you've got lots of courage to start work so soon after . . ." She paused respectfully. "Shows real class."

"Thank you," he said, typing "quick brown fox" repetitively, feeling her eyes, watchful, mooning with mothering.

"I just want you to know you have a friend in old Jan," she said in a throaty whisper.

"I appreciate that," he said, not looking up.

"Someone to confide in." She leaned over and touched his arm. "I mean it, Edward."

He nodded, not wanting to create a scene.

"Remember that, Edward."

"I need lots of space now," he said, turning to face her. He knew her offer was sincere.

"She was everything to you, wasn't she?"

"Just about."

It occurred to him that he must dissimulate, live the role of the grieving husband. Only with Viv could he truly be himself.

"It's dangerous to let someone be everything."

He felt their office relationship disintegrating, and he fought off the attempt at intimacy. Yet she was so utterly, undeniably female, physically, symbolically as well, underscoring his pathetic ignorance about the entire gender. Who are these people? He knew nothing about them, he decided, and had learned nothing. The female as a species might have been Martians for all he understood. Lifting his eyes, he inspected her. Perhaps she could provide him with knowledge, insight. Dispel his ignorance.

"And you?" he asked. He felt like a babe on her knee, a child to a mother.

"Me?" Her eyes flashed a predatory look.

"Have you many . . ." He paused, uncomfortable. He wanted to say lovers. "Boyfriends?"

"More than a fair share," she answered, and her brows knit suspiciously.

"Any of them in love with you?" It was, he knew, unthinkable to ask such a question.

"I hope most of them." She giggled with girlish pride.

"And you?"

"Me?" The attempt at coyness was transparent. Learn from this, he urged himself. Trust nothing.

"I love them all."

"I'm serious."

She looked at him, pondering.

"You really are."

"I told you."

She seemed suddenly confused.

"All right, then. Nobody special."

"Ever?"

"What's come over you?"

"I want to know."

"Know what?"

"About women in love," he said, pressing. "I want to know if there ever was anyone who moved you, moved you so profoundly that your judgment became blind. Hurtful."

"Hurtful?" Her eyes were big saucers, fierce, guarded, wary. "I never deliberately hurt anybody," she protested.

He could tell he had gotten to her soft center. She grew silent, tossing her hair with a motion of her head. Then the belligerence ebbed.

"Yes," she said, "I was moved once. For him I would have done anything. I mean anything. Given myself to him, body and soul. I would have died for him. That's what it's all about."

She stood up. Her pose of sexuality vanished as she exhibited her vulnerability. Actually, he decided, he liked her better this way.

"And what happened?"

She looked at him, her lower lip trembling. She seemed to be gathering the shreds of a flimsy pride. "Why do you want to know?"

"I've been damned nosy," he said. "You don't have to say. I'm just unstrung."

That part was true. Turning away, he looked out the window. But, oddly eager to show her wounds, she did not wait the decent interval to recover. They either tell too much or not enough, he observed, wondering if there was some universal truth in that. Lily had deliberately kept him in ignorance.

"It was the sweetest pain I ever felt. Problem is, it's like fire: very hot when it's going, cold when it runs out of fuel. They say such things can come only once in a lifetime, if ever. At least I had that. I've got no regrets."

He thought about what she had said. Had he ever been willing to die for anybody? Even Lily? Never. He was sure of that.

He felt her watching him, dreading any counter inquiries from her. None came. Perhaps she has no need to know about me. Maybe men are no mystery to her.

She ambled off.

The Congressman returned to the office in the late afternoon. He was irritable and annoyed. All outward concern for Edward's emotional state had vanished.

Edward handed the Congressman Harvey Mills's press release.

"It stinks," he snapped, frowning.

"I'll spruce it up before I let it go."

"There's a lot more that needs sprucing up here," the Congressman said, swiveling back in his chair and picking up the phone.

I may not be a good judge of women, Edward thought, but I know this son of a bitch.

As always, he stayed late, lifting his head from his typewriter to say good night to the rest of the staff, who left one by one. Even the Congressman poked his head into his office.

"It'll do you good," he called, placating him. "Get us back on the track." When he had gone, Edward continued to stare at his typewriter. He had not turned the release back to Harvey Mills for a rewrite and hadn't the faintest idea how to "spruce it up."

Harvey Mills came in. "All right if I check out?" he asked. He looked neater than before. A haircut, that's it, Edward thought. He wants my job. It wasn't paranoia, merely the recognition of a fact. So, his instincts had sharpened. It was a comforting thought. He seemed to have lost all sense of command over himself, over others. There's insight for you, he told himself.

"Sure, Harvey," he said.

"The old man like the release?"

"Loved it. Gets out first thing in the morning."

It would go as is. The Congressman rarely looked at things again, trusting Edward to get it right.

Jan came in again, freshly made-up. She was not wearing her coat and had not come in to say good night. He realized suddenly that his earlier conversation had set up an intimacy he had not intended.

"Buy you a drink?" she asked, reassembled now, her full body puffed to its outer limits. For a moment he contemplated it seriously, assailed by a flash of the old guilt.

"She's gone, Edward," Jan said.

"Gone?"

Actually, he was thinking of Viv, a new ripple for his conscience. It confused him momentarily.

The phone rang. He picked up the receiver and swiveled away from her. McCarthy's voice crackled over the background noises.

"There was something I wanted to talk to you about," Edward said.

"Sure."

In the pause, the noises grew louder.

"I'm at The Dubliner, across from Union Station. You know it?"

It wasn't far. He could cut across the park in front of the Capitol. Pondering, he swiveled and looked at Jan again, still offering herself. No, he decided, she wasn't part of it.

"I'll be there in fifteen minutes," he said.

"Maybe sometime." Jan shrugged, unable to conceal her disappointment.

22

From a booth in the rear, McCarthy watched Edward squint into layers of smoke and turn his head in a slow arc. The damages were showing now, he thought. The poor bastard had bitten the apple. McCarthy upended his shot glass of Scotch and chased it with a flat beer, just as Edward slid into the booth.

"What's your poison?"

He caught the man's indifference to his offer, the indifference of shock. Like a punch-drunk fighter. So the real world had settled back in, but it was not the original reality. Everything had changed.

"Same as you." Edward shrugged. Another symptom. Decisons were impossible, painful. Judgment had ceased. The man was up shit's creek without a paddle.

A blowzy waitress brought shot glasses of Scotch and beer chasers. As Edward observed the scene, McCarthy could see it was, for his visitor, a foreign world.

"The old ethnic tie," McCarthy said. "We Irish always feel uprooted. That's why we need each other."

Edward followed his gaze. "Like the Italians," he said. "My wife was one."

"Wops. Kikes. Niggers. Spics. Chinks. The family of man. At least with your own kind you know where you stand."

"Do you?"

The man sighed and watched the shot glass, his fingers caressing a metal ashtray. Brooding, McCarthy thought. Understandably. The man's world had closed in on him. Hell, I did what I could for the sad son of a bitch.

"Make peace with it, man," McCarthy said, knocking back his drink, wiping his lips with his sleeve, then chasing it down with a swallow of beer and wiping again.

"I'm doing okay," Edward said defensively.

He didn't look it. McCarthy wondered what the man wanted,

but he did not push. It would come. After all, they shared secrets. Not all, but enough to bond them. The Simpson woman was tougher, he decided. Burned the bastard. He liked that. Women were tougher, meaner. They always left men on the ropes. Like Billie. Let your guard down once, and they're all over you, chopping away.

While waiting, McCarthy had debated a position. He could dispense trite advice which would be utterly worthless, or he could tell him what he had learned, that a woman's betrayal had no known cure. He would find that out. Everything depended on trust. When trust went out, out went the props. The best you could do was, like him, hold yourself together and wait for the ice wagon.

You should thank me—he looked silently at the brooding man—for easing the pain a bit. Too much knowledge was the enemy. "Timmy's yours," Billie had pleaded on her knees in the motel room, making the sign of the cross across her bare breasts as if that were proof positive. "Timmy's his." Jim sat there on the bed, mute, head in his hands, hunched to hide his obscene nakedness. Yet even then, the real enemy was the woman—Billie. Jim, like him, was just an instrument. A dick. He had been dead certain then about Timmy's ancestry, and although the certainty had faded with time, the doubt lingered, spoiling it all forever. To make it worse, he was her image: blue eyes, fair skin, ginger hair, slight, small-boned. Wasn't a thing about him that hinted of himself. Or Jim. As if he had deliberately played on them both the trick of being created in her image.

"I've got some ideas that are bothering me," Edward said, clearing his throat.

Who hasn't? McCarthy chuckled to himself. "I did you a favor, pal. Leave it alone," McCarthy said.

"You don't really think about these things until later."

"That's the way it is."

"Things keep coming up."

"I kept it between us, didn't I?" Edward nodded, but McCarthy could not detect real gratitude. "That lawyer would have blown it out of all proportion. Wouldn't have done anyone any good. Fucking lawyers. Then the newspapers would have had it. Better for everyone. For her, too. And the kid."

McCarthy looked around for the waitress and held up two fingers, scowling at Edward who had not touched his drink.

"Do you good," McCarthy ordered, motioning with his eyes.

Obeying, Edward lifted his drink with shaking fingers. He took it in one gulp, gagged, and washed it down quickly with the beer, leaving a foamy mustache. You'd be taking doubles if I had told you the rest, McCarthy thought.

"I buried her yesterday," Edward said when he had caught his breath.

"Best place for 'em," McCarthy said, hearing his speech slur and feeling the cold grip of anger tighten. Drink could make him cruel. What in hell did this bastard want?

"We've been comparing notes, Mrs. Simpson and I," Davis blurted.

"Have you?"

"We have the keys. All we need is the place."

"Need?"

"Well, we believe," Edward stammered, "that it's important to know as much as we can."

"What will that prove?"

Edward ignored the question. "The point is, how does one go about matching keys to locks?"

McCarthy smiled. "They don't. Unless they're registered like Medeco. Or there's an army out there sticking keys in locks—say battalion-size. There are hundreds of thousands of doors."

The waitress brought two more shots. McCarthy stared at them in their wet circles, resisting. This time it was Edward who reached first for the shot glass, knocking it back, not gagging. He did not chase it down with the beer.

"Loose ends gnaw at you," Edward said.

"Is the Pope a Catholic? That's my bag."

"We've been discussing it a lot. Putting it together. They're only theories, only speculations, you understand." The color had risen in his cheeks, and his eyes were no longer shifting but were probing now. The man barely took a breath. "Look, we're both in the same boat, Mrs. Simpson and I. It hit us right in our guts. I mean, how do you explain it to yourself, no less to each other? We didn't know it was happening. We really didn't know. You can't blame us for trying to figure it out. There are things we should know. We *must* know."

McCarthy, saying nothing, looked at his drink, salivated, but held back, sitting on his hands. He began to perspire under his arms. He watched Edward swallow with difficulty, the Adam's apple bobbing in his neck. It'll only bring more worthless pain, McCarthy thought.

"So the two of you are piecing it all together," McCarthy said, knowing now that his warnings were for naught.

"Just trying to understand," Edward said. "Now, about the keys."

"Narrow the options. Look for accessibility, convenience. Time frame."

"We think they met in the mornings."

"Do you?"

"Someplace convenient to both our places."

"In between."

Despite himself, McCarthy was warming to the idea. "Never could resist a mystery." He reached for the shot glass, upended it, chased it with the beer, and ordered two more. Then he took out a pen and opened a cocktail napkin.

"Draw a circle. Say, fifteen minutes from both places. Then ten minutes. Then five. Divide the circles into manageable segments. Then work your way through the segments lock by lock. Look for Yales. Reject the others."

"This could take weeks, months."

"You asked me how. What the fuck's the difference? You got a lifetime."

"No other way?"

"You could find the damned address among their effects."

"We've looked."

"Then you missed it."

"We were very thorough."

"There's always something."

"We're not professionals." Edward hesitated. "They were the hares. We are just dumb foxes."

"You can say that again."

The waitress came again with two more drinks. Edward declined his, and McCarthy drank them both.

"And when you find it?"

"We'll take it as it comes."

"You don't know nothin', do you?" McCarthy felt his anger swelling.

"If it happened to you, you'd understand," Edward said.

"The barn door's closed. It's over. Leave it alone. The more you know, the more you'll shit. Accept it. They worked you over, and they got theirs. Dumb fate did your work for you. There are millions out there who'd like it done like that. Bam! Crash! Down the tube!"

"You don't understand."

He was seeing red now. "You think they were playing potsy? They were fucking you over!" He felt a howl come roaring out of his chest. "They didn't like the home cookin'. Not hers or yours. Don't talk to me about lost trust, commitment, relationships, honesty. When I was a kid, they talked about honor. Shit! You know what you're gonna find in that place? One bed and ten thousand dirty pictures and sheets stained with a million lost kids." He belched. "Except one." Hell, he had tried to do this fellow a favor, but he wouldn't leave it alone. McCarthy felt the rising tide of cruelty. "You've already been hit by a semi. You're about to get hit by a tank."

A frown furrowed Edward's forehead.

Poor bastard, McCarthy thought. Why the hell should he escape the full brunt of it? Share the pain, boys.

"She was pregnant."

"Pregnant?"

The man turned ashen and fell against the back of the booth as if he had been pushed. McCarthy's anger drained.

"Sit next to an Irishman in his cups, and he thinks you're a priest."

He watched as the man took deep breaths, puckering his lips. McCarthy was sobering now, the damage done.

"So," he said, cooling. "The more you know, the more it helps."

"Why . . . ?" Edward began.

"Loose ends." He shrugged. "I told you I don't like mysteries. The stewardess was also pregnant. It gave me an idea. The Medical Examiner ran the test just before we shipped her. A lucky hunch. Hell, it was only the day before yesterday. I might have called you." In a pig's ass, he thought. He got up unsteadily. Case closed. Enough for one evening.

"And the ends? Are they still loose?"

"For you. Not for me. Figure it out."

He started to amble away, unsteadily. Edward came up behind him.

"How long?" he demanded. McCarthy turned and faced him.

"About six weeks. Tell you anything?"

The man swiveled on his heel, moving again.

"Don't blame me," he shouted after him. "I didn't put the poison in the cup!"

23

Still in her coat, Vivien sat on a chair in the kitchen and watched Hamster sniff at the foot of the snowman, which had been yellowed by his incessant piddle. Dark patches emerged where the snow had disappeared, and the large lawn had a scraggly, unhealthy look.

When Hamster began scratching at the door again, her resolve hardened. Hamster was Orson's gift, his choice, and he and Ben had nursed him through puppyhood, which provided absolution for what she was about to do. Opening the door, she let him in. He shot straight to his dish, sniffed, licked the residue from the plastic, then turned to her, tail wagging, his round brown eyes moist with expectation.

"Sorry, pal," she whispered, bending and scooping him up with one hand.

With a firm hand, she had drawn this line in her mind. She hadn't been conscious of any pattern at first. Now it was clearly evident, and she relished the discovery. It wasn't simply a question of justice or even punishment. It was more like an exorcism. What had belonged to Orson, what reflected his point of view, his tastes, his alleged affections, his personal choices and effects, would be trashed. And the line had been advancing with each additional revelation. The Salvation Army had already carted away much of the physical evidence of his life in this house.

Returning home, she had noted immediately that the removal diminished the feeling of his presence. She could, of course, have burned these things. She regarded her decision not to as proof that she had not lost her sense of compassion or humanity. It was, after all, a bonanza for the Salvation Army: a Washington lawyer's smart preppy wardrobe, complete with more than a dozen pairs of shoes; his sports equipment—tennis racket, golf clubs; law journals, random files; writing materials; paperweights. She had stripped the walls of his study of prints, three carved duck decoys that had come down from some hunting relative, old pipes, his rack, even his coffee mug, the one that literally said His. Everything!

There were other things of his still remaining in the master bedroom: his jewelry (studs, cufflinks), shaving tools, cologne, and aftershave. Not another night must go by with such things in the house.

Now it was Hamster's turn, and she considered the act of disposal a true test of her resolve. She carried him out to the car and put him in the seat beside her. He liked to ride in cars, propped up on his haunches; his eyes roved the passing streets for fellow dogs at whom to bark a greeting.

When she and Orson went out of town in the past, they would send Ben to her parents' and board Hamster at a nearby farm. Often the people who ran the place would take "orphaned" dogs and try to find them compatible homes. It was not, she assured herself, like putting him to sleep.

As she drove into the dirt road that led to the farm, Hamster's body grew tense. His body shivered with fear as he huddled close to her.

"I'll try," the woman who ran the farm said. "But it's not as easy as you think."

"I'll pay for his board for as long as it takes."

"All right. But I can't give you any guarantees."

"I understand perfectly," Vivien said, writing out a check for a month's board.

Exile or death, she thought, experiencing the gnawing malice of her intent. She had deliberately kept the animal from going with Ben and her parents to Vermont. Perhaps later, if he could not be placed, she would develop the courage to put him to sleep, an idea that, despite all the ferocious intensity of her resolve, frightened her.

The telephone was ringing when she got home. She answered it, breathless from running, hoping it would be Edward. It was Dale Martin.

"We've been going over Orson's policies," he began after the amenities. "You'll be quite comfortable. Then there's the suit against the airline. . . ."

She listened with disinterest. Dale was also beyond the line.

"Are you there, Vivien?" Dale asked, after he had droned on without a response from her.

She felt compelled to grunt an acknowledgment.

"You'll be a very comfortable widow, I'm happy to say. The policies alone, including the firm's key man insurance, comes to a tidy seven hundred and fifty thousand dollars, and you'll undoubtedly get double that when the airlines pay off." He paused. "I know it won't bring Orson back, but it will ease your personal situation, financially speaking."

He seemed to be winding up the conversation, the part that she had been waiting for.

"I want none of it," she said firmly. "Put it all in trust for Ben."

"Will you say that again?"

She did.

"That's nonsense," Dale exploded, then softened quickly. "You're still overwrought, Vivien. You're not thinking rationally. We're talking big bucks."

"I want only the house and my own savings account." They're the only things that are really mine, she thought. It was she who had chosen the house, decorated it, lavished it with her care. "I'm going to sell it." It was impossible to remove Orson's aura completely. With everything else, the house, too, had to go.

"The market is lousy, Vivien. You won't get what it's worth."

"We'll see."

"Look, Vivien, I'm your lawyer—"

"I know. Just set up the trusts. I don't even have to be a trustee."

"You can't be serious. In the will, you are the sole inheritor. Orson set it up to protect you."

Against what, she wondered. Betrayal is not protection. Remain cool, she told herself. Remembering Orson's year of lies buttressed her decision. To take any money from him or his planning would insult her integrity, her self-respect. Accepting his money was like—she groped for the correct words—like validating evil.

"It's not a rational decision, Vivien."

"The client is always the boss." Those were Orson's words,

which further inflamed her. She wanted to expunge that, too. "Just do it my way," she said, and hung up. No debate was necessary. To placate her anger, she went upstairs and confronted the master bedroom. She threw everything that remained of his, willy-nilly, into compacter bags. Despite the denuding of his possessions, the room still reeked of him. She saw his indentation in the mattress. On the night table next to his side of the bed was a row of books he had liked to read to lull him to sleep. Men's books. Seeing them, she recalled how many of his books and records were still in the house. Some of them seemed even more personally his than his clothes. They would be the next to go.

She slid the bags into the compacter and listened to the crushing sounds, to bottles breaking, releasing the mingled scents of cologne and aftershave. Jewelry flattened. He had a little reading lamp for his special use, and she heard the bulb making a popping sound as the compacter's anvil came down. Finally, it was all in one solid rectangle, which she carried out and put in a garbage can. This done, she attacked the books and records, stuffing them into old cartons. She separated the books carefully. Most were his, but the records were mostly hers. It did not amaze her in the least how few of these items were really shared possessions. They had been two strangers living side by side, she thought bitterly as she carried the cartons to the driveway—another bonanza for the Salvation Army.

Yet, despite the fury and thoroughness of her efforts, Orson's presence was still tangible in the house. It was as if his persona permeated the air, like the lingering stench of smoke after a household fire.

By the time she had dragged the last carton outside, it was dark. Still, she was vaguely dissatisfied, and the tension, instead of dissipating, was accelerating. To calm herself, she poured out half a tumbler of whiskey and drank it down in a few quick swallows. It didn't calm her; instead, she began to sob uncontrollably, overcome with an emotion resembling grief. She knew it was not for Orson. Perhaps it was for the old lost life, which had been just fine with her. If it had been without the shattering complexities of love or passion or whatever emotional earthquakes could occur in this life, it was at least serene, calm, tranquil, safe. That was it. Recovering somewhat, she bent low over the sink and washed her face in the water. She felt unsafe, drifting. Who could possibly understand her state of mind? Only Edward.

Reaching for the phone, she dialed his home number. It rang into eternity. Then she hung up in despair. The population of her world was reduced to two. Two survivors. She felt some vague anxiety about his absence. He should have made himself available when she needed him, she thought petulantly. Then she remembered the question she had asked him earlier:

"If she had lived, confessed all, would you have forgiven her?"

"She didn't," he had answered, stating a truth which testified that all transpired events were inexorable and unchanging.

The telephone's ring stabbed into the darkening silence. Edward! No. It was her mother, and she felt a twinge of guilt at her disappointment. She had promised Ben that she would call. Where was Ben? she wondered. On which side of the imaginary line? It was painful to contemplate. Flesh of her flesh. Blood of her blood. If only he were not the image of Orson. A living reminder. Surely such feelings were unnatural. They made her feel very guilty. Yet, she could not deny them. Not to herself.

"Are you all right, darling?" her mother asked.

"Fine. Just getting things settled."

"You must be strong, Vivien."

"I am, Mother."

"Ben is fine," her mother said.

She listened as Ben's day was minutely described, as if each moment of his five-year-old life were precious and eventful. He would be in good hands, she knew. As her mother talked, her mind swirled with images of the clear, sweet winter air, the mountains majestic in their coats of snow, frosty windows, rosy cheeks, her father's pharmacy, where she had spent happy teenage afternoons dispensing malts and exchanging the kind of information that needed no computers to store or impart. Ben would surely thrive in that atmosphere. The image assuaged her guilt.

"Mommy!" It was Ben's voice suddenly intruding. She had hoped to avoid that. A lump sprang into her throat, preventing her from responding.

"Mommy?"

"I'm here, darling," she said, clearing her throat. "Isn't it wonderful up there with Grandma and Grandpa?"

"Will I go home soon?" The words wrenched at her heart. She heard an echo of Orson's voice, and it jolted her.

"You just be a good boy, Ben," she said, shocked at her own reaction.

"But when will I go home, Mommy?" Ben said. "I want to be with you and Hamster."

It was too awful to put into words, she knew. Too awful to confront. Too illogical and unnatural and hateful and obscene. I can't help myself, she wanted to cry out. When she spoke again, her voice was tremulous.

"Mommy has some things she must do"—she hesitated—"first." The extent of her hypocrisy and evasion startled her. Orson's legacy, she told herself. He had crushed her instincts, tangled her emotions. She heard Ben's voice, but she could not find the courage to respond.

"Are you all right, dear?" her mother asked in that gentle, concerned tone that had nursed her through childhood sicknesses and the routine traumas of a young girl's life, always a sure-fire remedy. But not now. With Ben off the phone, she regained her composure.

"A little strained, Mother."

"You shouldn't be there alone."

"I need this time, Mother." She caught the insistence in her tone.

"I'm not pressing you, dear. We'll keep Ben for as long as you like." Her voice dropped to a whisper. "He's fine. Really he is." She paused, faltered, cleared her throat. Vivien felt the psychic inspection. The woman could always sense danger. Hadn't she called immediately after the plane crash? The thought brought back the full impact of the betrayal, inflaming her again with a monstrous anger. The fury of it roared back on the winds of recent memory.

They had just been up for the Christmas holidays. Was it only a few weeks ago? It seemed like eons. The holidays? The joyous reminder retreated in her mind, stoking the ashes of the smoldering anger.

He had left the day after Christmas and had returned the day before New Year's Eve. Searching the pattern of past Christmas holidays, in which he stayed the entire time, she remembered that he had done this for the past two Christmases. Busy stuff at the office, he had told her, and it had meant nothing to her, hardly a blip on the screen of her security. He had been so devilishly clever, so devious. The full fury of her humiliation roared back at her. Orson had trampled on her most highly prized virtue: her sense of trust. He had had to deceive not only her and Ben but her parents, abusing their admiration and pride in Orson as a son-in-law. In a way, the deception had even encapsulated their town, Vermont, and New England, defaming the images and memories that she held so dear. And the Christmas spirit as well, its goodness and innocence.

"I think maybe you should register Ben in day school, Mother."

"Day school?"

"I think that would be best." She waited as the implication settled in her mother's mind.

"You don't think that would be disruptive?" Her mother's tone brightened. "Unless you're planning to come up and be with us?"

"I've made no plans," she said, conscious of her coldness.

"He's your child," her mother said with a sigh. "Please remember that." Vivien remained deliberately silent, waiting for her mother to continue, certain of her reaction. "Of course, I'll do whatever you say. I suppose it will be the best thing for him under the circumstances."

"Yes, it will, Mother." She drew a deep breath. Before she said good-bye, she said, "And kiss Ben for me." How often would she be saying that? she wondered.

She hung up and lay back on the couch, looking at the ceiling, fighting off the phantoms of guilt. Of course, she had Orson's memory to help her with that.

24

Edward was thankful that the streets leading back to the Rayburn Building were deserted. It was not danger that concerned him. He was already a victim. Inexplicably, his principal fear was that others would notice his shame. He had to see Vivien. Only Vivien could share this new knowledge. Only Vivien would understand. He passed a phone booth, started to dial her number, then aborted the call.

The information was too raw. It needed time to be sifted, mulled over, sorted out, perhaps softened. He did not want to overburden her with both the hurt and the complexity of dealing with it. It might have too many implications that would associate the pain with *him*, the way he now felt about McCarthy, who was, after all, only the bearer of the awful message.

There was also something terribly personal about the information—all those biological implications, the phenomenon of procreation. He had always been put off by the clinical details of conception. Yet between couples, he and Lily included, the subject and practice was unavoidable. Wasn't creating life, progeny, a central issue in a marriage?

By the time he reached his car in the parking lot, he could not bear the thought of going home. Home was no longer a concept that existed; it was hardly even a place. Tomorrow, he decided, he would give notice, sell everything but the clothes on his back. In his heart he felt a malevolent desire to set the place afire, obliterate all evidence of his life with Lily.

What McCarthy had told him had to be shared with Vivien. She could not, nor would she want to, be spared the knowledge. It was part of the truth. And wasn't the truth going to be the ultimate cure? He called her from a phone in the parking lot. She answered on the first ring, as if she had been waiting.

"I must see you," he said.

"Of course."

He was greatly relieved. She gave him careful directions to her house.

"Have you eaten?"

"No." Swallowing, he tasted the sour backwash of the Scotch.

"I'll pull something together."

"Brace yourself," he said before he hung up. It was unfair, gratuitous. She had offered no response. Brace herself for what? It seemed a male dilemma. Whose child was it? He searched his mind for answers, some definitive certainty. Finding none, he concentrated on his driving, observing that he had not yet reached the edge of sobriety.

In the dark there was not much he could see of the outside of the house, except that it was rather large, set back, and surrounded by tall, dark evergreens. He felt a twinge of jealousy. Orson was more successful than himself, obviously wealthier.

Before he could ring the bell, she opened the door and ushered him in. She seemed to survey him purposefully, inspecting him for hints of information. He let her do it, offering a shrug and a smile.

"It doesn't ever end," he said.

"Someday, maybe."

He took off his coat. Entering the living room, he looked for the bar. Some bottles stood on a cart.

"Help yourself."

"I've been on Scotch tonight. With an Irishman in an Irish bar, drinking Scotch."

He felt like blurting it out. Instead, he drank half of what he had poured.

"I've been separating the wheat from the chaff," she said, explaining what she had done about Orson's things, his clothes, and the dog.

"The dog, too!" he exclaimed.

"It was more his than mine."

"I know what you mean. I'm giving up the apartment."

If she had heard, she gave no sign, absorbed in her own enmity.

"Also the insurance. I've declined the insurance and everything that comes out of any suits. I'm going cold turkey."

It hadn't occurred to him as yet.

"It makes me feel cleansed," she said. He sat down. From the kitchen came the pungent odor of food cooking. "Meatloaf," she said, noticing his interest. "I'm sorry. It's all I had in the freezer." She had poured herself a sherry and sat opposite him, waiting. "I've braced myself," she said, offering a wan smile.

He plunged ahead. There was no point in small talk. First must come the overriding consideration. Finding out. Knowing. A relationship had been built on this mutual purpose. On that alone. Hadn't it? His questioning surprised him. He felt an odd tremor of longing, which he dismissed. Longing for what? For whom?

"I was with McCarthy, the detective. I wanted to know how to go ahead with this thing with the keys. You know—to find out how one goes about it." He was stumbling, inarticulate, feeling her eyes on him. He felt ashamed and wanted to tell her to look away.

"Dammit, Viv," he said impulsively, "Lily was pregnant. Six weeks with child."

To dispel her doubts, he went on, haltingly, to describe McCarthy's attitude, which could only be characterized as hateful. He was convinced the man's information was correct, despite the way it was proffered.

Her face registered the same total incomprehension as in her reaction to McCarthy's first revelation. Her body seemed to stiffen as she took the blow. But as he continued to talk, the outward tension eased, and her eyes narrowed, squinting at him as if some psychic myopia were inhibiting her comprehension.

"He really thought that by telling us about the possibility of their having an affair, he was doing us a favor," Edward said. "I guess when he saw we were going to peek under the rug anyway, he decided to show what else was swept under it. Something like that."

Without comment, she stood up and went into the kitchen. He heard the clatter of dishes and the refrigerator door open and close. When she came back, she brought tiny frankfurters on a plate, each skewered with a toothpick. A tremor betrayed her anxiety. She put the plate down on a cocktail table and sat again, in the chair farthest from him. Don't blame me, he wanted to say. She had clasped her hands on her knees.

"Whose child?" It was, unmistakably, a hard inquiry.

"I don't know," he said, the words choking.

He felt a squirming sensation, stood up, and began to pace the room. He felt her eyes following him. "Maybe if the Medical Examiner had taken blood tests. The real question is: Does it matter?"

"Of course it matters," she said, lifting her clasped hands and banging them emphatically on her knee. He stopped his pacing and looked at her. Was it possible that a child he had conceived had died?

"It gets us one step closer to the truth," Vivien said.

"Except that the real truth is hiding under a ton of earth."

It was another thing to hate them for—creating this uncertainty.

"Unfortunately," he said hesitantly, "it raises rather intimate and distressing questions."

She averted her eyes, looking down at her hands clasped around her knees.

"I'm a big girl, Edward."

"Well, then," he said haltingly, "we weren't planning a family. As a matter of fact, Lily was rather adamant. Very cautious."

"Was she on the pill?"

"No. She was afraid of side effects." To spare her further inquiry, he said, "She used a diaphragm."

"She could have forgotten. It happens sometimes. I'd forget to take my pill sometimes. But Orson was always there to remind me." Her lips tightened. "I would have been happy to have more kids," she said wistfully. "Five years is a long time."

"Lily never forgot," he said, feeling again the full fury of her betrayal. He remembered her sleep-fogged plaint, which he mimicked in his mind, "Not now, Edward. It's not in." At those times he had assumed that her thoughts were elsewhere. Sex was not one of her priorities. He had blamed that on her job and its increasing demand. A cold shiver shot through him. The last year was not a banner year for sex, he thought, his anger rising.

"If you'd rather we didn't discuss it . . ." Vivien said.

"No," he said, turning away, bending down to pick up a frankfurter. He didn't eat it but revolved the toothpick in his fingers. "We made love on Sundays. Then we read the papers." He emitted a snickering contemptuous laugh. "I won't dignify the term. We fucked on Sundays, quick, like dogs." The image riled him. "Like missionaries, if you get my drift. No pleasure at all for her. She did her duty. It wasn't always like that. Never quite like that. God, this is difficult." His eyes misted. "Probably my fault as well. You see, you can't summon up much enthusiasm when the other partner just endures it." He turned toward her. "You know what I mean?"

"Yes," she said. "I know."

He inspected her cautiously.

"You felt that, too? I mean, the same way as Lily?"

"Sometimes."

"Him, too?"

"I always showed"—she swallowed hard—"some enthusiasm."

"But you did have a child?"

"What has that got to do with it?"

"I don't understand."

"Conception doesn't need . . . enjoyment."

Was there a tone of ridicule in her voice?

"What I mean is," she said quickly, "it could have been your child. A diaphragm isn't perfect." She instantly regretted blurting it out.

"No, I suppose not," he sighed.

"So you see, it could have been yours."

"Technically."

"And biologically."

He shook his head.

"She'd get up, get out of bed, go to the bathroom. Go through the whole routine. That was a ritual. She was always careful about that. I feel certain—"

"But you weren't there. You didn't see her do it."

"No, I didn't. Wouldn't that have been . . . well, indelicate?"

"I'm merely stating a possibility."

"You didn't know Lily," he said. "She was totally organized. From the beginning. Even long before, when we first knew each other that way, she was cautious."

There was an air of unreality about what he was saying. He had never discussed such details. Even with Lily he would be circumspect, deliberately preserving the mystery, as if to discuss it clinically would brutalize their affection and detract from the spontaneity. But there had never been spontaneity. Again, he felt the gnawing shame of it.

"She could have been distracted. All the heavy pressure of knowing two men at once," Vivien said.

"But he also knew two women." He wondered whether it had sounded aggressive. "I mean, at the same time."

"I don't deny that," she responded defensively.

"Which proves that they weren't even faithful to each other. If they really cared, they would have . . . cut us off completely."

"Don't you see? That would have made us suspicious." She shook her head vigorously. "Maybe in the state they were in it didn't count. Not for them. More like a placebo for us. To lull us into feeling secure."

"Another deduction?"

"Yes. But it doesn't explain the child."

"No. It doesn't explain that," he said.

"I suppose we'll never know."

"How could we?"

He fought for control and discovered that he had crushed the little frankfurter, which he tossed back on the plate. "I'm sorry," he said.

"It's all right."

She went back into the kitchen. While she was gone, he poured himself another drink and drank it fiercely. Inside of him, the anger seemed indestructible, ready to burst out without notice.

She called from the kitchen, and he came in. She had set the table in the breakfast area, overlooking the rear lawn. Through the window he saw the snowman.

"I built that with Ben," she said. "It seems to be shrinking."

He had carried in his drink, upended the glass, and smiled at her across the table.

"Tough stuff," he said, "discussing this."

"It has to be said."

He ate compulsively while she picked at her food. A dimmer had softened the lights, leaving her face in shadow.

"But McCarthy did have a suggestion about the keys," he said after he had gulped most of the food on his plate. While she ate, he explained McCarthy's suggested method.

"Ingenious," she said with a faint note of sarcasm.

"It could take forever."

She looked up at him, but her eyes were lost in darkness.

After dinner she brought out snifters of brandy, and they sat in the living room. Sipping the brandy, his eyes searched the room.

"Seems like a pleasant place."

"It was."

They sat on either ends of the couch, her legs curled under her, his crossed in front of him. Their eyes met, and she quickly looked into the snifter while he continued to inspect her.

"You'd think he had everything: a nice house, a pretty lady to come home to, a son, a good living."

She looked up. This time it was he who turned away.

"Her life wasn't without its compensations."

"I'm not sure. Orson might have been a better bargain."

"Like Lily."

He put his snifter on the cocktail table and turned to face her.

"From the beginning," he stammered, "I wanted to ask."

"Ask away."

"Did you love him?"

"Did you love her?"

"You can't answer a question with a question."

"I certainly don't love him now," she said thoughtfully. "I don't even know who he was."

"I mean before."

"You mean the man that I thought he was?" She grew vague, as if she were suddenly rifling through some index file in her head. "Maybe. Maybe there was a moment."

"Only a moment?"

"You wanted an honest answer. I can only think in moments."

She settled back, took a sip of her drink, then put the snifter down beside his on the table.

"We were at my parents' house in Vermont, Orson and I. It was Christmas. No, the day after Christmas. Snow was falling, white and silent, a soft clean white blanket." Her face flushed. Was it too private for her, too intimate, to confront the vividness of the old memory? "You have to understand that Orson was a very proper young man, the model Ivy League gentleman. And you have to imagine the setting: the Christmas lights, the scent of burning pine logs, the sweet sound of the wood splitting and crackling, the feel of caressing fingers."

Was she deliberately censoring the image for his sake? Inexplicably, he felt pangs of jealousy. She appeared to be struggling to get the words out.

"What I gave him then, at that moment, along with the words of it, the obligatory I love you . . . was my being. Everything that meant my life I handed over to him. It was an act of trust. I gave my pledge willingly, eagerly, without strings. And when he said it as well, I was sure he meant it exactly the same way."

It was as if she were revealing some hidden sin, admitting to a crime against nature itself. Suddenly she became inert. "Goes to prove you should never, never give yourself away. You come into this world alone, you go out alone."

"So you did love him?" For some reason he felt vaguely disappointed by her confession.

"I committed myself to him. Isn't that what it means?"

He started to reach for his snifter, hesitated midway, then pulled his hand back. Entwining his fingers, he cracked the bones.

"Yes. That's what it must mean. It wasn't just saying it. It was believing in it. In its binding power. In its . . ." He searched his mind for a more precise meaning. "In its sense of sacrifice and selflessness. I must have felt that way, too, when I said it for the first time to Lily. Hardly as romantic as your experience. A restaurant in Georgetown, although I remember a spray of pink flowers, and I was looking into her eyes, drowning in them, I suppose. I haven't thought about it much the last few years, but when I said it, I felt the same way as you described. Everybody who says it must really feel it. It has got to come from the depths. Doesn't it?"

She nodded and sucked in a deep breath.

"I'll never give myself away again. Never." She said it firmly, lifting her glass.

"Never," Edward echoed. "Never."

Edward lifted his glass to hers. Both glasses reached out and clinked in a silent toast. They sipped, and their eyes locked. Hers appeared to him suddenly larger, deeper, darker, magnetizing. Perhaps it was the light, he thought . . . an illusion. The long moment became awkward as the silence stretched. Their gazes faltered, and they both looked elsewhere. He looked at his watch, but the numbers seemed blurred. He supposed he should be going, but he wanted to stay. To continue.

"It does seem like a logical idea," she said, breaking the silence.

"What?"

"McCarthy's. You know, checking locks against the key."

"Yes," he said, "logical. But time-consuming." His alertness became acute. Seize it, he urged himself. His heart pounded with expectation, and he grew excited as he remembered McCarthy's plan. The shrinking circles. It would take a battalion, McCarthy had said.

"I'd invest it . . . the time," she said haltingly.

"We could draw the circles, map out a route, and do it methodically. Why not? I'll get a map. We can work it out."

"But your job . . ." she began. "Maybe I could start working on it during the day while you're at the office."

"Yes," he said eagerly. "But what about you? Your son . . ."

"I told you. He's with my parents." She frowned, and he sensed that she did not want the issue raised.

"No," he said firmly. "We do it together." He slapped the table. "A question of priorities. There's nothing more important for us."

"Nothing," she said. He could observe her anger beginning to flare, feeding his own.

"And there is no shortcut?"

"McCarthy would know."

"They mustn't get away with it, Edward," she said, her voice rising. "Leave us like this, twisting in the wind."

The intensity of her fury brought McCarthy's words swarming back at him, stinging. "I didn't put the poison in the cup."

"They won't," he assured her.

25

In the morning, awakening from a drugged sleep, Vivien struggled to remember where she was. Orson's presence still lashed out at her. Would it ever go away?

Despite the absence of his things in the bathroom, his aura persisted. She performed her morning ablutions by rote, as she had done for years, brushing her teeth, washing the moisturizer from her face, brushing her hair, reaching into the medicine chest. Without thinking, she took a pill from the white plastic dial and flung it into her mouth.

"My God, he's dead!" she cried at her confused image in the mirror. Still, the old habit persisted, as if he had been standing over her. It was absurd. Not realizing, she had been taking them every day. The matter of Lily's pregnancy suddenly clarified itself, and she ran to the phone and dialed Edward's number.

It took a few rings for him to answer. He seemed out of breath and annoyed until he heard her voice.

"I've been gathering her things," he said, the irritation gone. "They're coming to cart them away. Everything. I'm never coming back here again."

"Where will you live?"

"A hotel. Anywhere. As long as it's not here."

She hesitated, then steadied herself as she formed the words, but she did not speak them. Surely they had achieved a level of intimacy that made it possible. She remembered last night. Once again it had validated the importance of their alliance. She would be merely offering another deduction to bring them still closer to the truth.

"Edward," she said tentatively.

"Yes."

"Have you still got her things? I mean, what she took on the trip. What was recovered."

"Yes. They're here waiting to be trashed."

"It's pure instinct—nothing conclusive—all part of the things we discussed last night, those intimate things. I'm glad I can't see your face." Her own was hot with a sudden flush.

"I don't understand."

"Perhaps you won't even when I say it. You said . . . well, you said that on Sundays . . ." She waited for his response.

"Yes, I remember."

"You felt certain that she used the device. You said she was quite disciplined about it."

"The diaphragm?"

"Yes."

There was a short silence as she waited for him to comprehend. Definitely a gender gap here, she decided.

"Now remember carefully. You said Sundays. Even recently."

"She was always fastidious about that." He paused. "Yes, even recently," he muttered.

"Would she have known she was pregnant?"

"She had a cycle like a clock. Once, two years ago, she was a week late. She had herself checked out." She sensed the dawning in him of this new revelation.

"Now look among the things that were brought up from the crash—her personal things."

As he searched, something nagged at her memory. A story by Philip Roth in which the diaphragm had become a symbol of commitment. Odd how her perceptions had multiplied, vibrating instincts and picking up distant symbols, as if she had lived in a thick soupy fog for years, all those years with Orson. In the distance she heard his footsteps. They grew louder. Then his voice came back.

"It wasn't there," he said. "It was in its usual place under the sink."

"You see?"

She felt strangely satisfied, knowing that she had achieved a level of intimacy with Edward that she had never shared with anyone, not even with Orson. On that subject she had always been reticent, even with Margo.

"But if she knew she was pregnant . . ." His voice trailed away.

Could she invoke the old cliché about the intuition of women? She decided against it. He might misunderstand. Where was her intuition when it came to Orson?

"Because . . ." She hesitated, not wanting to appear pedagogic about her gender. The problem was to frame the explanation in a way he would understand: Lily didn't want the essence of you to touch her anymore. Instead she said: "It was her way of being faithful." Waiting, she listened for his reaction.

"Sounds almost mystical," he drawled. "But I think I do catch your drift."

He seemed tentative.

"Call it a sisterly deduction," she said lightly. "It's the only explanation that makes sense." She paused. "And Edward, I believe it's important for you to know that it wasn't your child."

"Well, then, that's one mystery that we can dispense with," he said. "Now we can get on to the others." He seemed to be fighting away irritation.

"It was important to know, Edward."

"Yes, I suppose it was," he agreed. "The lying bitch."

"Don't you see? It wasn't your child that was killed. You can rest easy on that score." She had wanted to dispel his uncertainty. Wasn't that the point of the exercise?

"Thanks, Viv," he said gently. "You're right. I wouldn't have wanted to live with that."

Lifting his burden hadn't done much for her own. It galled her to know that Orson had fathered a child with a strange woman while she had yearned for another one, a companion for Ben.

"We'll meet later, won't we?" she asked. For a moment it had worried her that he might have forgotten or been turned off by this new bit of deduction.

"Of course," he said. "We have work to do."

For a long time she sat by the phone, trying to spark her resolve. She got up and walked through the house. Despite all the material renunciations, Orson's presence continued to make itself felt. She sniffed the air, catching the old scents of him. Listening, she heard the floor creak with the rhythm of his movement. His whisper, like a cold alien wind, tickled her ear, mocking and accusatory. "You bastard," she cried aloud, turning, arms thrashing as she ran through the rooms. In the kitchen, she shattered glasses, threw dishes to the floor, defying his sense of neatness and order. Opening a cabinet, she gripped a stack of plates, a wedding gift from his sister, and slid them over the rim. Panting, she leaned against the wall and stared at the broken shards.

"You fouled my home," she sobbed as she fought down hysteria. In the bathroom she splashed her face with tap water, diluting the burning salt tears. When her vision cleared, she watched her reflection in the full-length wall mirror. In the cruel, white light, her skin looked harsh, reddened by her rage. Is it really you?

She traced the line of cheek and chin, assessing what had once seemed attractive. Her long black lashes fluttered over hazel eyes, greenish now, newly washed. Like her father's eyes, always gentle, calmly observant, yet transparent in anguish.

Opening her robe, she saw her breasts, still high and firm. A "well-made woman" was the way Orson had put it. She stood in profile, her bare skin alabaster in this light, her silhouette curved and womanly, the patch at the bottom of her belly, jet black and curly. Compared to others, she had always perceived herself as reasonably attractive, yet something short of beautiful.

Sexy? For her there was only one reliable barometer, Orson's interest. One could not exactly call it lust. Sensuality between them had never been profound, and on the rare occasions when she was orgasmic, it seemed pallid compared with the descriptions of others she had heard or read. Yet she had never refused him. His demands were never urgent. But then, she had no real standard to judge his desire or enthusiasm. Sex between them had never been an issue, never a priority, never a point of contention. Was it something lacking in her, some secret well of desire that she failed to plumb? What had that other woman possessed?

Almost without her realizing, her fingers were trailing lightly over her nipples, which had hardened. Her other hand caressed her thighs, moved through the warm moist thatch of hair, touching skillfully, finding the outer edge of pleasure. She felt the beginning of a rhythmic pulsation vibrating inside of her, a strange, mysterious sensation. A vague image surfaced in her mind: male flesh, musky, urgent. Edward!

She turned away from the mirror in embarrassment. Quickly,

she stepped into the shower, washed her hair, and blew it dry, satisfied that it shined and cascaded with healthy attractiveness. Then she made herself up with more care than she had taken in years.

Dressing, she felt somewhat restored but offended by her earlier outburst and feelings of inadequacy. Fault yourself for ignorance, naivete, and gullibility, but not for some intangible female inadequacy, she rebuked herself. Never mind. They would get to the bottom of it somehow. She and Edward. By then she had totally dismissed her earlier fantasy.

She drove to the bank and withdrew the $9,700 she had saved from household monies over the last few years. She had never considered it a private nest egg, certainly not mad money. Orson had known about it, of course, and she had used it occasionally to buy gifts for him for birthdays and anniversaries, and for little surprises. It would not do at all to have asked for money to buy his own gifts or to use a charge account that, in the end, he would pay for with his own check.

"Cash?" the teller asked with an air of perplexed intimidation. Up to then she had not been certain. In her mind was the idea to transfer the money to a checking account in another bank. This was Orson's bank. She wanted no part of it.

"Yes," she replied. "Nothing larger than a fifty."

The cashier shrugged and counted out the money.

"That's a lot of cash to be carrying around."

She stuffed the bills into her pocketbook, ignoring the remark. Orson might have said it with the same inflection of condescension, and she enjoyed the sense of disobedience.

Before going home she stopped at the supermarket to buy steaks and red wine. She coped with moments of disorientation as she passed the cereal stacks and freezer compartments and resisted loading her cart with products which she had bought routinely for Orson and Ben. She wondered what Edward's favorites might be.

Although the routine of shopping was a familiar one for her, the experience today seemed uncommon; the familiar store seemed foreign. Even her usual clerk at the checkout counter looked at her as if she were a stranger, viewing her meager selection with disbelief.

"That all?"

"Afraid so."

Home again, she found the mess of broken dishes and began to remove the debris. Before she could finish, the phone rang. Edward? It was Margo Teeters.

"I took a chance, Viv. I thought you might be with your folks."

"No," she said calmly. "But they have Ben. There are some loose ends about the estate."

"Are you all right, Viv?" It must have seemed redundant, for she quickly added: "Well, then, let's do lunch. I can cheer you up."

"Not today, Margo," Vivien replied.

"What about cocktails and dinner? How about that?"

"I'm sorry, Margo."

"Just want to give you a lift, dear." Her good humor seemed contrived.

"Not up to it, Margo, really. Some other time."

"Well, let's set it up. I'm sitting here with my calendar. How's Tuesday?"

"I can't make plans."

She had not wanted to excite curiosity, but it was too late.

"What is it, Viv? You can't just brood. What are you doing with your time?"

"Just . . . waiting."

"Waiting? I don't understand."

Waiting? Now why did I say that? Vivien wondered.

"I'm fine, Margo. I just need time away. . . ." Away from what?

"I know I'm being pushy, Viv. I'm just worried, is all. You've had an awful shock. Awful."

"Maybe next week, then?"

"Maybe?"

Vivien hung up, searching her mind. Then she knew. She was waiting—waiting for Edward.

26

The two black men who had come to haul away the contents of Edward's apartment had looked at him through moist red-veined eyes, first with skepticism, then with greed.

"Everything but that," he told them, pointing to two large suitcases and a hanging bag in the corner. As far as he could ascertain, nothing he had packed could be classified as shared. Inside were a few favorite books: *The Collected Stories of Ernest Hemingway* and some of Simenon's Maigrets. Lily had detested Hemingway and had thought Maigret boring. He had mounted a spirited defense, he remembered.

As they carried the items out of the apartment, the younger of the men, perhaps prompted by a fit of conscience, approached him. The other man was struggling down the hallway with one of the heavy upholstered chairs on his back.

"That stuff's not junk," he said. "You could sell it."

"It's junk to me."

"He's gonna sell it anyway. And you're payin' for haulin' on top of it."

"Once it's out of here, it doesn't exist for me," he said. The perplexed man scratched his head. Sometimes pragmatism had nothing to do with economics. As the apartment emptied, Edward began to feel better, as if pus had been drawn from a boil.

"Look at all them shoes," one of the men whistled, seeing Lily's neatly stacked cache of shoes in plastic boxes.

"She had more than two feet," Edward quipped.

The man laughed.

"I didn't have my own shoes till I was ten."

"Life's unfair," Edward said and hated himself for it.

When they had cleared away everything but the suitcases and he had paid the haulers, Edward made one last call—to have the telephone disconnected. Then he carted away his suitcases and hanging bag and loaded them into the trunk of his car. As he drove away, a fleeting memory intruded.

"I love it," Lily had cried. It was more expensive than he had wished, but it was Georgetown. It pleased him to see Lily so happy. Newlyweds then, she was the fulcrum on which all life balanced. "Between us, we can make it, Edward." As a place to live, it hadn't mattered that much to him, except that she loved it and wanted it.

Now he felt an odd pleasure in chucking it all away, especially all the decorating gewgaws on which she had lavished so much time and thought. "Don't you think the couch is beautiful?" He had nodded, only because it was her choice. Every stick, every hue and shade that surrounded them was her choice. That was the way he wanted it. He did it freely, eagerly, absorbing her tastes as his own. "Don't you just love the carpeting?" she had asked. "Great," he had answered. The criterion was her approval, her wishes. What he had done was surrender his will to her. Now the idea revolted him. As Vivien had pointed out, to love meant giving oneself away. He shuddered at the extent of his surrender. For what? he asked himself. To be betrayed.

What Vivien had deduced about Lily's pregnancy offered mixed comforts. He and Lily had discussed children as a practical matter. She had never seemed to view motherhood with the same reverence that he felt, perhaps because she had experienced "family," taken it for granted, whereas he had been an only child and was orphaned now.

It would have disgusted him to know that she had been carrying his child by default, the result of some stupid technical "mistake." A child, in order to be loved, must be wanted. Also, the idea of his own dead baby drowned at the bottom of the freezing river was horrifying. Which left, as before, only the bitter pill of betrayal to feed his anger. She had deliberately conceived a baby with Orson, consciously or unconsciously. It was an inescapable conclusion. Perhaps she considered the genetic mix more suitable —with Orson offering superior qualities. This odd twist of speculation gnawed at him, gathering credibility as it fleshed out in his mind. Would she have carried it to birth, giving it his, Edward's, name? A lifetime of his love and pride lavished on a lie? To crown the cruel irony, she might have even named it Orson, an idea which opened new floodgates of rage. How would he have known? And, as always, he was sure to yield to her decision, probably intrigued by the odd name.

When the anger became too acute to bear, his thoughts shifted to Vivien and to how her deduction might affect her own struggle to confront the truth of Orson's betrayal. Would the insult also carry with it the connotation of her inadequacy? She had admitted a desire to have another child, and yet Orson had refused, preferring to have it with another woman instead. She might take some comfort in the possibility of accident. Such things were said to happen, although, knowing Lily, he doubted that.

She might be thinking, too, of the lifetime of deception that Orson might have held in store for her; he might have harbored this dark secret, revealing it only on his death bed, like in soap operas or Gothic novels, and leaving her to suffer in a lonely misery that mocked a lifetime of love and devotion. Orson, as revealed, was certainly capable of acting out such an evil scenario.

Before getting to the office, he stopped to buy some large colored maps of the area. He had called earlier to tell them he would be late. It was just after noon when he arrived.

"He's on the warpath," Jan Peters told him. "He made us tear up the release. Harvey had to write another."

Despite his foreboding, he was still surprised not to find the rewrite on his desk and rang for Harvey Mills to come into his office.

"The Congressman is on the House floor." He averted his eyes and cleared his throat. "He ordered me to send it down for him to approve." Lifting his gaze, as if he had suddenly gained courage, Harvey watched him through his glasses. Another warning, Edward thought, surprised at his own indifference. Dismissing him with a shrug, he shuffled through papers on his desk. The words shimmered incoherently. Swiveling in his chair, he looked out of the window. Mounds of blackened snow had crusted at the edges of the asphalt, offering a faint reminder of that fatal day. He felt disoriented, misplaced. The phone rang. He answered it, only after it became unbearably persistent. It was Anna, Lily's sister. He caught a tiny edge of contrition in her voice. Still, he regretted picking up the phone.

"Are you all right, Eddie?"

"Yes," he answered curtly.

"I want to apologize for Vinnie. He was upset. You know how he felt about Lily."

"It doesn't matter," he muttered, hoping it would hurry her.

"I had this idea, Eddie"—he could hear her draw in a long breath—"seeing that Lily and I were close to the same size." She cleared her throat. "I pooch a little in the belly." The attempt at ingratiation failed miserably. He withheld the expected polite chuckle. "Anyway, I'd like to have Lily's clothes." She waited. Again he said nothing. "Well, it would be a memory thing, too. She had such beautiful taste, and her wardrobe was fabulous, since she was in fashion and all. If you're not too mad at us . . . I was never your enemy, Eddie."

"No, you weren't." He felt compelled to say it.

"So you'll let me have them?"

Revenge, he thought maliciously. It came in mysterious ways. He wondered suddenly if Lily had confided in her. Sisters in league. They were always jawing together, he remembered.

"I'm sorry, Anna," he said.

"Sorry?" In the pause he heard her breathing grow more labored. "Listen, Eddie, this is Anna. Not Vinnie. She would have wanted me to have them. You know she would. It's the least you can do, seeing that you're going to get all that insurance." So they had already calculated that.

"I gave them away," he said calmly.

"So fast? You did that? You didn't even think that maybe I wanted them?" He would not have given them to her in any event.

"To what charity? Maybe I can explain . . ."

"To none. To the trash."

He wasn't sure whether her response was a cough or a gasp. He pictured the clothes on poor strangers, resisting a laugh from his gut.

"The shoes, too?"

"The shoes, too."

"You're a son of a bitch," Anna said. "Vinnie was right."

He was poised to tell it. Again, he held back, knowing that the telling would diminish himself further in his own eyes.

"You've got no heart, Eddie."

"Is that what she told you?"

Had she also confided the other?

"I'll never know why she loved you," Anna said. She slammed down the phone.

"Did she?" he asked into the buzz.

The Congressman did not return to the office until late in the afternoon. Edward, brooding and unproductive, had not noticed time passing. He sensed in himself a growing isolation from the present. Yet he was fully alert to the past, mesmerized by the images that floated by in his mind, like film running through a moviola: Lily and he running along a beach, the waves lapping and foaming around bare ankles. Acapulco honeymooning. Lying in a hammock on the Pie De La Questa, watching the awesome Pacific Ocean, getting high on cocolocos. (Had he babbled something then about forever yours, swearing it in his heart? Had she sworn it, too? Or was he imagining?) Lily and he strolling aimlessly in Georgetown. Brunch at Clyde's with Bloody Marys, then a walk along the old footpath beside the muck of the dead canal, holding hands. Lily beside him at night, her breathing steady and soft, enveloped in his arms, protected, secure. They had grown used to that style of sleeping, she on her side, her body angled, her buttocks against his belly, his arm stretched out in the space between her shoulder and neck, his hand cupped around a bare breast. Then, suddenly, it had ceased. Not abruptly. Subtly. Then they hardly touched at all. Lily fussed over his clothes and diet as if he were some big male doll. Once she had nursed him through pneumonia, sponging him down, administering medication, worrying over his body temperature.

Sometimes she had asked, lifting her head from a book or fashion magazine she had been studying, propped on pillows, big glasses slid halfway down her nose: Do you love me? And he had replied: Of course. Are you sure? Sure, I'm sure. How do you know? I know. Was it the intimacy of siblings or lovers? It crossed his mind that maybe she had one of those split personalities, two different people living in one. He shook his head, trying to rid himself of the old memories. In their place he saw Vivien, his alter ego now. And more. But he let that thought pass. Never, he told himself. Never, never.

It did not surprise him that the Congressman did not call him into his office. He would be pouting now, in a funk. The office was not humming with work, the staff was not churning with deadlines. The man was undoubtedly frustrated, fuming with subdued rage. There was no more compelling sense of anxiety than that generated by a politician running for office. Months earlier, Edward had submitted a report to the Congressman on the necessity of keeping his name before the public with a barrage of issue-oriented press releases, filling the hopper with bills and stepping up case activity with constituents tenfold.

"You sure we got the horses, Eddie?" the Congressman had asked. Edward felt strong then, ambitious, confident.

"Sure, I'm sure."

"To do it, I've got to have the backup."

"You've got it."

When a man had a secret oasis, he could trek any desert. His oasis was a mirage now. And he was tired and thirsty, and the sun was melting his eyes.

Taking out the maps he had bought, he unfolded them. To do what McCarthy had suggested, he had had to buy both a map of northern Virginia and a map of the District. He cut them apart and pieced together the specific areas he needed. He estimated the outer perimeters in terms of time and distance, drawing a circle, as McCarthy had suggested, then dividing the circle into manageable slices.

As he worked with the maps, Jan Peters came in, looking troubled.

"What is it?" He was hunched over his desk, studying the maps.

"There's a nasty-looking man outside. Wants to see you."

"Has he got a name?" He did not look up, although he could see the lower part of Jan's torso, fingers nervously tapping her thighs.

"He wouldn't give his name." She was obviously annoyed by his lack of concern. When he did not respond further, he saw her body come closer. She bent over the front of his desk. He could smell her sweet breath.

"What are these?"

"Just maps."

"The Congressman is working around you, Edward. He's

madder than hell. You're going to lose your job. You know he doesn't care about people."

Not as human beings, he thought. Ignoring her, he made marks on the map with his magic marker. He felt her hand on his arm, staying his movement.

"It's no joke," she pleaded.

At that moment, Vinnie burst through the door, a vast bulk, snorting like an animal, sending off waves of sweaty body odor combined with the stink of rotting wine grapes. Looking up, he saw Jan sidestep out of his way. She stood now with her back to the wall, a hand clamped over her mouth, her eyes popping with fear. Oddly, Edward felt no panic. Vinnie's meaty hand grabbed a handful of shirt just below his neck and lifted him out of his chair.

"Fuggin sombitch," Vinnie hissed as his free fist shot out and landed on Edward's cheek. The blow glanced off the bone. A large pinky ring opened a cut, and he felt the moist warmth of his own blood. Jan gasped out a scream.

"This bastard trashed my sister," he said, turning fierce eyes to Jan, who obviously had little choice but to endure the role of witness. Edward struggled to get free of the man's grip, but without success. Vinnie's free fist drew back and shot forward again. This time, Edward shifted his head, and the blow passed harmlessly into the air. Vinnie's heavy body lost its balance and fell over the desk, shredding Edward's shirt.

As a reflex, Jan shot forward and jumped on Vinnie's back, while Edward pinned down his arms. But the man was a bull, and all three fell to the floor. The thump knocked books and files off their shelves. As they struggled, Edward saw startled faces in the doorway and heard the Congressman's outraged voice.

"Stop this at once."

Vinnie continued to struggle, but they had gained the upper hand and the fight was going out of him.

"All right. All right," he shouted. Edward and Jan released him reluctantly. When he was still, they backed off. Vinnie lifted himself off the floor. The Congressman shooed everyone but Jan, Edward, and Vinnie out of the office and closed the door.

"Are you all crazy?" he asked. Vinnie had eased his bulk into a large leather chair, and Jan was staunching blood running out of Edward's cut cheek.

"I insist on an explanation," the Congressman said, his eyes roving, inspecting in turn each face of the participants.

"This man came running in . . ." Jan began.

"It's not your problem, Jan," Edward interrupted. "He's my brother-in-law."

"Fuck you," Vinnie croaked, lifting a fat index finger and pointing. "I'll get you."

"We can't have this," the Congressman said.

Edward knew then that there was no sense playing the charade. Beneath the guise of command, he knew the Congressman was scared. Little incidents like this had a way of getting out to the press, spoiling public images. He brushed away Jan's hand, which held a crumpled ball of reddened tissue. His fingers probed the swelling. The blood had thickened although it still oozed. He grabbed a wad of tissue and held it to his cheek. By then, Vinnie was calmer.

"Wasn't for him, she'd still be here," Vinnie said, his face puffed, his eyes filled with hate. "Now he's gonna get rich off her."

With effort, Vinnie pushed himself out of the chair. "It's not finished," he croaked.

"No, not finished," Edward said, noting that the Congressman's eyes had drifted to the maps. Far from finished, he thought. Vinnie glared at him, displaying the full measure of his hatred, then stumbled out of the room.

When he had gone, the Congressman looked at Jan.

"Leave us please."

Hesitating, she looked at Edward, who nodded. Moist-eyed, she walked toward the door.

"Not a word of this," the Congressman warned after her. She threw him a look of contempt, then softened, nodded, and left.

"Shit," the Congressman said after she had gone.

"I'm sorry," Edward said. With his free hand he tried to straighten his shredded shirt.

"Are you trying to ruin me?" the Congressman asked.

The question, of course, required no answer. Any explanation, however plausible, was useless. Invoking past loyalties and reminders of devoted service would have little meaning now. To both of them. It was as if Lily's scenario of deceit were unfolding from the grave, as if she were continuing to punish him for some unknown sin for which there was no forgiveness.

"I'm counterproductive now," Edward said, feeling little regret. His cheek pulsated with radiating pain, making his eye twitch.

"Maybe when you get over this . . ." the Congressman began.

It was, Edward knew, a statement meant to be interrupted, and he did so, obediently. "Maybe. In the meantime, I'd suggest you get someone else. Perhaps Harvey."

The Congressman nodded. Edward could see him winding up for hearts and flowers. Politicians were expert at eloquent farewells, flowery testimonials.

"Not now," Edward said. He had had quite enough hypocrisy for one lifetime, thank you. He began to gather up his maps. Then he put on his jacket and moved to the door.

"Edward," the Congressman called. Edward stopped in his tracks. It irritated him to know that he was still conditioned to respond. "He's not Mafia?"

A thin smile curled on Edward's lips. To a midwestern congressman, all Italians were Mafia. Edward shrugged, leaving the question hanging in the air. It was nice to know he had left the man with a touch of fear.

27

Vivien washed his wound with peroxide and pinched it together with adhesive.

"I'm a pharmacist's daughter," she said, watching him inspecting her handiwork in the bathroom mirror. It felt odd, being with a strange man stripped to the waist in the sanctum of the bathroom. More than strange, she knew. She could not deny the tingle of mysterious excitement. His shredded shirt and bloodied T-shirt lay in a heap on the floor.

"Not bad," he said, patting the dressing, smiling broadly at her in the mirror. His body was softer than Orson's, his chest hairier. Blushing, she noted how a thin line of hair trickled onto his belt. Orson had a small patch on his chest and larger pectorals, with better defined muscles on his upper arms. She was surprised at her absorption of these details.

Leaving him while he put on a fresh shirt, she went downstairs to broil the steaks. Despite the cold, she had set up a grill on the outside patio. In the quiet, she heard the faint rustle of pine needles. She turned toward the snowman, his size further diminished by time and evaporation. Thoughts of Ben intruded, which she thrust aside with a ruthless will.

"I'll do that," he called from the kitchen. He was buttoning his shirt. She arranged the steaks on the grill and came back into the house, just as he was putting on his jacket.

Earlier, he had explained briefly what had happened. It had shocked her to see him standing there in the doorway, blood caked on his cheek, a tattered shirt showing beneath his open coat. Under his arm he held a clean shirt. In his hand, inexplicably, he held a small tea rose, which he had taken the time to buy from a vendor.

"Something to chase a bit of the bleak," he said, obviously hoping it would make the sight of him seem less forlorn. She put the flower in a bud vase and put it on the kitchen table.

She gave him the grilling fork, and he went out onto the patio. As she tore lettuce and sliced tomatoes for a salad, she inspected him. Orson had never done the grilling. Orson, in fact, had rarely done kitchen chores. Watching him, intent on his work, squinting low over the glowing coals to get a better view of the steaks' progress, she grew curious about the way he and Lily had carried on with their daily lives, performed the mundane details of their existence. How did they divide the labor? Did he ever cook? Who set the table?

Her mind tried to form pictures of Lily in their apartment. Was she left- or right-handed? What color were her eyes? Did she have good teeth? She tried to imagine the sound of her voice. Was it high-pitched or soft? Were her fingers graceful or boney? Tapered like hers? Conscious of her fingers, she discovered suddenly that she still wore her gold wedding band. Not once since her marriage had she ever taken it off. Reaching for a bar of soap, she lathered her hands and forced it over her knuckle, ignoring the pain. Then she threw it into the trash, along with the leavings of browned lettuce.

He came in ruddy-cheeked. The steaks sizzled on a wooden board. She had lit candles and dimmed the kitchen lights. The little rose stood proudly in its vase. Rarely had she and Orson eaten their evening meal in the kitchen. The formality of the dining room was more to Orson's liking.

"Real cozy," Edward said as he sat down. She divided the steaks, poured out red wine, and offered the wooden salad tools. He dipped them into the bowl and lifted salad onto his plate. The smell of garlic butter wafted upward from the toasting French bread.

In the flickering light, Edward's face seemed altered, more angular. It was not just the swollen welt. When she had first seen him, he had appeared rounder. It could have been her imagination, since she had only the faintest recollection of their first meeting in the Medical Examiner's office. Now his presence seemed to dominate her perceptions.

"We'll have more time to do what we have to," he said after having told her that his job with the Congressman was over.

Beneath the appearance of apprehension, she was secretly pleased. "It doesn't worry you?"

"Not a bit. First, we have this to do. When it's over, I'll take it from there. Besides, what I was doing no longer interested me." He shrugged. "I'm free. There's nothing to hold me. I've got a few bucks saved, and there's severance." He speared a piece of steak and held it up as a pointer, nearly touching a candle's flame. "I agree with what you did about the insurance. It was an act of moral courage. I'm going to do the same."

"But you have no children." A wave of guilt about Ben surfaced, then passed. Would it ever be the same between Ben and her? she wondered, feeling sad.

"There's always charity. Or I can do what you did—set it up for your kid."

"That doesn't seem right."

"There's such a thing as poetic justice. He and Lily were in it together. She was carrying his half-brother."

So he was certain now, she thought with some comfort.

He bit a piece of steak from the prongs and began to chew, watching her. She wondered what he saw, how he would describe her. She wondered what sort of an impression he had of her. A confidante? A companion? A buddy? She pushed the thought away. It was too foolish to contemplate. Their alliance had only one purpose: to crack open the meaning of their spouses' mutual activities. Again, the knowledge of the elaborate deception charged through her. She shivered with anger.

"There are many who would think we're both crazy, not taking the money. The whole principle of insurance is to be compensated for pain."

"I might accept that," he said, "if the pain was in their dying."

"Sounds awful when you say it out loud."

"I know. That's just one more barb they left us with, one more resentment, one more dimension to disillusionment and hate. Before this, I could barely find it in myself. Now it's like something stuck in my tissues. Like lead poisoning."

She put down her fork. Her appetite had left her. Noting that he had finished his wine, she refilled his glass and topped off her own. They finished the remainder of the meal in silence.

He went into the living room and got his maps from the inside of his jacket pocket. When he came back, she had begun to clear the dishes. He helped her, then laid out the maps on the table.

Coming close, bending over his shoulder, she listened as he explained the logistics of the plan.

"We'll find it," he said firmly, looking up. His hand gripped her forearm. "You'll see."

"I'm sure of that, Edward."

He looked at his watch. It was nearly midnight.

"We should start early," he said, getting up. "I suppose I should be going."

She followed him into the living room.

"A brandy?"

"Maybe one."

He sat down and stretched out his legs on a hassock, and she brought him a brandy. Before he drank, his eyes roved the room.

"Grass is always greener." He shrugged, dipping his nose into the snifter. Then he drank and lifted his eyes to the ceiling. They glistened in the faint light, and she knew he was trying hard to prevent the tears from spilling.

It gave her another chance to study him. Physically, he was a thicker man than Orson, less imposing, shorter, softer. His curly hair was growing longer, making him seem younger. If she had met him casually, she wondered if she would have noticed him. He was so different from Orson. Orson exuded an air of self-confidence, containment, and authority. He shopped for his own clothes and turned himself out in a special way, as if his costume were designed specifically for his role. On Edward, she noted now, clothes hung, creased and indifferent. She had taken a special secret pride in Orson's craggy good looks and in watching other women's eyes on him light up with interest. Sometimes, a tingle of jealousy assailed her. Yet he had never been blatantly flirtatious. Never in her presence, she thought bitterly, hating him now—not for dying, for destroying her innocence.

Perhaps, underneath it all, all men were like that. Even Edward. She blinked her eyes, half expecting Edward's image to disappear. It remained, soft, vulnerable, not at all like your standard myth of manhood. Not weak, she added quickly to herself, noting the previous unreliability of her perceptions, or unmale. She noted that even the cleft in his chin had deepened. Her thoughts began to trouble her, and she was relieved when he slapped his thighs and stood up.

"I've got to go."

He had thrown his jacket coat over the back of a chair, and he moved to put it on. Orson would never have done that; he would have hung it up. All his jackets and suits were hung up on hangers, neat as soldiers.

"But where?"

"A motel somewhere." He shrugged. "It doesn't matter. Better than that place."

"That's ridiculous," she blurted.

"It's my choice."

"But I have all this room." Her arm moved about like a wand. "Believe me, I understand your hesitation."

"Do you?" His eyes probed her, and she turned away, addressing him while she looked out into the cold night.

"The house is mine, Edward. I picked it out. It's the only thing I really claim." A wave of panic crested, broke over her. I need you near me, she wanted to shout out.

"I'm in the guest room," she felt compelled to explain. "You can sleep on the couch."

"Like in old-fashioned movies." He smiled, felt awkward. Then he shrugged consent.

"It would make it a lot easier all around."

"I'll make up the couch."

She went upstairs to get sheets, a blanket, and a pillow. She heard the front door open and close, then the slam of a car's trunk. When she came down, his suitcase was on the floor along with the hanging bag. She made up the couch into a bed.

"I still feel funny about this," he said, watching her as she tucked in the blanket.

"I don't," she said, smoothing the blanket. Giving it a final inspection, she said good night and walked up the stairs.

28

"It will be like looking for a needle in a haystack," he told her. It seemed like a gratuitous warning, as if he were still testing her interest.

"As long as it takes," she said, pouring the coffee. Last night he had sensed the intimacy between them. This morning it frightened him.

He had slept well, with little disorientation, knowing exactly where he was. Before falling asleep he had listened to the sounds she made as she moved. Once, in the middle of the night, he had awakened. Straining, he imagined he could hear the rhythm of her breathing. He must have fallen asleep again while listening. When he awoke, he was certain that her own waking movements had nudged him out of sleep.

Dressing quickly, he took special care, wanting to look neat and presentable before she arrived. He felt like a teenager on his first date.

When she came down in the morning, she looked bright and fresh. Her hair was clean and fluffy, and she moved in an aura of a sweet lovely scent. It felt good seeing her.

"You smell good," he told her, feeling an odd thrill in the center of him.

"Just Arpege."

Peripherally, he felt her eyes probing him.

"You know it?"

"Not at all." It seemed curious for her to ask.

"I was afraid it might be hers," she said, averting his gaze. It gave him an excuse to move closer, sniffing. It felt very good to be close to her.

"Did you sleep well?"

"The best since . . ." He hesitated and then felt no need to finish the sentence.

"I'm glad."

To show her his sense of purpose, he opened the maps, leaned toward her, and pointed to the area where they would look first. The idea had expanded in his mind, and he felt the need to repeat the plan he had outlined last night. They would take it piece by piece, he explained. First, they would check all the apartment houses within the area that used Yale locks. That would narrow down the search.

"And then?"

"Where we can, we'll try them apartment by apartment. At some we'll have to enlist the help of a resident manager or a janitor. Someone usually has a passkey where the teeth match up. We'll have to play it as it goes."

If she had any doubts about the process, she said nothing.

"You still agree there is nothing more important than this?" he asked tentatively. He had walked a very thin line of logic, outlining what seemed a monumental, almost impossible, task. He wondered if she thought the idea half-baked.

"Of course."

"It's a psychological necessity."

"Absolutely."

Was mere consent enough of a commitment? Mostly he feared that something would intervene to abort the idea, force them from the task. Did the goals need restating? Would she lose interest or confidence in the idea? He must, above all, not show her any doubt on his part.

She drove his car. At each apartment within the area, he got out and checked the type of locks used. Where he was stopped at a reception desk, he would pose as a salesman from a key company. Since the information seemed innocuous, he managed to ferret it out quickly. Sometimes, when confronting an unmanned security system, he checked the lock with a copy of the key. Few were of the Yale variety, and those that he found did not fit, for which he was secretly thankful. It was still too soon. When he found an apartment house that used Yale locks, he went back to the car, and Vivien noted the address in a notebook they had purchased.

During the first day he came to some inescapable conclusions. In keeping with Orson's and Lily's sense of cunning and secrecy, they would not have chosen an apartment with a reception desk. Or even a lobby with a doorman. What they required was a place with easy access and no prying eyes. They would also need available parking, preferably a parking lot. They were, after all, on a tight schedule. He explained his reasoning. She nodded thoughtfully.

"Am I thinking like Orson?"

"Yes. He would consider details like that."

"He was methodical?"

"Yes. Totally organized."

"If he didn't think like this, this entire operation wouldn't wash." It was more a question than a statement, offered by way of reassurance.

"Yes, I would say so."

It had not occurred to him until they were heading home after the first day's excursion that his reasoning had narrowed the search.

Over dinner, at a small Italian restaurant in McLean, he reviewed the addresses of apartments that had Yale locks. He was surprised how many used them.

They ordered white pizza, pasta with clam sauce, and white wine. Edward noted that Vivien ate more heartily than Lily, who picked at her food. He observed, too, that her fingers were less languid in the way they moved, stronger. Physically, Lily was more wiry, more fragile looking, although on balance the comparison did not make Vivien seem less delicate.

The texture of her hair was different as well: Lily's had a silky quality, Vivien's had a natural curl, an elasticity that made it bounce when she walked. Eating silently, head slightly lowered, he had the impression that she was welcoming the inspection. He wondered if she was enjoying it, as he was.

Vivien's eyes were smaller, despite the difference in their size—Vivien was at least a head taller. Lily had large eyes, wide, dark pools set in well-defined bones, and an aquiline Mediterranean nose; Vivien's was smaller, fleshier. A tremor of rage bubbled up from his gut. Orson's women! When he lifted his wineglass, his hand trembled. A picture of Orson rose in his mind, a large floating face with ill-defined features. He wondered suddenly how his voice had sounded.

"What did he say?" he asked, his query oblique, as if he were ashamed to ask.

"Say?"

"I mean, what did you talk about?" Anger ebbed, although his curiosity hardened.

"When?"

Her eyebrows arched with confusion.

"Like now. If he were here instead of me, what would you be talking about?"

She shook her head, and her hair bounced.

"Ben, I suppose. Yes. I would tell him about Ben. I always told him about Ben."

"I mean talk. Between you. That's more like a report."

"Household matters, perhaps. He would tell me things about the office."

"Things?"

"Incidents." Her fingers tapped the table. "Actually, he never talked about the office much." She was looking down at her plate. "The food. We might have talked about the food. No—the wine. He was very interested in wine."

"Nothing more meaningful?"

"Like what?"

"Aspirations? Ambitions? What you both felt inside? Plans? People? Did you talk about people?"

"I did," she said brightly, as if she had found a hook on which to hang an adequate answer. Then she shook her head. "I'm sorry, Edward. We certainly talked, but I can't seem to remember what about."

"Politics, books, art, movies, television?"

"He seldom watched TV, and we rarely went to the movies."

"All right, then, the newspapers. Topics that you might have come across."

"I read the morning paper," she said pointedly. "Of course, he was already gone."

"Health. Did he talk about health? He was a jogger."

"On occasion," she said. "When he first started to jog, he talked about the cardiovascular system. He also took vitamins and talked about that sometimes. Not often. Sometimes when we were with other people, he talked about that."

"Money, then? Did you talk about money?"

"No. Not often. He simply deposited money into my account, and I took out what I needed. Like a household allowance. I saved nearly ten thousand dollars."

"I'm running out of categories," Edward said, slightly exasperated. "You're teasing me?"

"No, I'm not. Not all communication is based on talk, you know." It was a feeble defense, and he was sure she knew it.

"I'm getting a picture of a rather quiet man."

"He was quiet."

"You didn't play games? Cards? Bridge? Scrabble?"

"No. He hated games." She shrugged. "Sorry."

"Then what in hell made him so damned interesting?" He had raised his voice. A couple at the next table looked at them.

"To Lily or to me?"

"To both of you."

She sighed, sipped her wine, then motioned with her index finger, a kind of no-no gesture.

"We were a married couple. We shared a present, a child. It was never a question of interesting. He was part of a shared life. He worked very hard and liked what he was doing." She looked into her wineglass, inspecting. "Mostly he read law briefs. I read novels, best-sellers. He was a rising young Washington lawyer."

"All right. So he was successful."

Was it a stab of jealousy? She looked up at him, waiting patiently for the next question. She had, he admitted, submitted gamely, like a patient undergoing medical tests. The level of anxiety seemed to be higher on his side.

"I'm trying to be scrupulously accurate," she said.

"It sounds boring."

"But it wasn't." It was, he was sure, a protest to his conclusion, not a defense of Orson.

"Where was the excitement?" He kept his voice controlled.

"Excitement?"

It had become an abstract interrogation, and for some reason he felt she was decoying him off the scent, deliberately protecting some inner part of herself.

"Maybe I've used the wrong word," he corrected, his frustration rising. Again, she seemed to read his mind.

"How about contentment?" she asked.

"Sounds like something you do when you get old."

"Put it another way, then, Edward. I was satisfied. I had my house and family. I know, measured against Lily it must sound deadly dull. It's all right. . . ." She looked up at him, her eyes wide with apology. "I've had to defend what I had become before. I'm used to it. I know, I'm running counter to the times. Nor am I rationalizing because I did not choose to go out and fight the world. I'm all for the equality of women, but the hard fact is that I liked being a housewife. I liked my persona as "wife of." I liked the idea of having a man. My man. I never felt boring or submissive. Not then." She lifted her wineglass. "I thought he liked his life, too. Shows you." She took a deep gulp of the wine. "Maybe I imagined him." She laughed suddenly, eyes narrowing.

He paid the check, and they went back to her house. She was silent as they drove. When they came into the house, she straightened his couch bed, mumbled some perfunctory remarks about "being bushed," and went upstairs.

He knew he had offended her, and it upset him.

29

Sometime in the middle of the night her anger erupted. She had not slept. Resentment gnawed at her. How dare he try to assign blame? His implication had been quite clear. She was a boring little housewife, and Orson was primed, conditioned by a dull life, to climb into the arms of the first strange woman he encountered. Well, it was his wife. What the hell was her life like? Maybe she, too, was bored. Bored by him.

Putting a robe over her dressing gown and running a brush through her hair, she marched down the stairs. The lamp next to the couch flashed on as she reached the landing. Edward was squinting up at her, rubbing his eyes. He sat up. His torso was bare.

"What is it?"

"I couldn't sleep," she said, pacing, then alighting on the chair opposite the couch.

"Now me," she said. "There are things I need to know."

"Now?" Watching him, an odd note of comparison charged out at her. Orson always slept with pressed pajamas, which she had laid out neatly under his pillow.

"What did Lily talk about . . . with you?" It had come out more like an accusation, which she did not regret. "I'm expecting the same candor," she warned.

"Of course. . . ." He paused thoughtfully. "I've been thinking a lot about our life together, Lily's and mine. She was very much involved with her work—fashion. She knew all the designers, and she was always asking my opinion. 'What do you think of this Adolpho, that De La Renta, this Rykiel?' In retrospect, I evolved a whole series of automatic answers: A bit daring. Too overemphasized. No grace. Colors too primary. Comments like that. I wanted to look interested, but I really wasn't, you understand. I was proud of her, of course. But I didn't have a visceral interest in her work."

"And you? What did you talk about?" she persisted.

"My job. The Congressman. Snippets of office gossip. Again, in retrospect, her interest was probably as lukewarm about my work as mine was about fashion. Actually, she didn't really like politics. To her credit, she said so. I never told her how I felt about fashion."

"So what did you share?" She felt pugnacious, aggressive.

"We were absorbed in our individual work."

He seemed discomfited, and it gave her some satisfaction.

"We did go to the movies when we could," he said. "Ate in different restaurants. Twice we went to Europe—once we toured England, and we spent two weeks on the Riviera. That was fun. We did make plans for other vacations, and we read the travel folders."

"Orson and I would sometimes go to France on one of his business trips. I liked that."

"But it was outside ourselves, a diversion."

"Did you argue?"

"Not much." He shrugged. "Sometimes it would aggravate her that I wasn't more positive in my views—like when she decorated the apartment. I think she would have liked me to be more decisive."

"Why weren't you?"

"What mattered was that she was happy with what she got. I was satisfied with most of her decisions. What I mean is that much of what she did, well, it didn't matter as much to me. I was content . . ." He stopped short and looked at her, confused.

"There," she said smugly.

"Secure, then."

"What about happy? What ever happened to happy?"

"I suppose I was happy."

"So was I. You weren't bored?"

He stroked his chin, and the blanket slipped below his waist. She noted from the bit of haired flesh revealed that he was completely nude.

"No, I wasn't."

"You liked being married?"

"Yeah. I suppose I did. It was a lot better than being alone. Before I was married, I was alone a great deal."

"What about friends?"

"Oh, I had friends. But after we got married, we sort of narrowed the circle. Socially, things revolved around what each of us was doing. I guess the bottom line was that we had each other."

She watched his Adam's apple bob as he swallowed with difficulty.

"At least, I thought so. Yes," he said bitterly, "I thought so."

"You had someone in the whole wide world that you could trust."

He nodded.

"Someone you could commit your life to."

"Like the vows said: In sickness and in health. Till death do us part." His lip curled into a smile. As it formed, it became a snarl. "There's an irony for you."

"You never once thought that you had made a mistake? That it wasn't the least bit what you had expected?"

"No, I really didn't."

"That you had made the wrong choice?"

"No, I didn't. I liked coming home to Lily. I liked being with her. I liked looking at her." His voice lowered. He seemed to be forcing his eyes to stare at her. "Touching her. Sleeping side by side with her."

"It didn't sound like it . . . earlier—" she thought in graphic terms, but she couldn't bring herself to say it "—when you discussed making love."

If he sensed her sudden inhibition, he gave no indication. She felt an odd tingle deep inside her, a growing need.

"You adjust." He shrugged. "If you make too big a deal of it, you create problems. I lived with it. Not everything melts at the same heat." He looked toward her, started to say more, then pouted.

"Am I embarrassing you?"

"A little."

"You never looked at another woman?"

"Looked? Yes, I looked. That's human, isn't it? But I never went beyond that. It was an article of faith . . ."

Inexplicably, she felt relentless.

"Do you think she was frustrated? As a woman? A mass of unfulfilled inner needs?"

"Maybe." He said it slowly, watching her. "All of us are frustrated, one way or another. Nobody gets everything he wants. Or needs." Inside, his older view of his marriage was in flux. Like hers. A battleground.

Why did we marry who we did? she wondered. Had she overstepped, cast blame? By then her anger had dwindled, and she felt she owed him something.

"Do you think Orson was?" she asked.

His eyes widened. "How could I know that?"

"You're a man. What is it that men want?"

"I can't speak for all men," he muttered. "Only for myself."

"Well, then . . ."

He rubbed his chin thoughtfully. "In retrospect, I can see all the missed possibilities." She felt his eyes bore through her. "You don't know what you've missed until you miss it. Right?"

She shrugged, then nodded.

"What about you?" he asked. "Sounds like you were as content, fulfilled, and satisfied as a pig in swill."

"Now that's an ugly way to put it."

"Sorry."

Had she been, as he put it, a pig in swill? She wasn't quite as sure as she had been. Perhaps in a clinical way, if one used as evidence what was written in popular magazines, designed to make women feel inadequate, she could classify herself as discontent. As they say, the earth didn't move. But then she never truly believed it was supposed to.

"Can't we stop apologizing?"

"All right. But something was obviously missing somewhere," Edward said. The remark rekindled her anger.

"Maybe if they were alive, we could all sit down and discuss it—the four of us. Then we'd know why."

"I've upset you."

"Maybe something was missing in them. Ever look at it that way?"

She stood up. Would it always be like this, the chronic uncertainty, the gnawing presumption of inadequacy? Even when they came to the end of the maze, found all the paths? That was the ultimate fear: never really knowing the truth of it. She felt the urge to strike out at Edward, confront him with his abysmal lack of perception, his appalling ignorance. He was a man, dammit. He should have known. Couldn't a man tell when his wife was cheating?

"How could you not know?"

"And you," he snapped.

"I'm going up now," she said, sweeping her dressing gown around her.

Lying in bed, frightened and inert, she listened to the sounds of her pumping heart. There had been some promise in the idea, a ray of hope. Now a dark curtain had come down, shutting out the light.

"It's a question of finding out. Isn't that what we're doing?"

His voice was in the room. Rising on her elbows, she saw his outline looming over her. He had wrapped the blanket around his waist.

"Finding out what?"

She did not reach for the light.

"We agreed to be truthful," he stammered.

"I was."

"Too much so. It hurt me, too."

She softened somewhat and stole a look at him; the bare chest, the bulking silhouette. In the darkness, his features were vague, but there was no mistaking the hurt.

"I wasn't boring. I never felt boring."

"I didn't say you were."

"I was efficient, devoted, loyal and, yes, loving."

"So was I. You don't marry somebody for entertainment." Again, she felt the heat of her anger.

"I know that." He must have seen the rage rising, for his voice was lower, placating.

"When you describe it honestly, it does sound uninteresting. But it goes deeper than that. You're together to do a life, to make a family, to offer emotional support. Maybe we didn't discuss politics or art or movies or television or his law business. Not everything that passes between a husband and wife falls into a category. I mean, if he had a headache and complained about it and I gave him an aspirin, what would that come under? Nursing?"

"Vivien, really . . ."

"And what about support? Plain old-fashioned prop-up support. The kind that lifts you when you're down and joins the cheering section when you're up. I've done my share of both, but I can't count that under any category either."

"Really, Viv, I hadn't meant . . ."

But she was deep into it now, unstoppable.

"No. I didn't have any special interests outside of Orson and Ben. I didn't have hobbies. I didn't join clubs. You might say I was an outsider in a way, which might have made me somewhat dull, although I never thought of myself as dull. This was a part of my life reserved for wifing and motherhood. I can't help the biological clock. Some women just breeze through it happily. I thought I was one of those." For a moment she waffled; a wave of self-pity crested, broke, then went past her. Still her anger was not fully vented. She tried to penetrate the shadows between them.

"I know what you're really after." She grew suddenly cautious, then angry again. "Men and their . . . their things. That's the standard for everything. You want to know about our sex life."

"It's just one factor. A piece of the puzzle, I suppose."

"I never once refused him. Not once. Pallid, placid little Vivien. Always available. Only he wasn't too peachy keen most of the time. He wasn't always, as they say, hot to trot. I suppose you can blame me for that as well." She paused, feeling a sly malevolence rise inside her. "I'd like to know more about your little woman. Did you move the earth for her?"

"No, I didn't," he said, "if that's what you want to know."

His answer calmed her. There was no mistaking his sad regret. Wasn't it, after all, a prime measure of manhood to be capable of giving a woman satisfaction? Or was that another old-fashioned shibboleth to keep women lying, faking passion? As she did. What bothered her most was the indelicate way in which men treated the process, the act. Orson was, at first, gentle, caring. It was lovely to nestle in his arms, to feel him deep inside her. Something had changed later. In him? Or her? She couldn't be sure. Nevertheless, the exchange of flesh was still an act of faith between them, a renewal of the bond. Did it always have to be measured in ecstatic pleasure?

Perhaps it was futile to berate this man, torture him further. It may be, she thought, that the chasm of understanding between men and women was simply impossible to bridge. Reaching over the space between the beds, she touched his arm.

"I'm sorry," she said. "Maybe it's also a category. Classify it as blowing off steam. I never did with Orson."

"Maybe you should have."

All anger had seeped away.

"There was just nothing to fight about. Or I didn't see it. Funny, how much more aware I am now. A little late. Too soon old und too late shmart, as the Pennsylvania Dutch say."

In the darkness she felt the grip of strong fingers on her hand. With his other hand he was stroking her arm, and her skin broke into goose bumps. But she did not pull away. He moved across the space to her bed and held her. She felt the warmth of his flesh against hers, her nipples hardening against his bare chest. His arms encircled her, and she brought hers around him, stroking his back and shoulders. He was trembling.

"What is it?" she whispered.

"I don't really know."

Her fingers stroked the nape of his neck, and his reached into her hair. Shivers shot through her. The inevitable comparison surfaced in her mind, the different touch, the different aroma, the softer body. His hands fondled her breasts. Was he, too, inspecting, comparing? She desperately wanted to know what was going through his mind at precisely this moment. If she asked, would she get a truly honest answer? She did not ask. In men, sex seemed an imperative, an uncontrollable urgency. At this point Orson would be spearing into her, beginning the inevitable primal stroke.

They stretched out on the single bed. Holding her gently, he made no move to enter; his hands gently explored, as if he were frightened her flesh might tear at the slightest movement. She held him, caressing him as if he were a small boy. Like Ben, she thought. When she kissed him, his lips were firm and warm, his probing tongue gentle and caressing.

Often with Orson she had concentrated with all the power of some inner force, waiting for the signals to begin of the ecstasy that rarely came. Yet with quiet, enduring patience, she had listened for his impending shudder, anticipated by a storm of shortened breaths and heated flesh, as he moved with relentless energy to what she assumed was the imperative moment of joy. Always, it was mysterious, a ferocious, private, male experience. Sometimes, when he had rolled off her and his steady breathing indicated that he had slipped into an alien world she wondered if what had occurred had anything at all to do with her.

Now she felt that her mind and body were opening to some new knowledge over some path bushwacked out of tangled jungle. Edward's hand stroked, his fingers probed as she opened to him. She could feel the blood coursing through her body as she explored him, touching the hard male part of him, the silken skin, and feeling his quickening heart. For long moments he ceased to move, suspended in space and time, letting her caress him until his own rhythmical movement began and she became the caressed.

In him she felt none of Orson's urgency, none of the domination. A pact of equals, she decided, as they held each other without discomfort in the narrow single bed, their bodies adjusting, fitting together like pieces of a jigsaw puzzle of a barely comprehensible picture. It was, surprisingly, she who took the initiative, drawing him into her, deep inside, holding him there as the intensity of her need erupted.

She had not looked for signals, and when they came, they startled her. She felt gripped by a powerful inner hysteria to which her body surrendered, frenzied, mindless. Yet she knew that wherever it took her, he was there with her, she was not alone. He was reacting to her and with her. She let it happen, floating in its moist vortex, abandoning herself to wave after wave of pleasure, sure that his body was responding in kind.

It took a long time for them to quiet down. When he started to speak, her fingers reached out and touched his lips.

"No."

She wanted no explanations, no post mortems, no excruciating analysis, no rationalizations, no deductions. Why had this happened with Edward and never with Orson? She was afraid to know, afraid that, whatever it was, knowledge would diminish it, make it disappear. Something had changed inside her, and it would reveal itself soon enough, she decided.

30

Edward shared her fear. Emotional scrutiny, translated into words, had the power to distort perceptions. Wasn't it enough to feel? To be moved? Talk might change the delicate calibration. Go with it, his mind told him.

It was as if Vivien had probed deep inside him, found something that belonged to her in his heart and he had urged her to take it. He knew that it was not a one-way transaction, but he dared not inquire; he was fearful that what he had from her was stolen, not freely given.

Whatever it was, he would not give it a name, would not hold it up for identification. Neither did he want it labelled or defined. Giving it a name would either trivialize it or, worse, put it in the category of aberration.

For three weeks their actions held to an unvarying pattern. It proceeded, naturally, by silent mutual consent. They would rise early, always a joyous awakening for him, locked in each other's arms. Awake first, he would gently kiss her closed eyes and feel the tickling flutter of her lashes. Then her lips would nuzzle his face, her knowing fingers would roam his flesh as his caressed, searching for the triggers of her special joy. Soon they pursued each other with frantic abandon. Each final phase, when their bodies closed in the primal embrace, was a restatement of their passion, a celebration of ultimate joys and fulfillment.

Yet when they stepped out of bed, it was as if they had entered into an untracked void, an environment of menace and danger. It was that sense of infinite uncertainty that gave meaning to their search. It took on a mystical aspect, like the hunt for the holy grail which would miraculously unlock the secret of life. Without knowing, without finding, nothing between these two separate aspects of their lives would ever connect.

At breakfast they studiously avoided the subject of themselves.

Yet they watched each other, like animals circling with wary inspection, always with caution.

When they talked, it was with measured words, with the focus always on their objective as if that other part of their lives did not exist. They drove from apartment building to apartment building, following the relentless preconceived pattern, never varying, writing down each building that used Yale locks. Paradoxically, each notation somehow seemed a diminishment of themselves, generating an awesome, all-encompassing fear that, once it was found, exorcism would be achieved, and there would no longer be anything to hold them together—like being between the devil and the deep blue sea.

Compulsively, they persisted in questioning each other about the other life, as if it might hurry the process of understanding. Lily. Orson. Memory became more clinical, less visceral, and oddly repetitive. In the end, comparing their marriages was like comparing different kinds of apples. They were similar in taste and texture, but decidedly different.

When they did not eat at the little Italian restaurant in McLean, they ate at Vivien's house. Neither would dare suggest varying the routine.

By the end of the three weeks they each knew more than they might have wished about the material facts of each of their former spouses. Yet they continued to probe, both of them knowing that the real mystery remained, the ultimate questions were unanswered: Why had they been betrayed? Why had they been unable to detect it? Why had they married who they married? In the evening after dinner they went up to the guest room and made love. Quickly, along with their clothes and inhibitions, they shed all the formalities and insecurities of their other life. Flesh was their medium of communication. It was like living life in a euphoric limbo. Except for the fear of its ending abruptly one day, being with her in this way was the closest thing to paradise he could imagine.

At times there were intrusions, which heightened their fears. Her parents called more often from Vermont. When was she coming for Ben? Soon, Mama. But when? Soon. It was another thing not to be discussed. Dale Martin, too, called often about the insurance, trying to talk her out of her decision. That pressure was more easily deflected. Once the lady from the farm where Hamster was boarded called.

"We're not having too much luck."

"Keep trying," Vivien said. "I'll send another check." It occurred to her that it might be better to put Hamster to sleep, but she did not press the point. Not yet. Soon.

It became apparent that "soon" was an answer applicable to everything, the ultimate tentative. Even for Edward.

"When do you think we'll have the information we need to begin to check the keys?" she asked.

"Soon," he told her, looking at the map.

He hoped soon meant never. Another question begged an answer from her, but he would not ask it because its meaning had been distorted by their experience. Do you love me? And if she said yes, would it have any meaning at all? And if it were no? It comforted him to know that either answer would ring hollow and untrue. Why then was it important to know?

When the backlog of other questions became too much to bear, he had only to look at her, feel the quickening of his pulse beat, sense the enormity of her power over him. At night, in the narrow bed, holding her, embracing, caressing, merging into the oneness of a single being, all questions disappeared. All doubts fled. All fears subsided.

Practical considerations became vague and less defined as each day passed. Such mundane items as money had little impact on them. He had filled out a forwarding card at the post office and had received his severance check, which he had cashed, adding the money to the pile that was in the top drawer of the guest room dresser. They made no attempt to separate the monies, taking only what they needed. Whatever bills came, she paid by money order.

They were always within earshot, if not within visual communication. Mostly, they were within touching distance. And their eyes locked often. They allowed themselves only a single outward symbol of tender sentiment. Every few days he would buy her a fresh single tiny rose for the bud vase. "Must never let one die there," he told her. "Never."

Their universe had narrowed to the sparest economy of space. They moved in four rooms: kitchen, bathroom, living room, and guest room, where the space further narrowed to a single bed, one dresser, and one closet. Where it was possible, doors closed off other rooms, like the master bedroom and Ben's room. They rarely used the den, Orson's place, except to pass through, but only when necessary.

They sat close together in the car. He usually drove, and they weaved through traffic with no sense of the pressure of time or annoyance.

When the dreaded intrusion came, he rejected it at first as an illusion. Then it became undeniable.

They were being followed.

He did not have to formally transmit the apprehension. In their state of heightened awareness, nothing untoward could be hidden from one another. It had happened at the beginning of the fourth week, in the morning. He had been conscious of the car following almost from the moment he had left her street. His eyes kept darting into the rearview mirror, then shifting to the side mirror. She had turned in her seat as he swung the car into turns, up side streets, and parked in the lot of a shopping center.

Two men were inside the car, and they stuck to the trail with dogged tenacity.

"What do you think?" she asked.

His immediate thought was Vinnie.

"I'm not sure."

More than simply danger, it triggered in both of them the fear of the real enemy . . . change. She had moved closer to him on the seat, her hand gripping his thigh.

For the rest of the day they continued as they normally did, checking apartment houses, making notes. In the evening they came home and peered out the front windows of the darkened house. The car was there, hidden beyond the lighted circles of the street lamps.

"See that?" he whispered, spotting the sudden glow of a cigarette's ash.

"But who? And why?"

He could not give her an adequate answer.

He remembered what the Congressman had asked: "Is he Mafia?" The idea had been patently absurd at the time. Now he wasn't so sure. Vinnie had enough hatred in him to kill. Or to arrange a killing. It was far afield from his experience, but surely possible.

They went to bed and clung to each other, and although they made love, which moved them both as before, he felt that the pattern of their special existence had been tampered with. In the middle of the night he rose and went downstairs to look out the window again.

"Still there?"

She had followed him down.

"Still there."

In bed again, he felt her trembling. She lay with her head in the crook of his arm, and he stroked her hair, wondering if this meant the beginning of the end. Embracing, they drifted into sleep.

The phone woke them. Another intrusion. Their eyes opened instantly, but neither of them made a move to answer it. Nothing that came from outside their world could be the harbinger of good. That was one deduction that did not require words to define. But the ring persisted. Finally, it was he who picked up the instrument.

"Davis?"

The sound of his name startled him. Who could know he was here? How could they know?"

"It's McCarthy."

"You."

He looked at Vivien, whose frown mirrored his confusion.

"It isn't my fault. I'm really sorry about it. But you see, it had to be put into the records. The thing about the pregnancy, too."

"You're not making yourself clear."

His last view of McCarthy resurfaced in his memory: sour smelling, stinking drunk, his features distorted by some secret anger. To Edward, he was running true to form as the bearer of bad tidings.

"They're investigating certain aspects of the crash," McCarthy continued, his voice transmitting his resignation. "It's all very complicated. There are a million details to be checked out."

The crash? What has all this got to do with us? Edward wondered. Not now.

"There was no way to hold anything back. Not from them. Not that there is any hard evidence about anything."

"Really, McCarthy . . ."

He wanted to protest this intrusion, invoke invasion of privacy legalities.

"I'll find a way to make it up to you."

"Make it up? For what, for crying out loud?"

His voice sounded ominous, and his hand gripped Vivien's shoulder.

"The FBI. In a crash of this magnitude"—official jargon crept into his voice—"every facet must be investigated. Since identification was my official responsibility in connection with your respective spouses, I had to give them everything. Everything. They know everything."

"Everything?" Who could know everything? he thought facetiously.

"So they'll be around. I'm just calling to sort of alert you so you'll keep cool, that's all."

"They think we had something to do with the crash?"

Vivien rose on one elbow, watching his face in horror.

"They have to consider the possibility. Just tell them the truth."

"We don't know the truth," he sputtered. That's just the point, he thought.

"If it means anything, I told them they were barking up the wrong tree."

"You know we're completely innocent."

In the silence, he heard a faint crackle. He wasn't sure whether it was the telephone line or the man's voice.

"Nobody's innocent," McCarthy said, the crackle disappearing as the line went dead, leaving a buzz ringing in his ears.

31

Any attempt to hold together their routine now seemed fruitless. They sat in the kitchen, sipped coffee, and watched the rising sun slanting through the trees. It was a clear, cold morning. The snows of January had melted, and the snowman had almost completely disappeared, swallowed by the earth. The only evidence of its brief, transitory life was a battered hat and an old pipe lying on its side in a patch of brown grass.

Something was going to change, and they both sensed it.

The digital clock showed exactly nine as the doorbell rang. They exchanged glances.

"Just tell them the truth," Edward said, his whisper frantic as he rose to answer the ring. His step felt heavy, and he imagined that the floor creaked.

The two men entered, noncommittal, professional. Each wore a three-piece suit and sported a deliberately self-effacing demeanor. One was gray-haired with moist blue eyes and broken veins showing through thin skin on his cheeks. The other was younger with black curly hair, clear eyes, a tight face, and unsmiling. They seemed to have worked out their roles in advance: the gray-haired guy world-weary and laid-back; the young turk a tense eager-beaver.

They flashed credentials, and Edward made a show of studying them. Vivien had followed him, and they all settled into seats in the living room, static characters in a quirky play. Like the illusory search for the lock that fit the keys, its logic was suspect, although its purpose was now clear. They had come to separate them, destroy the elaborate contrivances that had brought them together.

"This is an investigation with enormous ramifications," the older man said. "We have got to explore every avenue, every facet—" he paused—"every motive."

"I understand," Edward said.

"Of course," Vivien agreed.

"No stone must be unturned," the older man said.

"There are many people to be satisfied: the airlines, the industry, the insurance people, the government. You must understand. We're just doing our job."

The older man scratched his head amiably.

"We've been following you, you know."

"How could we not know?" Edward said, looking at Vivien.

"In our business we must be very thorough," the older man said. "We're just conduits. Other people will want to know. The root of the problem is: Why did the plane crash? Was there foul play? Was it an accident? Was it human error?"

"You haven't found out?" Edward asked.

"Not yet," the older man said, looking at his partner. "For that reason we must delve into areas that might seem . . . well, very personal."

Edward nodded, but his guard was up. He exchanged troubled glances with Vivien.

"We've done a great deal of preliminary investigating," the older man said apologetically. He nodded, and the younger man looked into his notebook, flipping the pages. Edward's stomach knotted, and Vivien's complexion became ashen.

"There are lots of different ways to interpret actions. I'm sure you understand."

"Yes," Edward said, turning to Vivien. "I'm sure we both understand."

"If you'd like, we could talk to you separately," the older man said politely.

Again, Edward looked at Vivien, but it was Vivien who answered for both of them.

"No. We're in this together."

"And we have nothing to hide. From you—" Edward paused—"or each other." He wondered suddenly if that were true.

"That's good," the older man said, rubbing his hands. He took out his notebook and opened it. Then he produced a ball-point pen and nodded to the younger man, who assumed the role of interrogator.

He began with names. Mrs. Vivien Simpson. Mr. Edward Davis. Then he recited dates of their birthdays, marriages. "Just routine confirmations," the older man interjected.

Then the younger man crossed his legs and looked at each of them in turn, as if to establish some modus operandi for the interview. For some unspoken reason, Edward assumed that he would be the mouthpiece for them both.

"Did either of you have any knowledge that your respective spouses were involved in an illicit relationship?" The question was flatly put, with what seemed a perfect sense of neutrality.

"None."

"Not the slightest suspicion?" He looked at Vivien.

"I told you," Edward said.

"Not the slightest intuitive idea?" It was quite obviously a question for Vivien.

"We did not know," Vivien said between pursed lips.

"And the pregnancy?"

"Of course not."

"You're certain?"

"Of course I'm certain."

"Did either of you know each other before . . . before the crash?"

"No, we didn't," Edward said. "We met for the first time in the Medical Examiner's office." Vivien nodded.

"Approximately four weeks ago?"

"Yes. That was the first time," Edward said.

"You're positive about that?"

"Absolutely."

"Then you met together at an all-night coffee shop?"

"Yes, we did."

Looking quickly at Vivien, he noted the confusion in her eyes.

"The next day at your apartment?"

"Yes."

"Then in front of the Rayburn Building, where you drove to the deserted parking lot at the Jefferson Memorial."

Edward's pores began to open. His mouth felt parched.

"Is this all necessary?"

"As I explained, we're only the conduit."

"But the implications . . ." Edward began.

"What implications?"

"Well . . . that we were engaged in some kind of conspiratorial plan." In a way that was true, he realized.

"Is that the conclusion you draw?"

"An implication, I said. I'm concerned about the conclusions of others."

"Why is that?"

He looked helplessly at Vivien. Tell the truth, McCarthy had said.

"Never mind."

The younger man looked at him for a moment. Seeing that no answer was forthcoming, he spoke again:

"Mr. Davis, three weeks ago you had all of your possessions moved out of your apartment. Am I correct?"

"Yes."'

"And where did you store these possessions?"

"I didn't."

"Did you sell them?"

"No. I . . ." He hesitated. "I just had them thrown away."

The older man scrawled something in his notebook.

"Then you moved into this house?" the younger man pressed. He looked at Vivien, who averted her eyes.

"There it is again . . ."

"Another implication, Mr. Davis?" the younger man asked.

"Well . . . yes."

"Why don't you simply answer the question, Mr. Davis?" the older man said pleasantly. "It's just factual information."

"All right. I moved in."

"And you, Mrs. Simpson, you've removed all of your husband's personal possessions?"

"Yes," Vivien snapped.

"And your child. Where is he?"

"At my parents' home in Vermont." Her face flushed. "And my dog, a gift from my husband, is being boarded."

"Yes. We know all that, Mrs. Simpson."

"Then why are you asking?"

"I told you. It has to be aired."

"Why?"

"So that every facet is explored," the younger man said patiently. "Really, if you'd like, we could wait until a larger investigation ensues. That's your choice."

"Vivien, we have nothing to hide. Nothing," Edward said.

There was a long pause. The two agents exchanged glances.

"And are you now cohabitating at this house?"

"Cohabitating?"

"Living together, Mr. Davis," the younger man said.

"I don't see what that has to do with anything," Edward protested.

"Maybe nothing," the younger agent said. "One would think the house has, well, inhibiting memories."

"That's disgusting," Edward muttered. He wanted to explain about the guest room but held his tongue. Besides, he was certain they knew that, too.

"Just seems outside the pattern was all I meant," the younger man said. He looked at Vivien. "Considering you had him cremated when he did not specifically request it."

"That, too," Edward sighed.

"It's obvious," Vivien said. "They're looking for motives. They're trying to establish that we knew each other before the crash, that we destroyed them and everything that reminded us of them, that somehow we had something to do with it. How would you put it?" She turned to the agents. "Revenge for profit? Something like that?"

"It's crazy," Edward said. "We're rejecting the insurance. Every cent of it."

"Yes, we've heard about Mrs. Simpson's instructions." He paused, inspecting Edward's face. "Your decision is news to us."

"It's the truth," Edward pouted.

"We're not here to establish truth, Mr. Davis. That is for others to determine."

"But the way it's being put . . ."

"Can we get on with it?"

Edward didn't answer.

"You've given up your job, Mr. Davis?"

"You apparently know the answer to that as well."

"Yes, we do."

"And to everything else?"

"Not everything, Mr. Davis. We were hoping you might lead us to the apartment they used. It's obvious, though, that your method would take forever. That's why we had to see you now. People are demanding answers."

"And we're suspects," Edward said.

"Until there are answers, everybody is suspect."

Surely they were mocking them, dishonoring their sincerity? His mind raced with rebuttals. What did it matter? Their private world was caving in around them. The ultimate irony. It had not been private at all.

"What did you expect to find there? In the apartment?" Edward asked. It had been a central question at the beginning. Not a question really, he thought, more like a focus. Now it had become the goal that held them together. He felt the panic of impending loss.

"As I said earlier," the older agent said with a tinge of exasperation, "we must explore every facet. In this matter there is the technical side and the human side. We haven't the expertise for the technical. Our job is to look into the human aspect."

"Why were . . ." the younger man began.

"Aren't you going to answer my question?" Edward interrupted.

"All right," the younger agent said blandly. "We aren't really sure what we'd find. But the question I was about to ask is: Why were you looking for it"—he paused—"with such methodical zeal?"

Edward shot a glance at Vivien. How could that question be answered?

"That's between us." The four of us, he thought.

"It seemed a very clever plan," the younger agent said. "But too time-consuming."

That was exactly the point. Was there really another?

"I'm glad we didn't do your work for you, then," Edward muttered, his outrage rising. Before either of the agents could reply, he said: "And you're really not sure about the crash, whether any crime has been committed?"

"We told you that up front," the younger agent said.

"Suppose," Edward said, summoning the effort to hold back his rage, "that you do find a crime was committed—a bomb, perhaps, or some other device or method."

"We'd be back," the older agent said.

"Accusing us?"

"Probably," the older agent said, "if the evidence fits the theory."

"So you're working backwards."

"You might say that," the younger agent said. Both men remained cool, soft spoken, and deadly rational.

"Are you here to make us confess to something?"

"Well, you could make it easier on all of us."

The older agent's eyes sparkled with amiability.

"Why us?" He looked at Vivien. Her earlier confusion had disappeared, and he could sense her intensity.

"Three possibilities," the younger agent said without seeking approval from the older one. "Greed, love, and hate. All powerful motives."

"You're off the wall . . ." Edward began.

"I want to hear it, Edward," Vivien said.

The younger man smiled.

"Greed as a motive is weakened by Mrs. Simpson's instructions to her lawyer and your alleged rejection. Could be a red herring, but we're inclined to dismiss it. As for love and hate, revenge and elimination. Take your pick. You don't seriously expect us to believe that your . . . your relationship . . . is of recent vintage. The visible evidence suggests a long-standing relationship. Two sides of the same coin. People just don't get entangled this swiftly."

"So you're experts?"

"We've seen enough of it."

"Which would you say, then?" Edward sneered. "Love or hate?"

"I wouldn't hazard a guess."

"Nor me," the older agent said. He stood up. "I think we've taken quite enough of your time."

The younger agent aped his action. Neither held out a hand as they let themselves out the door, closing it quietly behind them.

Vivien and Edward sat in silence for a long time, stunned by the intrusion.

"They have a point, you know," she whispered. He felt the urge to protest but said nothing. When he looked at her, she turned away.

32

That same day Vivien put her house up for sale. They also discontinued their search for Orson's and Lily's apartment.

The agents had brought with them the cold wind of reality, however absurd the premise. It did cross her mind that the possibility existed for criminal accusation, but that had not been the main point. Love or hate. Take your pick. It had put the matter between them in perspective.

There was no point in searching for the apartment. Ridicule had, in a way, destroyed the premise. It had been an excuse, a dependency. It would take forever, the agents had said, which was the unspoken reason for the search.

What they needed now, she decided, was to escape their memory completely, destroy the influence of their past lives, obliterate them once and for all.

From the beginning, from the very moment that her conscious mind grasped the totality of her involvement with Edward, she had distrusted it. Perhaps it was her New England upbringing which glorified self-discipline, revered reticence. The pleasure, the ecstasy, the sheer joy of it was undeniable, and she had surrendered to it briefly. But hadn't she surrendered herself once before? Never again, she had vowed. Never never never. People had a tendency to repeat mistakes, and the emotions were an unreliable barometer, she told herself. The FBI agents had made that clear as well. They had questioned the speed of her involvement, something which she had asked herself. Entanglement was the word the agents used. Could it really happen so swiftly? Hate had brought them together, not the other. Love could not possibly grow out of hate! Logic told her that their relationship was merely a common defense against the fear of inadequacy. It had set off some bizarre mechanism that had, temporarily, she was certain, unleashed the floodgates of sexual passion.

Whatever the reason, she could not deny the feeling, the communication of the senses. In his presence, in his arms, she had felt alive with a new sense of herself. She was not faceless, not the lump of unfeeling flesh she had been with Orson. Again Orson, resurfacing in her mind, mocked her as always. Still, she had never been so aware, so conscious of her body and of the full range of her senses. Her intellect, too, had never seemed sharper, never more exploring. Even her thoughts were eloquent, her explanations to herself, articulate. If questions and mysteries persisted, they would be resolved through tough and honest reasoning and logical action. In the end, nothing must stand in the way of her complete independence.

She had also agreed with the agents about the house. It reeked of Orson. It was an illusion to think there was any sanctuary here from his presence. It was impossible to get his stink out of the walls, the floors, from the mute and mundane objects. Edward had shown more courage, more resolve, by dumping everything.

Looking for a quick sale, she deliberately priced the house low. The brokers she called were quite pleased to take it on. Edward had already cut most of his lines with the past. It was her turn now to take the final steps.

She called her parents in Vermont.

"As soon as the house is sold, I'll be going away," she told her mother.

"Where?"

She ignored the panic in her mother's voice.

"I'm not sure."

As she spoke, Edward stood beside her. They had decided to go somewhere where all possible reminders of the past could be expunged—maybe a foreign country or some totally different environment in the states.

"You mean just leave Ben with us for an indefinite period?"

Leave Ben? But wasn't Ben an inhibitor of her independence? Why were all these crazy emotions warring inside her? She had no prior experience with these ancient battles. Her other life was safer, more secure. Damn Orson, she cried to herself, leaving her stranded like this.

"I'm not sure, Mother. It's just an idea. Besides, all Orson left in insurance will go to Ben."

"That's only money, dear. Ben is your child."

"And Orson's . . ." She wanted to say more but checked herself. How deep was the power of hate, she thought sadly. Had they destroyed her sense of motherhood as well? Could things between them ever be the same?

"He asks about you often, Viv," her mother said.

"And I think of him." Her voice caught. She disliked this new Vivien, but she hated the other one. "I haven't made up my mind."

"Orson would not approve of this," her mother said. "He would have expected you to carry on with your responsibilities."

"Would he?" Her anger felt like molten lead, overwhelming her.

"Yes, he would," her mother persisted.

"To hell with Orson," she cried.

"I'll pretend I didn't hear that, Vivien."

"Don't pretend, Mother. I'm finished with pretending."

There was a long silence at the other end of the phone.

Vivien felt the tears well behind her eyes and spill over. Her shoulders shook with restrained sobs.

"We love you very much, Vivien. That goes for Dad and Ben."

"I know, Mother." She managed to say it without conveying her agony. Then she hung up.

When she went upstairs, Edward was waiting for her. He took her in his arms and kissed her cheeks.

"Salty. You've been crying."

She nodded.

"It will all come out fine," he said. "You'll see."

Her heart thumped. "Don't you ever say that to me," she cried angrily. "I will not be patronized."

"I hadn't meant—"

"But you did. You have no special gifts of prophecy. The next thing you'll say is trust me. I've heard that before."

"So have I."

She wondered if she had overreacted.

"I might have been testy, but I won't apologize."

Yet she did not disengage. Then his caresses soothed her, and they made love. Sometime in the middle of the night she shook him awake.

"I have to leave this house," she said, shivering. "I still feel his presence here."

He tightened his embrace. "As long as we're together," he said.

His response frightened her. To still further comment, she kissed his lips. No sense raising painful issues just yet, she thought.

In the morning she wrote a note to Dale Martin, telling him she was considering going away and reiterating her desire to set up the trust fund. She told him to mail any papers to her present address, as she was planning to leave a forwarding address.

The next day they visited some of the apartments that they had seen earlier. They found a small efficiency that did not have a Yale lock and arranged for the rental of a bed and dresser from a furniture rental firm. The apartment was on the ground floor of a small building that was surrounded by mature trees which blocked the light, but it was the only place they could find where they could move in immediately. She had filled two suitcases and a cosmetic case, leaving all her other possessions to be sold or carted away when the new owners arrived. She did not look back when she left the house. Sentiment for the past, she told herself, was the enemy. She was in transit to a new life.

"No regrets?" Edward asked when they had unpacked. They had bought a minimum of dishes and pots and pans from the hardware store and stocked the refrigerator with basics. They had bought linens and towels in a nearby department store. They did not order a telephone. And, of course, they brought with them the little bud vase and filled it with a fresh new rose. There was nothing from the other life now except their clothes.

They spent every moment together. And although they did not question their relationship in conversation, as if it were a pact between them, they both felt the sense of transition. Of impermanence. Neither had the courage to confront the dread specter of commitment. It was enough to feel, she decided. Wasn't it?

They had not bought a television set or a radio, no newspapers or magazines. Sometimes, when the days were bright, they drove along the Potomac and then walked along the paths of the parkland that lay beside the George Washington Parkway. Since there was still a chill in the air, the trails were usually deserted, and they could savor the delight of being totally alone with each other. They had shrunk the world to their own specifications.

Although the bed they had rented was double sized, they clung to each other all night, using a minimum of space. And they still made love as if they were the last ones on earth.

Despite the delicious feeling of euphoria, the sensation of drifting on calm waters on a sweet sunny day, Vivien did preserve for the moment some vestiges of practicality. The house would be sold. This would provide enough money for them to pursue another life, which remained vague and undefined. Beyond that, she felt no desire for material possessions. Since they possessed each other, what more could they desire?

There was also the matter of talk between them. She remembered what he had said: What did you talk about? Between Edward and her, options of talk, like their existence, were deliberately narrowed. Even when she described her earlier life, the life before Orson, her childhood and girlhood, she would measure her words against her memory of old conversations with Orson. Had she told Orson that? If she was to excise the past, she had to also excise everything that went before.

Finally, to spare herself the tension of the editing, she eliminated from her thoughts anything that referred to her past life, her past self. There was only the now. Only Edward.

"Can you make believe? No. Not make believe. Truly believe that all life began at the moment of our meeting." So that, in the end, despite their mutual caveats and prohibitions, the only discussion between them could be what they felt toward each other. There was only themselves to contemplate and their now circumscribed world of the present. The past was irrelevent and the future uncertain.

"When did you first feel, you know, this sense of attraction?" she would ask.

"When I first saw you. And you?"

"It was later, at the coffee shop I felt it."

"Did it come as a bolt from the blue? A flash of light? Some explosive cosmic force taking possession of you? Something like that?"

They would be naked, clinging to each other. The weather had hit a rainy spell, and they rarely went out, except when it was necessary to buy food. Outside, the rain splattered against the windowpane. Days and nights merged. Conversations, like a moon-pulled tide, ebbed and flowed without any sense of time passing. Always the same theme surfaced, disappeared, resurfaced, like bobbing flotsam. Life lost all purpose other than themselves, knowing themselves, understanding how this had happened.

"Yes, something like that." She touched his cleft with her fingers, tracing a line down his neck.

"Was it something tangible? Physical only? Did you feel a yearning, an urgent need?"

"Yes, of course."

"Something beyond the flesh? Beyond biology? Like you had lost a piece of yourself and suddenly found it? Something like that?"

"Yes, something like that."

"Can you be sure? Try to say it. I want to hear it in your words."

He would become inert, thoughtful. She studied him minutely: where his flesh creased when he smiled; the direction in which his chest hair curled, like a windblown wheat field; his flesh, alternately rough and smooth; the secret places of his manhood; the way his skin cooled and popped into goose bumps. And the sounds taking place within him, the pumping, whooshing, gnawing sound of his physiological life, the body alive. But his thoughts were mysteries to be plumbed, only hinted at by words, expressions, movements, all guarded and reflexive.

"Like . . . ?" She would watch him struggling, journeying in his mind. Listen, she begged herself. Make no judgments. Do not commit.

"Like . . . punching through the clouds, finding blue sky."

Not that. Beside him, she would tense up, stiffen. A plane! He had described an airplane, which meant that he had not completely exorcised her, Lily, that she was still alive inside him. And since the image was clear to her as well, Orson, too, remained.

"No," he would correct, perhaps understanding the image. It was awesome, being beside him, listening, touching, but not truly knowing the inside of his thoughts.

"Say it another way." She hungered for explanations.

"Like a pile of dry tinder, something hidden and unseen, a

mysterious life force, suddenly becoming hot, bursting into flame, lighting up a totally interior world that we didn't know existed. All we knew was what we could sense, the source of the flame."

"Where did it come from?"

"From inside us."

"And you feel it now? This heat? This power?"

"Yes."

"And will it burn forever? Always?"

"Yes."

What she yearned for was some part of herself to detach, fly out of her being, hover over the room like a beam of light, probing his thoughts, then hers, evaluating, like some all-seeing, all-encompassing computer that could calculate truth and feelings and track its eternal validity, test and compute the furthest range of its power. She wanted proof, absolute surety.

When they kissed, she imagined that, with some magic special maneuver, he could suck her inside him, absorb her into his bloodstream, into his mind. But when her eyes opened, she was, of course, still outside him. And when he entered her in other ways, she willed herself to open, not just her body, everything! To draw him into her, absorb him inside her. Wasn't it the only way she could always be certain of him, to foreclose on any future betrayal? Only then, with him absorbed into her, could she be certain of his permanence.

She had resisted it from the beginning, from the moment that her brain required a description of what she felt. Love? To declare it, even secretly to herself, meant a further diminishment of its currency. It was clichéd, overused, abused by countless lies and seductions. It had lost all value, all meaning. What she dreaded most was that he would send it first out of the silence.

He did.

"I love you."

Instead of some physical expression of validation, she got up, walked away, paced the room, her arms hunched against her body.

"You don't mean that," she said.

Her reaction startled him.

"That's what it all boils down to. However you describe it, that's the way I feel. I love you. It is everything. I love you."

"You can't . . ." She groped for some way to stop what Orson had also once said to her. Between them, it would always be the ultimate comparison. The sluice gates of memory were opening, spilling out. "You said it to her." Her voice rose with anger and frustration.

"It wasn't like this."

"Then it is empty to say it."

"But it's what I feel," he said.

"Did you feel it then?"

"It doesn't matter."

"Yes, it does." She wanted him to feel what she felt, the feeling beyond words, the feeling of eternal possession, of selflessness, of a love so pure and refined that nothing could shatter it, a love that defied betrayal. And words. "Don't you see?" she cried, wringing her hands.

"No, I don't. I love you. I want to devote my life to you. What more can I say? There is nothing in life that I want. Nothing but to be with you, to hold you, to be near you. However you describe it, it comes down to that."

"You can't know for sure. Not so soon."

"I know."

Still, something inside told her it was not enough, that they had not yet struck the essence of it. She would force her anger to cool, then would come back to him, embracing.

The focus of everything had narrowed down to that one tiny center of intense heat, like the heat of the sun, captured into a single tiny beam through a magnifying glass. What she wanted, needed, longed for was the ultimate assurance. No matter what transpired in a life lived, however age would paint her, whatever her failings—whether she was bored or excited, comforted or irritated—whatever circumstance might buffet her, change her, sicken her, stunt her, embellish her, whatever her faults or flaws, her attributes, her capacity to enjoy or give joy, to enlighten or diminish, the ultimate value of their relationship would remain as pure and untrammeled as refined gold. Purer than that. More lasting than that.

How was it possible to declare such a thing, to promise it irrevocably? The best that could be pledged was this feeling now, at this single moment of time. Could she promise more than that?

No!

In the end she would be alone, unloved and unloving. What she craved was impossible to achieve, nor was it possible to erase the memory of the past. Soon she would have to eliminate the last reminder of the past, Edward himself. That would leave her with the only person in the world to whom her future would belong, the only person she could ever trust with her life, permanently, eternally.

Herself.

33

Three weeks after they had moved into the apartment, Vivien's house was sold. Twice a week she had called the broker from a telephone booth and received a report on the sales effort.

Edward accepted the news more with concern than unmitigated joy. They had talked of going away and, at the beginning, had explored endless possibilities. Since they had both cut away all moorings, any place in the world would have suited them.

The nature of the game was to be together, as they were now. Beyond that was the void.

Yet, regardless of how he studied her, there was always a point beyond which he could not penetrate. At times she drifted, grew vague and brooding, then she would surge up in intensity and passion. She alternated between reflective silence and curious probing questions.

"Do you think you know me, really know me?"

"I'm not sure," he replied.

"Just testing. I don't think I know you."

"Not consciously."

"What does that mean?"

"That we probably know each other deep in our subconscious. Really well. Totally."

"I don't believe that for a minute."

"Then why do you . . . make me feel so physically complete? What makes that happen?"

"Chemistry."

"But why you?"

"I don't want to think about it. Just feel. That's all I want to do. Just feel. No past. No future. Only to feel what I feel."

"And what is that?"

"It has no definition. And if it did, it wouldn't matter."

"But it must have some definition. Surely there are words to explain it."

"There are no words for that."

It seemed a refrain, and he longed for her to frame her feeling for him in direct and simple language. He wanted her to put it flatly, nakedly. Perhaps a simple "I love you," despite all its clichéd meanings. He did not ask any other assurance beyond that.

But he did not press her; he accepted her own special definitions and those that he would concoct at her urging. What was happening was beyond any of his experience. Perhaps it was, he told himself secretly, beyond the ability to articulate, something infinitely ethereal and spiritual, a perfect melding of desire and mutuality. He had never known such perfect joy.

On the surface, they existed in this finite world: a room, a bed, space, the present. To him, the past was dead, unmourned. Sometimes, merely to test himself he tried to dredge up old images. When they came, the definition was so feeble that it barely had the power to preserve itself, like a Polaroid picture that did not take.

Nothing intruded on the glory of the present, which was being with Vivien. Vivien was all life, an entire world, her body eternity, her spirit an indestructible force inside him. How could words convey that? He lived in a cocoon of fulfillment and ecstasy.

"I do love you."

Sometimes she would be playful.

"Just that? But how do you know? How are you sure?"

"I know."

"That's no answer."

"I feel."

"That's no answer."

"I'll give you proof."

They made love, passionate, intense, culminating as they crested on a single wave, the all-perfect legendary ninth wave.

"What does this prove?" she asked when they had cooled.

"That the body is the cathedral of the soul."

She laughed.

"I want to worship in your cathedral."

"Forever?"

"Of course forever."

"Do you love me?" she pressed.

"More than that."

But while coping with her questions, his questions had their own special perils. Why had this happened? First had come the random selection of joined lives: he and Lily, she and Orson, then the coming together of Lily and Orson. More random selection: betrayal and death. Each phase had triggered the other, expanding the mysterious connections, culminating finally in he and Vivien.

Why?

Between the frenetic love-making, they began to expand their verbal excursions. It was all part of the basic investigation of themselves. They talked of their general interests, favorite foods, flavors, seasons, colors, actors, political ideas, a panoply of sensations that might be a clue to the spark that set them off and joined them. Nothing fit with the smoothness of a jigsaw puzzle. There were always wrong angles, jutting tabs, bad fits.

"Ordinary people, that's us," she would say when it became apparent that whatever worldly talents or interests were inside them were unremarkable.

He would tick off the obvious categories of assets, and she would respond.

"General education?"

"Fair to middling. No marketable specialties."

He had majored in political science, she in psychology.

"Blood and breeding?"

"Not thoroughbred, but good sturdy stock."

"Physical aspect?"

"To others, well, sort of pleasant."

"And to you?"

"Surpassing beauty."

"It's in the eye of the beholder."

"And I'm the beholder."

"So am I."

In other words, he thought, nothing special, except to each other. He would have to look elsewhere for answers. Give it time, perhaps a lifetime, which suited him fine. A lifetime with Vivien, like this, was all one could wish for.

There were moments when he truly felt that they had reached

some nadir of communication, transcending experience and gender, as if they had achieved a cloning effect. Yet he still could not find the words to describe it, except in that way, which sounded more wishful than actual. However he wished it to be, he could not truly get inside her mind. And she could not get into his.

Which was why the subtle changes he began to detect began to worry him. Sometimes he was awakened by her soft sobbing, but when he asked her the matter, she would say: "Just happy."

Which satisfied him for a time. But when it persisted and he pressed her, she would answer finally: "It will go away."

"What will?"

"This. Us."

"Never." Again he would proclaim his feelings.

"It's not enough," she would sob. "It's transitory. It will disappear, disintegrate. You'll betray me. Perhaps I'll betray you."

"Nonsense." He tried to joke her out of it. "I'll never let you out of my sight." He meant it, envisioning a life like this, with every moment together.

"It's true," she said.

Despite the foreshadowing, he was stunned when it happened. He had gone with her to the title company, and the settlement had gone routinely. She received a certified check for nearly $200,000, which she slipped into her purse.

"This is it, the last of it," she told him in the car. As he drove, he watched her. The lines on her face were smooth, betraying no anxiety. When their eyes met, hers turned away. Something strange was happening inside her. At first he had thought it was his own paranoia reacting. Wasn't love a form of paranoia? With that to sustain him, he tried to dismiss his growing concern. Was she drifting away from him on strong but invisible currents? He could not bear such thoughts. Nor could he imagine what life had been or could be without her. By then, Lily had become merely a name, a non-person, someone he had seen in a movie who was briefly engaging but forgettable.

When they got back to the apartment, at first she sat on the bed, trancelike, lost in herself. He puttered in the kitchen, making them coffee. His hands shook. His heart pounded. The sense of menace was pervasive. Last night they had, as always, clung to each other. But something was happening, something ominous.

"What is it?"

"Nothing."

"But I feel something, and it frightens me."

"I know."

When he brought the steaming coffee mugs, she waved hers away, and he put it on the floor beside the bed. Watching her, he backed away and sat on the floor against the wall, sipping the hot liquid.

"I'm leaving," she said, drawing in her breath, her eyes moist but alert. The words seemed to break something inside him. His ears buzzed with crashing sounds. He hoped his body would explode. His mind told him to eject his thoughts, to empty itself of everything, to vanish.

"It would always be between us," she whispered, her words crashing into his consciousness like clanging cymbals. Yet he wondered if she had existed outside his imagination.

"But I thought . . ." he stammered.

"I just can't live with the danger, Edward."

"What danger?"

"That it won't last, that it will go away."

"Then you can't love me, that's why you don't say it."

"And if I said it? What would it mean? They're just words, Edward. Just words."

"What about feelings?"

"I don't trust them. Inside me they will always seem like a lie. I can't live with this fear. It will corrode me. The only certainty I can find is myself, in myself. You see . . ." The tears bubbled over her lower lids and slid onto her cheeks.

"But I thought we had smashed the past."

"You may have. I can't. There is still one thing left to do."

"Me?"

She nodded.

He continued to sit, paralyzed and inert, unable to find any spark of life in himself, extinguished.

He watched her rise, take out her suitcases, and begin to pack. It was too unbearable to watch, like observing a gaping wound in himself, blood flowing freely, his life slipping away.

When the knock came, he could not relate it to anything outside of himself. When it persisted, he looked at Vivien and saw her fear. There was no escaping its urgency. He crossed the room and opened the door. It was McCarthy.

"I found it," he said. "I found their place."

34

Outside, it was warmer. The afternoon sun threw shafts of light through the still barren branches of the trees, defining the expanding buds. She could detect the unmistakable signs of the earth's thaw, and it filled her mind with memories of past springs in Vermont.

She had let herself be persuaded, not by words, but by the nagging feeling that she must not leave until all the tangles of her past life had been broken. It had taken every ounce of her courage to make her decision to leave Edward, and there was little left to resist. In her mind it would be a ritual, the final cremation.

It had been an idea that had loomed large between them with its promise of exorcism and revelation. But hadn't she already had her exorcism? Hadn't she faced the ultimate reality of womanhood, exploded the last remaining myth of the necessity of male attachment? What she had concluded was that it was better to be self-contained, better to control her own destiny without the encumbrance of this powerful magnetism that made her dependent on something outside herself. There were signs, too, that the magnetism had fulfilled its purpose, leaving her with its inevitable consequences. That, too, would have to be eliminated.

She sat in the seat beside McCarthy. By silent consent, Edward sat alone in the back.

"It's not far," McCarthy said.

She had disposed of her key but was not surprised when Edward had produced his, confirming what she had intuitively sensed.

Although McCarthy looked ahead impassively as he drove, he spun out a monologue without interruption.

"Must have had a practical streak, your wife did, Davis. I traced it through a cash purchase she made at Woodies—a box spring, mattress, sheets, and pillows. Nothing more. Got the employees' discount and had it delivered to J. Smith, Eighteen

Twenty-five Parkend Street, Arlington. Had it right about the time frame and distance. J. Smith. If you want to be anonymous, J. Smith is your best shot. More J. Smiths than anything else in the telephone books of the U.S. Actually, I had it a couple of weeks ago, but I held on to it." He paused and cleared his throat. "I really brooded on it, but coming so soon after that FBI thing, I thought it might be a little too much to take. Lousy, the way they moved in on you like that. Just one more road to take. In this business that's the way it is. You got to admit the logic in it, though, especially . . ." He took a deep breath but still did not look at either of them. "Hope they didn't shake you up too much. Hell, you two together was a surprise to me, too. I knew you sold the house, Mrs. Simpson. Then, when you settled today, I figured you might be cutting out somewhere. I hope I'm doing the right thing. But somehow I feel that if you don't tie up this one loose end, you'll always have some lingering feeling of mystery. Not knowing, you know, only half knowing, can be a tough thing to live with. Hell, it's none of my business." His eyes darted to the rearview mirror. "You forgive me, Davis? I'm a shit when I'm drunk, although I guess you should have known that . . . about the pregnancy. Should have told you at the time. My fault. This is also my fault. Don't try to put it together. Nothing ever happens by accident, even in my business." He laughed suddenly, making a croaking sound. "I never did tell the Feds where it was, being a sneaky bastard. Anyway, you'll be happy to know that they got to the bottom of the crash. Something about the deicing solution not being enough to keep the ice off while the plane waited on the runway. Simple as that. It's the simple things that foul you up every time." He squinted at the windshield and brought down the sun visor to shut off the glare of the slanting sun. "Not far. I didn't go in. As a matter of fact, I'm not going in. This is not for me. It's out of my system now." He pulled up in front of an older garden apartment project, not unlike the one they had chosen themselves.

"Around the back," he said. "Ground floor. I'll wait here."

Edward got out of the back and opened the door for Vivien. She remembered the project. It was one of those they had inspected on the very first day. She speculated on what might have happened if they had stumbled on it. Would it have foreclosed on what had come after? Or was that inevitable?

They did not speak as they walked around the back of the building. The apartment, Number Two, had its own entrance. Like theirs, mature trees blocked off the sunlight. It was also a lower-middle-class community, working people whose lives were played out in constant economic stress. A perfect place for anonymity, she thought: few children, hardworking single people or couples. It was a factor that neither of them had considered, perhaps deliberately.

The door to the apartment showed signs of age and long usage. Multiple paint jobs had made a valiant but unsuccessful attempt to cover the chips and chinks. Below the bell lever was a place for a name card, but none was in it.

Like the name they had chosen, a sense of anonymity pervaded the entrance. With pale, trembling fingers, Edward fumbled with the key, inserting it finally. Before he turned it, he looked up at her.

"Doesn't seem important anymore," he said with sadness. When she did not answer, he turned the key. The lock clicked open, and he pushed at the door with the palm of his hand.

Feel nothing, she urged herself as she followed him inside. With the single window blocked by the trunk of a close-growing tree and the last fading rays of a winter sun throwing sparse light, the apartment seemed enveloped in a smoky haze. It took some moments for her eyes to focus.

When she was able to see clearly, her gaze swept the room. The walls were painted in a nondescript dingy color. Like theirs, it was a single room with a small Pullman kitchen and a door that led, obviously, to a bathroom. Jutting out from one wall was a mattress on a box spring, neatly dressed in a fitted sheet and two matching pillows. At its foot was a folded pink blanket.

In terms of space alone, the sense of emptiness was pervasive, almost stifling. Her eyes darted toward Edward. Yet she sensed that something existed in this room that transcended the Spartan setting. It might be only fantasy, spun out of her knowledge of what had taken place here, but Orson's presence seemed to rise out at her, enveloping her in a gauze of compelling power—not the shuddering eerie presence of a haunting ghostly spirit bent on vengeance and disruption, but more like the cry of a helpless, vulnerable tragic child, pleading for compassion.

She felt the hate and anger seep out of her.

A gurgle of response started in her throat, but she remained silent. Behind her, she could feel the faint rustle of Edward's movements, his breath shallow and steady. Was it a sign? Did he feel what she was experiencing? As she turned toward him, her sweeping vision caught the glint of crystal, probably from the last single ray of declining light. Beside the mattress, at first hidden from her view, was a small bud vase. In it were the remains of a single sweetheart rose, its dry petals resting sadly on a weary wizened stem. Only then did a sound rise from her lips—not a stifled cry of repressed pain, but more like a bleat of a young lamb saved from slaughter.

"We must forgive them," she whispered. He turned, hesitant at first, then let himself rush into her waiting arms.

"Of course."

In the sweet silence between them, she heard her words. Uncertainty, too, had vanished.

"I love you," she whispered.

"And me you . . . for always."

"At least for now," she said.

35

When they came back to the car, McCarthy looked at them with questioning eyes. None of my business, he had told them earlier. But he had made it his business, Edward thought, for reasons unknown except to himself.

They came back to the car with arms around each other's waists. Through the engorging fullness of his happiness, Edward could still observe the detective's sense of surprise and curiosity. He considered the man's dilemma with wry amusement and resolved to toss him some tiny crumb of knowledge. But when he searched himself, his knowledge was confused, his understanding murky. Instead of the burst of sunlight, the explosion of understanding that is supposed to accompany an epiphany, he felt numb, drained of insight. What had changed inside Vivien was as womanly and, therefore, as mysterious as ever. His love, need, attraction for Vivien had been quite clear and uncomplicated for some time now. Memories of Lily were as thin as dust, and strong gusts were swiftly blowing even the tiniest particles from his mind and memory.

He decided not to exhaust himself with any further explorations. It was enough to believe that he had captured some lost part of himself, however the process was labelled.

"We must forgive them," she had whispered, illustrating the full depth of a woman's journey to obliterate scorn. Was she able now to trust his love? His loyalty? His commitment? He would spend his lifetime proving that she could.

They slid into the rear seat, embracing, touching, silently conveying their urgent relevancy to each other. Looking up, he saw McCarthy's eyes observing them in the rearview mirror. Offering a broad smile, McCarthy's gaze swept back to the road.

"Please stop," Vivien said suddenly. "There." She was pointing at an outside telephone booth in a filling station. Without comment, McCarthy pulled in front of it while Vivien fished in her handbag for change.

"Here," McCarthy said, leaning over and offering a handful of change.

She took it, looked up into McCarthy's eyes, and thanked him.

"I have to call my parents and speak to Ben," she said as she slid out of the car. She looked back at them briefly, her eyes glistening, her smile fuller than he had ever seen it. A serene, happy face, Edward thought as she entered the booth and began to punch the numbers.

"Satisfied?" McCarthy's voice was calm, his inquiry gentle.

Edward nodded.

"They're all sisters, aren't they?" McCarthy said.

"In a way."

"Never understand how they hook us, reel us in. Hook hurts going in, hurts going out. Doesn't it?"

"Maybe someone should ask the fish."

"All right, I'm asking."

Edward felt the brief bite at wisdom, a nibble at the edge of insight.

"People fall in love," Edward said. "Can't be helped. Like the fish. Right place. Right time. Right bait. Makes them crazy. Don't try to figure it out."

"Love," McCarthy sighed. "They probably invented it. Think it excuses everything."

"Doesn't it?"

"Maybe so." He rubbed his chin in contemplation. "They may know something we don't. It *was* Eve who ate the apple." They laughed, and were still laughing when Vivien came back to the car.

"What's so funny?" she asked.

"Oh, nothing," Edward replied and gave McCarthy a knowing wink.

Vivien looked at each of them in turn, and seemed perplexed, but shrugged it off and said, "Ben's fine. I said I'd be there tomorrow night. First I have to pick up Hamster. I told them all to be prepared for some surprises." She turned toward him and took both his hands in hers. "Okay?"

"Never gonna let you outa my sight," Edward sang softly.

She looked back at him mischievously, then moved her lips to his ear.

"I hope he's exactly like you," she said.

"Who?"

"Our baby."

His heart lurched, and he turned to face her.

"Mother Nature has spoken. She could be fooling, but I don't think so."

"I'll take her word for it," Edward said. "She usually knows what she's doing." Vivien moved into his embrace.

"Especially now."

"Especially now," he agreed.

DISCARD